BLACKBEARD'S FAMILY
BOOK 4 OF:
THE VOYAGES OF
QUEEN ANNE'S REVENGE

JEREMY MCLEAN

POINTS OF SAIL
PUBLISHING

Points of Sail Publishing
P.O. Box 30083 Prospect Plaza
FREDERICTON, New Brunswick
E3B 0H8, Canada

Edited by Ethan James Clarke

Cover Template by Kit Foster

This is a work of fiction. Any similarity to persons, living or dead, is purely coincidental… Or is it?

DEDICATION

Thank you to the fans who are reading this now who've stuck by
in the long wait for this book to be released.

TABLE OF CONTENTS

1. STABBED IN THE HEART
THROUGH THE BACK

"We should strike now. We know where he'll be, and it's the perfect chance to kill him without a huge battle." Herbert sat forward in his wheelchair, one arm leaning on the table in the *Queen Anne's Revenge* war room. His other hand was in front of him, palm open and motioning in supplication to his pirate brethren.

"Although I defended you in the past to be fair to everyone, Herbert, you must know you're biased in this decision." Anne, the *Queen Anne's Revenge* quartermaster, sat stoically, her posture perfect, arms resting on the chair. She had a slight investment in the outcome due to her own past with their enemy, Calico Jack, but her tone and muted expression painted things otherwise.

Herbert lowered his head, more in frustration than shame, and looked up at Anne from under furrowed brows. "My emotions may be compromised, but my faculties aren't. I'm not wrong."

William, his arms crossed as he too leaned forward in his chair, stared at the wooden boards of the ship as he said, "I am inclined to side with Herbert." William gave Anne a sidelong glance, then added, "My apologies, ma'am." He couldn't help but channel his former royal guard nature when speaking with Anne.

Anne's clenched jaw betrayed her annoyance at both of William's comments. She didn't enjoy being outnumbered but also didn't enjoy being reminded of her former royal status. "And what if the information we were given is incorrect, hmm? What if we head to Tortuga and his crew is there waiting for us?"

"Impossible," Victoria said, shaking her head. "My informant doesn't make mistakes, and he wouldn't betray us. Besides, Calico Jack frequently visits Los Huecos to check on his commander Silver Eyes before travelling to Tortuga. Then, after he's had his fill of his baser inclinations, he heads back to his base of operations in Nassau. I know this from my time on his crew."

"Also, *ma chérie*," Alexandre, the *Queen Anne's Revenge* surgeon, chimed in, "it should be noted that when on land, Calico Jack would not travel to all places with his entire crew. A covert assassination should prove effective, provided he doesn't know we are *arrivant*."

Anne sighed, her responsibility as quartermaster wavering against the mounting offensive from her crewmates. "I suppose you may be right. But," she said, turning her gaze to her husband, Edward Thatch, "what does the captain think?"

Edward's hands were clasped together in front of his face, his fingers entwined and his elbows resting on the table. He had listened to everything in silence, his eyes trained on a map in the middle of the table, but not focused on any of the shapes.

He eventually looked up at all the eyes staring back at him, suddenly aware of the entire room waiting for him to make the definitive decision. He unclasped his hands, leaned back, and stroked his long black beard.

Herbert spoke again. "If we let this opportunity slip away and do nothing, we will eventually come to regret it. This isn't like before. We'll do this together, and we'll do it right this time."

The others nodded in approval when Edward turned his gaze on them. All of them agreed with Hebert's declaration. Herbert met Edward's gaze, unwavering, letting Edward know that he wouldn't hesitate in following him into the unknown battle ahead.

"Set course for Tortuga."

"You found him?" Edward questioned the breathless crewmates. "You're sure it was Calico Jack?"

The crewmates both nodded at the same time. "No doubt, Captain. From what William told us 'bout his looks and the manner he carried himself, this was Calico Jack."

"How many were with him?" Herbert asked, wheeling himself over to the commotion.

The sky was darkening above Tortuga and the *Queen Anne's Revenge*. The crew had only just finished settling the ship at anchor a ways from the harbour. The three masts' sails had been furled, and the halyards secured to the vessel, and the crew was ready for the long night at rest.

"Far as we could tell, it was just him an' two others what came to the tavern. They entered after a time and were bein' served food and drinks just as we left."

"That means we don't have much time. How many were in the tavern?"

"Not more than twenty."

"Then we proceed as planned," Edward said as he turned towards Herbert. "Get your pistol ready, Herbert, we're ending this tonight."

Herbert couldn't help but smile, but his eyes soon misted, and he cast his eyes downward. He turned away from Edward. "Sorry, Captain," he said, his words catching in his throat.

Edward issued a few commands to the nearby crewmates to prepare the ship for departure and bring the crew up from below before coming back. Then he knelt next to Herbert.

"No need for that now," he said.

Herbert nodded as he wiped his eyes. "I know, Captain, I'm not sure what came over me. The deed's not even done yet."

Edward nodded. "True, but we both know that this is revenge years in the making. It may not bring your legs back, but if it can bring closure, it's no wonder one would be overcome by the magnitude of it."

Herbert looked up at Edward, his eyes still shining in the waning light as the wind of the sea blew against his short brown hair. "Tonight changes everything. Tomorrow will start a new life for me. You have my thanks, Edward. Without you, this wouldn't be possible."

"Not so. You made a choice to join a bunch of pirates under the condition that we help you in your vengeance." Edward placed his hand on Herbert's wheelchair. "You are the architect, I'm just the hired help."

Herbert and Edward both chuckled at that, but then Herbert shook his head in defiance. "No, you're family. And I've told you before that this family is my strength. It's the only reason I've gotten this far."

Edward's face warmed, embarrassed, but happy to have Herbert make such a declaration. "Let's kill Calico Jack then, shall we, brother?"

"Let's," Herbert said as he clasped Edward's forearm. Edward grabbed Herbert's forearm back and shook it to seal the informal bond of vengeance.

Christina, Herbert's sister, rushed up from below deck over to Herbert and Edward, with Anne trailing behind her. "We found him?" Christina asked expectantly. After a quick nod from Edward and Herbert, tears filled her widened eyes, and she fell to the deck on her knees next to Herbert. Her arms wrapped around him, and she shoved her face into his chest, her strawberry blond hair draping over him. Herbert's chest muffled her sobs.

Herbert wrapped his arms around his sister, and his tears came back at once. He consoled her, but knew that she was crying for the same reason he had; this was joy, and possibly relief.

After a moment, the other crewmates rushed up from the depths of the ship and began preparations to leave Tortuga at a moment's notice.

Christina regained her awareness with the noise of the

many feet pounding against the weather deck. She got to her feet and wiped her tears away, a quick transition to the determined, anxious look of a woman ready for a fight.

The crewmates who had found Calico Jack returned with the men who were going to help with the plan. Ten men in all would help while Edward, Anne, and Herbert would carry out the other half of the plot.

"Do we all know our parts to play?" The crewmates nodded. "Then show us the way, men," Edward commanded.

"Captain," Christina said, stepping forward before they could leave. "I know that I'm supposed to stay here and prepare the ship for departure, but I wish to join you." She stood defiantly, her fingers balled into fists. "Please."

"Christina—" Herbert began, but Edward's hand on his shoulder stopped him.

"Rest assured, you will have your chance to extract your pound of flesh from Calico Jack," Edward declared. "But we need you here. Without Herbert, you are our best helmsman."

Christina's gaze fell, and her fingers dug into her palms for a moment. Nassir, the negro shipwright, came over beside Christina and wrapped his massive arm around her, pulling her in close. She looked shocked at first, but when she gazed up at him, her features softened. They shared a bond of loss over the years aboard the ship, and it carried a weight that a captain's command simply could never hope to rival. Next, her wolf companion, Tala, nudged her fist with a whine. Christina looked down at her, opened her palm and scratched her friend on the nose.

When her gaze came back to meet Edward's, she wore a false smile and misted eyes. "I'll hold you to that promise," she said.

"Understood," Edward replied.

As the departing crew began boarding a longboat for shore, Edward stopped to talk with William, the boatswain in charge of the ship while Edward and Anne were away, and Jack, the musician.

5

"Keep the men in line and entertained," Edward said, leaning in with a soft voice. "Tensions are high, and we can't have any mistakes. Not tonight."

William gave a stiff salute, and Jack nodded. "Understood, Captain," William replied.

"I'll bring out the fiddle tonight," Jack added with a smile. "That should lighten the mood a touch."

Edward gave the two men a few more explicit orders about when to be ready, and whom in the crew to use at which stations, before turning around to join the others still boarding the longboat. Before he could disembark, another crewmate came up behind him and gave him a forceful slap on his back.

Edward let out a grunt as the stinging on his back coursed through his spine. He glared at the Mayan prince he knew to be behind him, and the prince smirked back at his captain.

"Pukuh, I thought you to be sleeping at this hour."

"I would not miss this," he replied. Pukuh's smile faded, and he gave a stern look. "Do not underestimate this man, Calico Jack. According to my father, when he was known as Benjamin Hornigold, he was a fearsome man to his enemies, and the years seem to have hardened him." Pukuh's light accent belied the harsh tone he employed.

"Not to worry, friend, we have our best opportunity here and now, and I wouldn't let my guard down during such a crucial time."

"You would not let your guard down? How was it I hit you on the back a moment before then?" He shot Edward an impetuous grin.

Edward shook his head. "I knew you were there, but it seemed like you could use a boost of confidence after losing your arm. Perhaps if you were in good form you would have been able to sneak up on me," Edward tried his best to add a fake tone of pity to his words, but he couldn't help but grin at his own jesting.

Pukuh playfully punched Edward in his arm before he exchanged another few words of encouragement for the battle to come.

The crew watched as their captain and the shore party entered the longboat and paddled to shore. They were mostly silent, imparting strength in solidarity for the task ahead. Everyone knew who their captain was about to face, and the weight of what it meant when they would come back with the enemy in hand.

Edward noticed Alexandre and Victoria on the quarterdeck, near the helm. When deciding who would be part of the team to face Calico Jack, Victoria had chosen to stay behind. By her demeanour, though she portrayed a mask of strength, Edward believed she didn't wish to confront Calico Jack, the man who had tortured her, again.

Though the torturer had been different, Edward knew the feeling well. It was that feeling which forced him to keep a flask in his pocket at all times.

The longboat docked at Tortuga's harbour, and from the sounds that met the crew's ears, it was the beginning of a night full of drunken revelry and debauchery. For Tortuga, it was a Thursday.

Edward commanded a few of the crew to find the men who had taken leave at the shore and bring them back to the ship. Thankfully, everyone was expecting to leave on short notice and agreed to stay close to the harbour, so he didn't expect there would be any issues finding the men.

The sound of pistols, battle cries, and lamentations, coupled with the occasional cracking of breaking glass, echoed across the dingy stone walkways the crew traversed on their way to the tavern where Calico Jack was waiting for them. The smell of hard liquor, ale, body odour, and piss wafted towards them, mixed with the scent of the ocean and nearby grass and tropical trees. Years of dilapidation and neglect meant that the smells simply compounded on top of one another, and the air was forever tainted by the musk of the pirates and rebels that inhabited the lawless island.

When they were three buildings away from the tavern, the

crewmates who had found Calico Jack pointed out the tavern in which he was to be found. With a quick check of readiness, Edward continued towards the tavern.

"Hold, Captain," Herbert said, stopping at the back of the group. "I cannot enter the tavern. I shall wait around back."

Edward's jaw went slack for a moment. "Why?"

"I know I was but a child when I was on his ship, but there is no mistaking my condition. My wheelchair will stand out like a sore thumb, so it would be best if I remain outside not to disrupt the plan you have in mind."

Edward looked deep into Herbert's eyes and saw no sadness in them. He could only see the same determination as before staring back at him.

"Understood," Edward said. "You stay with him," he added, pointing to one of the crewmates. The crewmate nodded, and he and Herbert went around the back of the nearby buildings to where they would take Calico Jack before bringing him back to the ship.

The rest of the crew proceeded to the tavern, and gradually entered in groups. The last group consisted of the two crewmates who had found Calico Jack initially, and Edward and Anne.

The inside of the tavern smelled another level worse than the outside of Tortuga. With little ventilation, the foul odours concentrated in the confined space and permeated the walls and air of the establishment. The twenty or so patrons, now bolstered by the ten from Edward's crew, packed the quarters and made the space uncomfortably hot. It also didn't help that, although expected given the gravity of the situation, Edward felt tense and on edge.

"Where is he?" Anne asked, staying hidden behind Edward's large body until she could get a line of sight.

"In the corner on the left," one of the crewmates answered, being sound of mind enough not to point as he did.

Edward and Anne both tentatively glanced in that direction, only briefly catching a glimpse of Calico Jack and his mates.

Edward almost felt that he could sense the man's presence, as though his reputation weighed on the hot, stuffy air. Even so, he wasn't sure if it was merely nerves, so he asked, "Is that him, Anne?"

Anne's face scrunched pensively. "I cannot tell. There are too many people here."

"At worst, we point a pistol at another pirate. Let's find somewhere to sit."

Edward, Anne, and the two crewmates found a few empty chairs and a table to sit at, and shortly afterwards a husky woman brought them all pints of ale without their asking. She let them all know they would bring them food should they have the coin to pay, though not letting them know what the food was or how much it cost.

Edward took a few coins from his purse and tossed them her way. After a check of their quality, she nodded in approval and left to the back of the establishment.

Edward looked around at the other patrons. Many of them were men, some young and foolish, and some old grizzled seamen, but there were also a few women of the night, as well as a few middle-aged female bruisers who seemed to be sharing stories with the seamen. He noticed that he was growing accustomed to the smell, and it, like the noise surrounding them, faded into the background. But, as the sounds faded, his nerves finally caught up with him, and he suddenly felt ill.

Thoughts he wanted to keep buried crept into him, gnawing and itching. *Not now. Please, not now*, he begged, but he could already feel his skin go cold, and his hand trembled. His chest felt as though a cannon was sitting on top of it.

Edward swallowed and moved his hand into his breast pocket. The thick air now seemed an ocean of mud on his body. He thought all eyes were on him, and he was moving too slow, too unnaturally, to look normal. He forced against the mud, and it made his hands shake with the effort. The thought that his weakness was showing only made the trembling worse, and it took all his strength to twist off the cap of his flask. He brought the flask full of rum to his lips and took a long and deep drink from it.

The sharp and bitter harshness cut through his other pains like a blade through flesh, and he sighed in relief. The rum gave him no pleasure in its taste, only respite from the weight of the mud around him. This was his only way to control it, but the mud was hardening as each day passed and required more to wash it away as well.

Edward could feel Anne's gaze on him, and he glanced over at her. She had a look of concern on her face. He lifted the flask up in the air and did his best to grin as he said, "Liquid courage," but the grin felt hollow even to him. He took another deep drink from the flask.

The woman who had served them the ale returned with a few plates full of what appeared to be some sort of stew with meat in it and old bread. She didn't say another word to them and left to serve other people.

None of the crew even entertained the thought of trying the food, and so Edward leaned forward after pushing his plate aside. The others at his table followed suit.

"The back room is a bit far from where he is. We'll need to act fast while our crewmates are doing their part."

Anne and one of the crewmates nodded, but the other leaned in further. "Captain, I know we wus supposed to wait a bit before startin' the ruckus, but I think Ca— I think our man is close to finishing his meal."

Edward's eyes widened slightly, and he glanced over to where Calico Jack was sitting. From what he could tell, the men at the table looked relaxed and took small bites of their food and infrequent drinks of ale.

"It's time," he said.

Edward rose from the table and locked gazes with one of his crewmates in another part of the tavern. The crewmate scratched his nose, showing he understood what to do next.

Edward casually walked towards the back corner where

Calico Jack waited, followed closely by Anne and the two crewmates they were with. As they moved, the crewmate whom Edward had given the signal started an argument with another mate.

The other patrons hooted and hollered, cheering on the arguments and adding to the insults tossed at each other and tossing actual objects at them as well. The air in the tavern was changing swiftly as the excitement of a brewing fight riled everyone else up.

According to plan, when Edward and the others were a few feet from Calico Jack, the shouts and taunts changed to fists. Most of the patrons were all paying attention to the fight now, and none were looking at Edward and the others.

To ensure nothing went wrong, a few other crewmates started fights with other patrons in the bar, and in a matter of seconds, the entire right side of the tavern had turned into a riot.

Edward, Anne, and their companions took advantage of the commotion, pulled pistols from their coats, and pointed them at the back of Calico Jack and his mates.

"Calico Jack, I presume you wouldn't enjoy a bullet to the back, so don't move," Edward commanded.

For a moment, there was complete silence from the man in front of Edward. He glanced over to the other mates on the other end of the table, the ones whose faces he could see, and noticed that they looked wholly and utterly calm. They appeared as though they didn't care in the slightest that they had pistols trained on them, and the looks unnerved Edward even more than he had been, despite the drink hitting him at that moment.

"So, you're finally here, son," Calico Jack, the man in front of Edward, said over the commotion on the other side of the tavern.

Even above the commotion, Edward knew the voice was a familiar one. He couldn't place it, but Calico Jack raised his hands, rose from his seat, and turned around, and then he knew why the voice was familiar.

"Dad?" Edward said, his mouth going slack as he stepped back in shock.

"Ed?" Anne called.

Before Edward could recover, his father slapped the pistol away and punched Edward in the gut. Edward doubled over in pain but was pulled up by his hair and put in a chokehold.

"You disappoint me, Edward," his father whispered in his ear.

Edward felt a sharp pain shoot into his lower back and travel all through his body, and then there was a sudden empty feeling. He felt warm blood gushing out of the wound.

"Let him go!" Anne shouted, firing her pistol at Calico Jack.

Jack ducked out of the way, but Anne's shot was wide and more a warning. "I think not, little queen," he replied. He pulled a small hunting horn that appeared to be made of tarnished gold from his pocket and blew into it.

The tone from the horn was piercing and like no other sound Edward had ever heard. It shook his whole body with the noise it made, and after it went away, there was silence. Silence, not because Edward temporarily went deaf, but because the patrons in the tavern stopped fighting.

Edward couldn't move his head, but looking over, he could see all eyes on them. The men and women who had not a moment before been beating each other to a pulp were now staring at Calico Jack in a sort of religious reverence. Edward's crew had stopped as well, though from confusion rather than whatever the sound of the horn had wrought.

"By the sound of the Golden Horn!" one of the men in the crowd shouted.

"By the sound of the Golden Horn!" another continued the chant.

Edward hadn't heard the chant himself but had been informed by Anne about its significance to Benjamin Hornigold, Calico Jack's former alias. *His father's* former alias. It was a battle cry used by those pirates in league with Hornigold in a failed war years ago.

Soon most of the patrons were shouting the same battle cry as they descended upon Edward and his crew. After each chant, they took a step forward in unison, as though under a trance.

"By the sound of the Golden Horn!"

"By the sound of the Golden Horn!"

"By the sound of the Golden Horn!"

Anne's eyes were wide with terror at the sight of all those men and women walking as one towards them. She reloaded her pistol, but didn't know where to point it, whether at the man who had sounded the call, or the crowd that had answered it.

Edward's father pushed him away, and he fell into Anne's arms. His legs were weak, and he had difficulty moving. The drink and the loss of blood were taking its toll on him, and he could feel the void creeping up on him.

"You would have had me if you weren't so weak," Jack scolded. "Try again when you grow a spine."

In front of Calico Jack, his crewmates stood as an honour guard, shielding him from any harm. All the while, the crowd was still chanting and getting closer.

Edward put all his strength in his feet and pushed Anne towards the back of the tavern. The crowd didn't pounce on them, they simply forced them back with each step they took. They were letting them go, but Edward didn't know for how long that would remain so. They needed to run.

Anne kept her pistol trained on the crowd, shifting its muzzle from one person to the next as she backed towards the tavern's kitchen. In the kitchen, the men and women who worked the tavern continued the chant in the tight corridors. Their eyes stayed trained on Edward and Anne, but it felt as though they were looking through them.

Edward and Anne stumbled out of the back exit of the tavern to the alley, where Herbert and another crewmate were waiting. Herbert's eyes looked like saucers at the sight of Edward.

"What happened?" he shouted.

"By the sound of the Golden Horn!" Behind them, the chant was getting closer.

"There's no time!" Anne yelled back. "We're getting out of here. Someone help me with Edward."

Edward tried to get to his feet to help his wife and crew escape, but he'd lost his strength long ago. His head became leaden, and his eyes closed. As his world faded to black, the image of his aged father stabbing him in the back burned in his mind.

2. RESOLVE

Edward awoke with a jump and a pounding headache. By the time he was sitting upright, the pain in his backside flooded over him. He grabbed his left side where the wound was and turned over to avoid lying on it again.

"Welcome back, *mon ami*," a familiar French voice called behind him.

Still deep in pain, Edward lowered his head and peered through the crook in his arm to see an upside-down Alexandre sitting behind him. He smiled in his hollow way and turned his head slightly to match Edward's orientation before waving to him.

Edward lifted his head and glanced around. He was back on the ship in the surgeon's own room. Various bottles filled with coloured liquids dotted secured shelves alongside every manner of medical equipment and textbooks from across the globe. The strange concoction of medicine and decay hit Edward's nose, and he remembered part of the reason he'd never liked the room.

Edward noticed his body weight shifting back and forth rhythmically. "We're sailing?" he asked.

"*Oui*," Alexandre replied. "After the run-in with your *père*, it was decided to leave before trouble follow us."

The pain left Edward in a flash as he remembered what had happened. His father had been in that tavern, and had stabbed him, his own son, in the back. Worse still, his father was Calico Jack, and Benjamin Hornigold before that.

His father had been alive all this time. His father had been alive and hadn't come home.

'Your father is in the Caribbean, Edward.' Those had been the

15

last words of John, the former quartermaster of *Queen Anne's Revenge* and an old friend of Edward's father. *He knew,* Edward thought. He didn't like to dwell on that moment, as he had been tortured for days on end afterwards, and so he'd forgotten its significance. *He knew where my father was, and who he was, all along.*

Edward's hand shook as the pain returned, and not just the physical.

"I need a drink," he sputtered as his eyes became hazy.

After a moment of shuffling behind him, Alexandre handed Edward a glass. Edward took it and gulped the liquid down. After finishing half, he stopped and shoved the glass back.

"Rum," he demanded.

Alexandre produced a flask in an instant as if he'd predicted the desire for hard liquor before Edward had asked. Edward cared not for the surgeon's ways and took the drink. In a matter of seconds, Edward guzzled down half the flask's contents before he had to come up for air.

Edward's hand still shook as he lowered the flask. He took in ragged deep breaths, trying to bring air back to his lungs, which felt, to him, so desperately empty. His head and heart pounded in his chest, and he couldn't make sense of the feeling of dread washing over him.

He finished the flask with abandon and lay there on his elbows for a time. He had trouble thinking and didn't know how much time passed. The drink hit him hard and fast, his loss of blood no doubt contributing to the swift onset. The haze clouding his thoughts changed to a different kind, and ever so slowly, Edward felt he could breathe once more.

Edward looked to his right to see Alexandre there, watching him. Alexandre's eyes were dull and cold, as usual, but Edward thought he could see an expectant look on the surgeon's face. Alexandre must be awaiting some sort of explanation for what just happened.

"Stop staring at me, you damn Frenchman, before I cut your eyes out." Edward cared little for his harsh words now that the drink was affecting him.

Alexandre rose from his seat and walked away without a word. Edward shuffled over and rose to his shaky feet. Turning around, he noticed Victoria, Calico Jack's—his *father's*—former plaything sitting there watching him.

"Did you know too?" he shouted before tripping over his own feet. He grabbed onto the frame of the door nearby to steady himself.

"Know what?" she replied, clearly irked by Edward's accusation, but giving him a chance to back down.

"Hmph," Edward scoffed. "Whoring yourself out to him must have made you privy to his secrets."

Victoria crossed her arms and flashed him a vile look. "Watch what you say next unless you want to lose the chance to have your own son come to try and kill you," she said, nodding towards Edward's nether regions.

Edward laughed a chuckle at first, and then full-blown laughter as he leaned against the door frame. He covered his eyes with his hand as he laughed, rubbing them as they misted, from the humour or the sadness he knew not.

"He tried to kill me," Edward let out between breaths. "My own father tried to kill me. And not just once. He sent me for the keys to this ship, knowing I could die trying. He knew just how to prick me to make me jump the way he wanted."

Edward lowered himself to the sole of the deck, his back resting against the open frame of the door. The pain from his wound was a dull sensation now, dissipated in the haze and spinning that the drink and blood loss brought him.

Time lost meaning to Edward, and he vaguely felt as though he were floating or being carried before lying in his familiar bed. The gentle rocking of the waves and the spinning in his head lulled him to sleep.

The sun hit Edward's eyelids, waking him from his slumber.

Reflex forced his eyes open and then closed again from the glare. He blinked quickly to adjust himself to the sudden brightness and rose from his bed.

His head was pounding, and his body aching. He sat doubled over on the edge of the bed, holding the sides of his skull to hold back the beating, but it was no use.

"Finally awake, then?" Anne asked near the captain's cabin window.

Edward glanced her way, the light from the sun behind her setting alight her auburn hair. He could barely see her face because of the luminance, but he could tell she was frowning from her arms folded in front of her chest. As soon as she moved, the sun shone directly on his eyes again.

"Agh," he shouted as he looked away. "Dammit, woman, you're killing me."

"No, I'm afraid the drink is to blame from your woes," she replied. She walked over to a barrel secured in the corner of the room, lifted the top of the cask and dunked a cup inside. "Here, drink this," she said as she walked over with the cup.

Edward took the cup and drank the contents. The water, mixed with enough rum to sanitize it, felt good on his tongue.

"We've landed in Puerto Plata for a quick restock and regrouping. The sun will set soon, and we need to decide where to go from here and what to do about recent... revelations."

Edward looked up into his wife's pained eyes. They seemed on the edge of tears, mourning for his situation.

"We're quite the pair, aren't we?" Edward said, casting his gaze on his half-filled cup. "Both our parents want us dead."

Anne lifted Edward's chin up. She still had the glow of the sun surrounding her long red curls. "They aren't our family any longer." Anne stroked Edward's cheek, running her hand down his long black beard before giving it a light tug. "The men and women on this ship are your family now, and they're all that matters."

Edward nodded and forced a smile for his wife. Her sentiment made his heart swell, but it wasn't enough to quell the storm bubbling beneath.

Anne gave him a kiss on his forehead and sat down next to him, not saying another word, but holding him as he continued drinking the water.

"Could it be he just didn't approve of the beard?" Edward joked, giving Anne a sidelong glance with a grin.

Anne looked a bit shocked at first, but chuckled after a moment. "Perhaps you should cut it off and try again?"

Edward laughed with his wife and then gave her a peck on the cheek before resting his head on hers. For a moment, they sat in silence together, embracing each other in solidarity and strength.

"This doesn't change anything," Edward said eventually. "The only thing that's changed is how I must now seek out answers from him. He still abandoned me, abandoned Herbert, tried to kill all of us with foolish trials, and more directly. He's not the man I once called my father."

Anne pulled away from Edward and cocked her brow. "You can't mean that you're still going to kill him? Edward… "

Edward opened his mouth, but for a moment, the words wouldn't come. "I… I know in my mind that if I want this family to survive, and if *I* want to survive, he needs to die." He stared at his cup for a moment. "What I'll do when I face him next, I cannot say. But I need to face him."

"Then I'll stand by you when that happens. *We* will," Anne said, placing her hand on Edward's.

Edward smiled, this time more genuinely, and held his wife's hand. They once more sat in silence as Edward finished his water. After it was empty, Edward let go of Anne's hand and rose from the bed.

"Could you gather the senior officers to the quarterdeck cabin? I must tell everyone of my intent."

Anne nodded, gripped Edward's hand for another second, then rose to her feet to leave the Captain's Cabin. Edward watched her as she left, and just before she exited the room, she glanced back his way and smiled at him.

Edward let out a long sigh after Anne left the room, and he lay back in his bed. The weathered boards of Caribbean pine above him suddenly felt unfamiliar and no longer like his home of the last few years. Even the bed appeared lumpier and uncomfortable, though he admitted to himself that the stab wound could be to blame.

He had to get up. He couldn't dwell on his thoughts for long. He could feel the creeping sensation coming at the back of his head, and his legs began to itch.

Edward got up and dressed in his standard attire, save for his tricorn hat. He left that behind, but donned his longcoat, given that night was approaching. Following a visual inspection in a mirror, he left the captain's cabin.

He headed through the gun deck to the ladder leading to the weather deck. On his way, several crewmates tipped their caps and inquired about his health. He gave a few short words telling them not to worry and that he was doing much better now.

On the weather deck, a cold salty wind hit Edward's face and hands on his ascent. The sun was just hitting the horizon, but its warmth had all but vanished.

Edward passed by many a crewmate, some lounging, some testing the myriad rigging ropes and knots, and others conversing about what had happened. Their voices grew silent as Edward approached before quickly returning with concerned tones passed along by well-worn phrases asking of his condition.

After repeating the same words he'd said to the crewmates below deck, he laughed off their concern, ensuring that all knew he was in good spirits despite the opposite being true. After wading his way through the throngs, he entered the quarterdeck cabin—the war room, as they called it.

Inside the war room, a smell of musty tomes and gunpowder wafted his way as he entered. The room had its fair share of old books and maps littering tables and cabinets, lending their essence to the ship's wooden architecture.

At the main table, a large oval table stood beneath an ornate chandelier, and on an equally lavish red velvet carpet covering most of the room. Around the table, Anne, William, and Alexandre were sitting in chairs, as Victoria read one of the books on the port side of the room. Christina, her arms folded, leaned against the starboard side of the cabin next to her brother, Herbert, who sat in his wheelchair facing parallel to the entrance to the room.

Upon hearing the door open, all eyes turned towards Edward, and Herbert turned his wheelchair around to watch Edward enter. Herbert's eyes and expression were inscrutable, a mix of confusion or pity or anger which Edward couldn't pin down. He chose to ignore it.

He walked over to his high-backed chair on the other side of the oval table as the heat of all those eyes bore down on him. After sitting down, his back as straight as he could manage with his wound, he stared down each person in the room for a few seconds before lingering a touch longer on Herbert.

"We missed our golden opportunity in Tortuga. There's no use in dwelling on my mistakes, so let's focus on correcting them," Edward said. He turned to Victoria, who still had the book she was reading in hand. "We go back to the original plan and dismantle Calico Jack's empire. Where was Silver Eyes located, Victoria?"

Victoria opened her mouth to respond, but Christina interrupted her. "We're not to talk of what happened?" she said, her hand half-raised in the air, emphasizing her incredulity. "Are we living in some fantasy where you expect us to ignore that we're talking about your father?"

Edward clenched his teeth. "What of it?" he seethed. "Does it change what he's done to us all? Does it change the undeniable fact that he wants us dead?"

"It changes you. Doesn't it?" Christina asked, her tone of anger shifting to concern. "We all know that part of the reason you went to sea was to find your father. It may not have been the focus, but it was always there. And now you find out that the person who's been pulling your strings, who abused and nearly killed everyone in this room, including your wife, and more, is your father, alive and well? Which also means he truly did abandon you as a child." The room was silent, and even the sound outside the cabin couldn't penetrate the tension left by Christina's plain levelling of the facts. "You mean to say you're still willing to kill him, despite knowing he's your father?" She glanced at the others in the cabin. "Come now," she called. "I cannot be the only one who has doubts."

After another moment of silence, Herbert looked up at Edward. His expression had changed, but Edward still couldn't read him. "I also have questions," he said first, "but, Edward, if you say you're still going to see this through, then I won't doubt you. You've taken us this far, and I'm sure that this only makes you want to confront him even more."

"You can't expect him to kill his own father, can you?" Christina shouted. "Are you mad?"

Herbert turned in his wheelchair to face his sister directly. "Christina, shut it. This is bigger than you or me now." He turned back around, considering the matter done.

Edward stared at Herbert for a moment, trying to read him, but gained nothing. "I plan on seeing this through to the end, as promised."

Herbert paused for a few seconds and then nodded. "That's good enough for me," he said.

Christina clenched her jaw tight enough to bite her tongue, and then stormed out of the room, slamming the door behind her.

Herbert's expression didn't change from before, and he didn't even glance over his shoulder when the door crashed against the frame. "Shall we move on then?"

Edward began the discussion and proposed again that they should move back to the original plan and go after either Silver Eyes or Copper Legs. The only one they had reliable information on was Silver Eyes, so they decided to go after him.

Copper Legs was always on the move, so it was hard to pinpoint her location at any given moment. From their information, she was never too far behind where Calico Jack was, but everyone agreed that it was too dangerous to go back to Tortuga.

After making the decision, they gathered the crew, and Anne proposed a vote. With a few deft words and Edward's reassuring presence, the crew seemed placated and didn't bring up the recent revelations. Edward was happy to not have to broach the subject in further detail over and over and hoped this would be the end of it.

With the vote cast, the crew slept, awaiting tomorrow when they would set sail. Edward, however, was restless.

He tossed and turned in his bed as the gentle rocking of the ship did its best to lull him to sleep, but a nagging feeling pricked the back of his mind. Warning chills travelled down his spine as though he saw a subtle grey cloud out of thousands.

Herbert had acted strange, and Edward had to check on him to alleviate at least one of his worries.

He stepped out of bed and donned some basic clothes. Anne roused with the rustling, her hand reaching out to the empty space where Edward was supposed to be, and she was instantly awake and alert. Her eyes soon found him in the dim light of the moon filtering through the windows in their cabin.

"Edward, are you well?"

Edward smiled, though he wasn't sure if she could see. "All is well, I simply feel I need some of the night air," he said, walking back to the bed and leaning over to give his wife a kiss. "I will be by your side again soon, worry not."

Anne said nothing, and Edward didn't wait for a reply. He rose again and went to open the cabin doors. Before he was through, Anne finally called to him again. "Edward?" she said in a near whisper. Edward stopped and looked her way. "You know I love you, right?"

To Edward, her wording conveyed a message of support as well as a declaration. "Of course," he replied simply. "You know that I, too, love you?"

Anne grinned, reassured by his words. "Of course," she mimicked.

Edward smiled again and closed the door behind him, heading into the gun deck.

On the gun deck, the thirty twenty-two-pound cannons remained secured in place with heavy lines attached to the back of them and to the side of the ship. Nary a crewmate was in sight, save a few men keeping watch and having a lively but quiet conversation about which mate's wife cooked the best pie.

Edward passed by them with a nod of his head when they looked his way. The lot returned his gesture with a "Captain," before returning to the debate over spices and pie preparations.

In the infirmary, Alexandre and Victoria were still awake, speaking in French while preparing what Edward thought was medicine. He steered away from the open door, not wishing to turn into a subject of whatever concoction they were making.

He headed down the ladder into the orlop deck to the crew's quarters, brig, and various other parts of the ship just above the waterline.

No matter where Edward looked, he couldn't find Herbert, nor his wheelchair. He wasn't sleeping, he wasn't conversing with the crewmates awake in the communal area, and none awake were able to give a hint of where he was either.

His worry deepened when he noticed Christina sound asleep. The two were never far apart, and even their sleep patterns often matched each other. Only in times of distress would Edward sometimes find Herbert on the weather deck, unable to sleep, as Edward often was.

Edward rushed up the ladders to the gun deck and then to the weather deck, grabbing one of his coats hanging on a hook before heading into the frigid air above.

On the weather deck, several crewmates were milling about, talking with each other and keeping their eyes open for any suspect activity around the port. They were also in charge of ensuring the ship was ready to leave at dawn before switching with the other crewmates sleeping below.

Edward couldn't see Herbert anywhere, and even a quick

glance in the quarterdeck cabin proved fruitless.

"What'cha lookin' for, Cap'n?" one of the crewmates on watch asked.

"I'm looking for Herbert," he replied. "I need to talk with him about something, but he's not on the ship as far as I can tell."

"Aye. He went inta town not an hour ago, I'd wager. Said he was tryna gather some last-minute supplies. Had a big pack with him as well."

Edward's face must have contorted into a look of massive shock, as the crewmates around began to ask if he was well. Herbert was planning on leaving on his own, Edward was sure of it. Leaving the ship in the middle of the night just before he was to helm it, and with a large pack full of supplies, no less. It was so unlike his usual activities, there could be no other explanation.

"I am well, gentlemen, return to your duties," he said after a moment to regain his composure. "I think I'll find our man Herbert and bring him back. The hour is late, and he needs to be fit and fresh for tomorrow."

With a few final words to the crew on board, Edward stalked towards the town of Puerto Plata with purpose. There were only two places Herbert could be: either somewhere in the port, talking with ship's crews to seek passage, or in an inn for the same purpose. He didn't have much time before they lost Herbert, so he had to work fast.

Edward started by going ship to ship himself, asking the crew still awake if they had seen or talked with a man in a wheelchair. Many affirmed they had spoken with such a man who had been seeking passage to Tortuga, and even offered a fair bit of coin for it too, but was turned away because Tortuga was a lawless pirate haven.

Dammit, Herbert. What are you thinking?

Tracing each ship's account of where Herbert went next, Edward found a man who pointed towards town. One ship's mate said he directed Herbert to a local inn to talk with his captain about passage, as they would be sailing close to Tortuga at dawn.

Edward thanked the crew of the ship and rushed to the inn in question. Thankfully it wasn't far from the port, and he was there in a matter of minutes.

Inside, the inn was a typical, ordinary establishment with a large interior parlour in which guests could eat and drink. At this time of night, there were scant men in the room, with only a few at a table and another couple in the corner, as well as a man Edward assumed was the owner's son tending to them.

Edward quickly found the familiar back of Herbert's wheelchair, a large pack, stuffed to the brim, slung over the back. He was conversing with the sailors at the table, a jovial discussion to be sure, and one in which Edward was sure Herbert had already secured passage, going by the tone.

Edward took a breath to calm himself and take stock of just what he was going to do. He could force Herbert back to the ship, but to what end? If Edward thought about it for but a moment, it was clear Herbert was trying to save him the pain of facing his father, as well as secure revenge. However foolish the plan was, stopping him needed tact.

Wait... What exactly is his plan? Infiltrate Jack's crew to get close to him and assassinate him? Jack never saw his face in Tortuga. He could do it... and then die in the process. But everyone else would be safe...

Edward's thoughts turned to his beloved Anne and the rest of his crew. His father was the cause of many of their miseries, and by asking them to fight, they would be putting their lives on the line to solve his family problems.

Maybe Herbert has it right, Edward thought, a plan forming in his mind.

He walked towards the table, grabbing a chair along the way, and went up beside Herbert to sit down with the rest of the men.

"So," Edward said as he sat down, and all eyes turned towards him, "have you secured us passage to Tortuga, my friend?" Edward looked at Herbert directly for a moment, and after the shock left Herbert's eyes, Edward gave him a single nod, hoping to convey his plan with that subtle gesture and his open question.

After another moment, and a grin, Herbert nodded back. "Ah, yes, gentlemen, I owe you my most sincere apologies. My friend here, Edward Teach, was also seeking passage, if you would have us both. He could help in sailing as well. You will find no more skilled a sailor than he, I can assure you."

Herbert repaid Edward's hope tenfold—the years they had spent together, the talks they had had, the promises they had made to each other. They had built a relationship of trust and awareness of the other. Edward had known there was something off about Herbert's earlier words, and Herbert knew what Edward had wanted to do at that moment.

"As long as he can pay the price, then your friend is more than welcome," the captain replied. "We've no fear of where we've gone before. We hunt whales, and those beasts have nothing on those prancing rogues in Tortuga."

Edward found out the price of passage, paid it, and after some introductions, he did his best to make a good impression on his new host. Though, with the price of passage, Edward doubted it would matter what kind of man he was.

Another hour passed, and the captain and his men finished drinking and eating and left for the ship to prepare.

"And, Captain, as discussed, and as was included in the price we paid, your crew's discretion is most appreciated," Herbert said.

"You've no need to have your boots quivering, young master Blackstad. I'll be sure to let my crew know that we've no stowaways or new crewmates aboard today. Only old mates that've been with us for years," the captain replied with a wink.

Outside the inn, the captain, his crew, and Edward and Herbert all made their way to the harbour. Herbert was slowing down in wheeling himself forward, prompting the captain to turn around and check on him.

"You and your men go on ahead, we'll catch up," Herbert

said. After a moment to give them some room, Herbert shot Edward a nasty look. "I was doing this for you, you bastard. What are you doing?"

"Tch," Edward spat. "I know what you're doing, and you're getting yourself killed, that's what. I'm here to save you from yourself."

Herbert's face softened. "From what just happened, I know that means you won't be taking me back to the *Queen Anne's Revenge*."

"No," Edward affirmed.

"So," Herbert began, then stopped wheeling himself forward for a moment. "Are you sure you can do this? I know I said I before that I wouldn't doubt you, but my sister was right. This changes things."

"It means that I need to do this more than before. My father has done so many wrongs, killed so many of my men. I can't put this burden on the crew any longer."

Herbert had a stern look on his face. "If Roberts were here, he would tell you that your father's sins are not your responsibility and share some scripture to prove his point. You are not your father's keeper."

"That is a nice sentiment, but not practical. If I allow my father to continue what he's doing unimpeded, then that would be a greater sin."

Herbert nodded. "I guess I have no more objections," he said. "We should catch up if we're going to make it. The price I paid was to leave well before dawn."

Edward and Herbert began hurrying towards the harbour. "Just as a curiosity, how do you plan on masking yourself from Calico Jack and his men? They know your face now."

Edward smiled. "I have a plan for that," he replied.

Edward stepped out of the barber-surgeon's room aboard their temporary ship as it was sailing towards Tortuga. His face no longer held the mass of black hair with which he had become known. He was clean-shaven, aside from the nicks here and there left by the barber's blade.

Herbert sized up his captain without his beard and appeared unimpressed. "I don't know if I can get used to this," he said. "You look but a boy now."

"Then that means it'll work," Edward replied.

"I suppose." Herbert stared at the blank canvas that was Edward's chin for a moment more before looking him in the eyes. "Ready?"

Edward nodded. "Ready."

3. COURSE CORRECTION

Unease forced Anne awake. The pre-dawn air and a feeling of unease chilled her to the bone, needling her with her every movement. Edward was not next to her in bed still, and some of his last words echoed in her mind.

"I will be by your side again soon, worry not."

Soon had come and gone as far as Anne was concerned, and something had felt off about the way he was acting. He was more restless these days, but a different kind of restless. Frequently it was one of cold sweats and gasps for air. This had been an inquisitive restlessness. A search for answers.

But what was the question? Anne pondered.

She sat up, cleared her mind, and let the rocking waves guide her breathing. Meditation was an early lesson in mindfulness she had been taught when learning to fight. A healthy mind and a healthy body went hand in hand, but meditation had other uses as well. She reflected on the day's events, tumultuous as they were, to find out what was plaguing her husband so she could trace his steps.

It didn't take her long to come to an answer. "Herbert," she said aloud.

Anne rose from the bed and donned her clothes, and it was then that she noticed Edward's cutlass hanging from a chair, firmly in its scabbard. Its presence wormed more worry into Anne's mind. It meant, if Anne was right, that Edward was confident he was going to be coming back and forgotten it, or that the golden blade was too conspicuous and he couldn't be seen with it.

Anne swore under her breath and rushed to the weather deck. There, the crewmates on the night watch were talking

30

amongst themselves. Their shift would end with the earliest rays of the morning light, which were quickly approaching.

"The captain has gone ashore, has he not?" Anne asked as she approached the men.

The men dropped what they were doing for their quartermaster. "Aye, ma'am, he went not two hours a'fore."

"And Herbert before him, I imagine?" she said, annoyance evident in her tone.

"A... Aye," the crewmate replied, fear breeding hesitation.

"Dad dammit!" she cursed. "Drop everything you're doing and search the harbour for them. Ask every ship if they took notice of a man in a wheelchair and a fearsome man with a black beard."

"Ma'am?" the crewmate asked.

Anne folded her arms. "Herbert and the captain are about to abscond to pursue Calico Jack on their own. We haven't much time if we mean to stop the fools before they leave the harbour," she explained. "Now go!"

The crewmates on deck hopped to their feet and rushed off the gangplank to the harbour. They quickly split up and began asking the men milling about preparing to leave for their captain and helmsman.

Anne gazed upon the harbour to both sides of the *Queen Anne's Revenge*. Ships dotted the angled harbour, each with crews preparing to leave, each of them a merchant or trading vessel and each, unlike a pirate ship, needing to be on the move early to ensure they met their predetermined shipping times and made the money they were promised.

Anne's faculty of memory was a work in progress. She didn't have perfect clarity that Alexandre seemed to possess or the recall that Christina had built up over time, but she was close. After a few minutes, she was confident that at least two ships had already left the harbour. She scanned the horizon but couldn't see any others. If Edward and Herbert had been on one of those ships, there was no chance of finding exactly where they were going.

Blackbeard's Family

Anne soon received her answer by the hand of an errand boy and in the form of a letter addressed to her.

Dearest Anne,

With the recent revelations, I can no longer in good conscience allow the crew to take part in this family matter. Herbert and I plan to end this ourselves. When you hear the news of our enemy's passing, come to his former base of operations. It will be safe then.

You'll be safe then.

I love you,

Edward

Anne crumpled the paper and tossed it in the ocean with a huff. The errand boy, waiting to see if Anne wanted to send a letter herself, looked afraid and confused. She handed him a coin and sent him on his way.

She walked over to the edge of the ship, looking over the port side and up and down the harbour. Her gaze eventually caught one of the crewmates searching for Edward, and after a moment, their eyes met, and he stopped in his tracks. She motioned a circle in the air, telling the crewmate to gather the others and return to the ship. He nodded, letting her know he understood before going about his task.

She turned around and rested on the port railing. She closed her eyes and tilted her head back, letting the sea breeze flow over her.

"What now?" she muttered aloud.

There was only one choice that didn't involve them rushing into an obvious trap—the only one that could help before heading to Nassau, and possibly to help Edward as well.

"On to Los Huecos then."

"This is foolish!" Christina shouted, accentuated by a slam of her fist on the war room's ornate table. "My brother's obviously going to Nassau to kill Edward's fa—" Christina paused, the word hanging on her tongue like a curse she dared not utter. "To kill Calico Jack," she finished.

"And what if they plan on heading to Tortuga instead?" Anne countered. "What if both of us are wrong, and we step into enemy territory no closer to recovering Edward and Herbert?" Her tone held a hint of the anger Christina was displaying openly, betraying her genuine emotions like a grey cloud on the horizon. Anne's ire was there, just as the approaching storm, but she had control over it, unlike her junior.

Christina barreled onward, not pausing to think over her words. "Then at least we can finish the job in their stead." She reeled back as soon as the words left her mouth, as though she knew it was a fool's errand, but she kept going to save face. "It's no different if we head to Los Huecos. There we face certain danger in attacking Silver Eyes, and have no clue if that's where Edward and Herbert are heading."

Anne levelled her simmering gaze on Christina, the gouging look of royalty that forces the haughty to kneel lest they wish to be impaled. "Then you are more a fool than I took you for," she said flatly, letting her eyes do the talking. "Sit down," she added softly, but the words fell with the thunder of a command in the still air of the room.

Christina locked up for but a moment, her expression souring in the face of Anne's dangerous gaze and her own foolish comment, and then sat down in her seat with a thud.

"We head to Los Huecos not just for the off chance it is one of the three spots Edward and Herbert could be going, but because it's the safest option we have. Nassau is Calico Jack's base; we have no support there, not in numbers or knowledge." Anne kept her gaze on Christina, though she was slumped in her chair. "Thanks to Victoria," she said with a wave in her direction, "we know the island's original inhabitants have been forced under Calico Jack's thumb. We can use that to our advantage. The best that could happen is we help Edward and Herbert in whatever it is they're trying to do next and join up with them there. The worst is that we keep Calico Jack's allies occupied for them."

Christina had crossed her arms as though she were protecting herself from Anne's attacks. Her face bloomed the flushed look of an embarrassed youth.

Anne let out a sigh and relaxed in the high-backed chair Edward usually sat in. "I won't lie to you," she began, her tone softening as though she'd just remembered she was talking to a young woman, not an adult, "Edward and Herbert are most likely trying to assassinate Calico Jack." She let the words hang, like a silent prayer for the plan to succeed, as she eyed those in the room—from Alexandre to Victoria, and over to William before finally resting back on Christina. "If we go to Tortuga, we die. If we go to Nassau, we die."

Christina shuffled in her seat a bit before grinding out, "I know, Dad dammit. You don't have to rake me over the coals for it." After the shuffle, she absent-mindedly grabbed the wooden rose around her neck, a sure sign to Anne, and possibly most in the room, that she was agitated.

The rose, so delicate in its craftsmanship, was a memento from Ochi, Nassir's son, who had passed in a battle years ago and caused a rift between Nassir and Edward. Anne took the remembrance of that time as a clear sign that she couldn't allow what happened then to happen now between her and Christina. The crew needed unity now more than ever.

"You're right, I don't," Anne replied. "But I do need you on my side. I can't manage this crew without a helmsman."

It took a moment for Christina to notice the unasked question. When she did, she looked up at Anne, then over at William, as though she were wondering why her and not him.

Anne shrugged. "William will be busy as quartermaster when I take on the role of captain until Edward returns. And while I know a bit of reading clouds and steering the ship, I'm no match for you or your brother." Anne spun a convincing lie with just the right amount of frustration filtering into her voice to match the audience's perceptions of her.

The truth was that Christina was still wet behind the ears and needed practice without her brother there for guidance. She was like a rider taking the reins for the first time. At first, if the horse is ill-tempered or not used to the rider's voice or touch, a familiar hand can prove useful. If the rider isn't left alone, before long, that familiar hand turns into a crutch. Christina needed to take the reins alone to gain the confidence necessary to tame the beast that was the *Queen Anne's Revenge*.

The lie worked, and Christina's face lit up with joy as a smile spread across it. "I'll do it!" she said, brimming with bravado. "I'll be your helmsman!"

4. CAPTAIN'S ORDERS

Over the few days' travel from Puerto Plata to Tortuga, Edward and Herbert ingratiated themselves with the crew of whalers and sailors on the *Hunter* through demanding work and a good share of stories.

Their tales of hollowed island puzzles, savage natives ready to sacrifice an outsider, and run-ins with a Spanish galleon and pirates took on a note of tall tales in the ears of the humble, honest men aboard their host vessel. They listened attentively as Edward and Herbert went back and forth, telling their version of events, laughing as the two men bickered over the finer details, and all the while shaking their heads at the foolishness of it all.

It made a difference that Edward and Herbert both neglected to mention they were captain and helmsman. They also didn't correct the men's thought that they had been travellers aboard a different ship in each tale.

The men laughed all the harder when one of their own snidely remarked that the two were bad luck if it were all true, and jested that if any hint of a storm showed they should be cast into the ocean to save themselves the trouble.

The laughing stopped when Edward removed his sweat-soaked shirt in the middle of travel one day, showing off his multitude of scars across his large barrel of a chest and muscular back. That night, the attentive audience was a bit quieter when Edward told of a wounded man who sniffed a mysterious poison that gave him speed and strength beyond that of an average man.

During the travel, Edward's sudden shift from being a captain of over a hundred souls to a lowly deckhand jarred him in an at first confusing but ultimately relaxing way. Not having responsibility over dozens of men at a time, juggling being a kind yet firm measure of authority, lifted a weight from his shoulders he hadn't known was there.

At the same time, he had to catch himself several times before he chastised his new crewmates and issued orders beyond his station. Each time it was minor, but he had to bite his tongue lest he sour the relationship between the men giving him passage and they did indeed throw him and Herbert overboard.

Herbert, it seemed, enjoyed the lack of responsibility even more than Edward, and for a good reason, as the crew expected exactly nothing of him. A few gave him dark looks the first day when he got in the way of more than a few men milling about tending to ship's duties, only holding back from swearing and smacking him because he'd paid his way. After warming to the duo, it turned to simply ignoring him as he stared off at nothing on the horizon.

Edward mused to himself that he wasn't the only one with a hidden weight that needed lifting.

It also took Edward a goodly amount of time to adjust to taking orders. More than a few times, the captain and first mate of the *Hunter* had to repeat orders to him, even shouting his fake name, Teach, louder for him to come to his senses.

It was a valuable lesson and one he was glad he learned now on a ship they'd paid passage for rather than when aboard an enemy ship where their only protection would be their false identities.

When they arrived in Tortuga, it was with a warm cup of whiskey and a smile and a wave from each of the ship's crew. Edward was glad for the time in many ways, as soon, he suspected, there would be no smiles to spare.

"There it is," Herbert commented delightedly.

Edward's gaze followed Herbert's outstretched hand as he pointed towards a ship stationed in the harbour. It flew the familiar flag of one of Calico Jack's crew, a white, symmetrical skull with crossed swords underneath it, but the burnished copper trim around the edges of it denoted that it was for one of his subordinates. The flag flapped towards the two men as though it were a supple young lady beckoning them closer, but Edward knew the lady to be a siren in disguise, and so he steeled his mind appropriately.

"Herbert, whatever happens next, don't question me. Understood?"

Herbert looked over to Edward with a confused, half-cocked expression. Before he could ask Edward what he meant, Edward spoke again.

"I need you to promise me first, then I'll tell you what I plan to do. I don't want to have to order you as your captain, but I will."

Herbert glanced back at the flag, then down briefly to the dock, his chin soon setting as hard as a lock. He gave Edward a nod and said, "Understood."

"From what we've seen from Calico Jack's crew, and from what you've told me, they value strength above all else."

Herbert stroked his chin. "That is true. Before Cache-Hand could become part of their crew, he had to capture a Spanish galleon. A near-impossible feat. It makes one wonder what strange acts the others had to do to prove themselves to Mad Jack."

Edward grimaced at the casual mention of his former enemy, the pain of each inflicted wound returning to him, along with memories of dead crewmates' warm blood on his hands and the sick smell of death in his nose. A thousand thoughts like silent needles stabbed his skin and mind, and his hand and heart began to shake. He reached inside his breast pocket with laboured movement, grabbing the flask held there, and hastily took a large drink from it.

Herbert was at a loss for words as he watched his captain

drink. After a moment, he sputtered out a meek, "Sorry."

Edward forced a smile just as laboured as his hand's moving, then chuckled. "You have nothing to apologize for. That was for what's about to happen," Edward said before taking another drink. He then turned to face his friend and crewmate directly. "I'll be blunt," Edward began, "Calico Jack's crew doesn't like cripples. If we both want on that ship, we need to prove to them you're not going to be a burden. We can't expect them to allow you passage with some coin, and they will have a helmsman currently, so they have no need of another."

"So, what do you propose?" Herbert asked.

"We ask them what we need to do to be a part of their crew, and whatever they ask for, I'll do the work of two men." Edward pointed towards himself with his thumb, full of the confidence that comes partly from being a foolhardy young man, and partly from frequent imbibements.

Thinking the matter settled, Edward headed towards the ship. "That's not a very good plan," Herbert shouted after him.

"Have you a better one?" Edward replied over his shoulder as Herbert rolled up next to him.

"No, I suppose I don't," he replied with the sulky tone of a chided child.

Edward leaned a bit closer to Herbert, trying to talk secretly over the din of the surrounding town and harbour. "Also, I think it best if we were brothers for this. More reason for us to stay together than just being friends. We'll be the Blackstads, travelling and trying to find work as sailors but not finding luck."

Herbert touched his nose and grinned. "I see, brother. So... why are we trying to join so obvious a pirate ship?"

"Better a wolf than a sheep," he replied with a shrug.

"I suppose that's as good a reason as any."

Edward and Herbert passed by many rough-looking sailors preparing to leave in the early morning. The hour was late, and these were not merchants who lived by the hours of a well-wound clock but were pirates who struck in the mid-day when ships aplenty were found in the vast and plentiful trade routes along the Caribbean Sea.

However, Edward was interested to see there were more than a few men like those they had been with earlier, a few whaling ships looking for hardened men who weren't afraid to face down a beast half the size of the ship they were about to travel on. A few others were merchants Edward suspected served as middlemen to ill-gotten gains, closer to pirates than merchants, but with a foot firmly in the trade business. They had gained the respect of the pirates who frequented these parts, whether through might or connections Edward could not tell.

Upon reaching the pirate's ship, the mates bringing cargo aboard gave them wary glances. All of them were battle-hardened; the faint grey-white of faded scars and the dark lines of sliced and reformed skin protruded and poked out from behind woollen longshirts and beneath messy cleft hair. More than a few had tattoos blackening part of their necks or faces, a brand of their well-worn travels for some, and, from his dark complexion, a tribal honorific for another. Edward read the words "Hold Fast" across one man's knuckles, saw constellation across the back of another's hand, and on the dark-complexioned man were segmented lines in a stunning wave-like pattern across half his face.

Edward leaned down slightly and whispered to Herbert. "You still have those hidden implements in your chair, yes?"

Herbert nodded. "Aye, along with a few other surprises our friend Nassir made for me. I'm never too far from something with which to defend myself."

Herbert spoke of the *Queen Anne's Revenge's* shipwright, who doubled as a wheelchair expert when it came to Herbert's condition. The most recent addition was hidden compartments only he could reach with weapons at the ready should Herbert need them, and apparently that wasn't all.

"Good," Edward said. "We may have use for them."

Edward and Herbert continued their advance to the gangplank of the ship. It was a two-masted light brigantine with a single deck, and Edward estimated about thirty or so cannons aboard. It would be fast and efficient in any fight, and with a skilled commander it might even give the *Queen Anne's Revenge* a challenge. Emblazoned in large white letters on the side was the name of the ship, *Black Blood*, a singular contrast with the words written as they were neither black nor red, but it got the point across. The ship and the men aboard it were not to be trifled with.

"What d'ye want?" a gruff man asked as Edward and Herbert approached. He held his hand aloft in front of him, stopping the men.

The man wasn't tall but built like a rough sailor used to the harsh rigours of a ship at sea with all the right callouses in all the wrong spots. He also had the marks of battle across his face, arms, and no doubt all over his body. His face looked a weathered mess of white scars, pocks from some childhood condition, and broken and healed bones. He couldn't have been that much older than Edward, perhaps in his thirties, but he looked much older.

"We're looking for work and heard you were looking for a few good men to join you on the seas," Edward replied.

The man spat on the pier. The mucous glob stayed mostly intact as it splayed on the grubby wooden planks. Edward and Herbert's gaze followed the spit and the motion of the man's head as he looked back on them. "That's a lie," he said flatly. "No one 'ere would'a told ye ta try joinin' us, less they want ye dead."

Edward noticed the man's hand lower and rest on his hip, near the hilt of his cutlass. He could feel the air around him thicken with eyes watching him more intently now.

Edward inched his own hand to his hip and felt nothing. He remembered he was unarmed, his golden cutlass left behind because he had forgotten it.

A bead of sweat formed on his forehead and rolled down the side of his cheek.

"Nigel, fuck off with that, would ye?" a gruff woman's voice called from the deck.

"But ma'am, we best be leavin' soon if'n we're gonna catch the bastard what done in Jeremiah."

The owner of the voice strode to the port side of the deck and leaned on the railing, her right arm resting lazily across it while her left held steady on her hip. The look was casual, but Edward saw a coiled snake ready to strike at a moment's notice. She could jump over the railing to the deck, or just as quickly pull a knife from behind her, and any number of things in between.

"He's not going anywhere a few minutes won't change. Bring them aboard," the woman said before eyeing Edward and Herbert up and down. "If you're able," she added before casting a sidelong glance at Herbert's chair and walking away from the railing.

The man guarding the gangplank stepped aside, letting Edward and Herbert board. Herbert went first, and Edward helped push him up the steep incline and force his wheelchair over the lip of the deck. He landed on the sole with a loud snap of wood on wood, gaining the attention of the other crewmates who had been paying them no heed until then.

Now on deck, Edward was able to get a better look at the woman who appeared to be in charge—Grace 'Copper Legs' O'Malley, by Edward's estimation.

Her coal-red hair was cropped short and, if not for her attractive features, would have made her look more a boy than a woman. Her body was voluptuous and well figured, with plenty of meat on her bones and quite different from the women on his ship, but from what Edward could tell, it was all muscle.

"My, my, you are a big one, aren't ye?" she said as she eyed Edward up and down, her voice drawn out with a hint of Gaelic on the edges. Her accent was faint, as though weathered away after years away from home. The barest hint remained like single boulder on a sandy beach.

She walked around Edward, poring over him, studying his

features beneath his loose clothes. Though she was far shorter than he, and shorter than most of the men aboard, her gaze made Edward feel exposed. A woman he should be wary of was measuring him against some unknown weights.

Edward clenched his jaw and returned the gaze. He needed to project strength, match her, and beat her at her own game to impress her. He needed her to need him more than how little she would feel she needed Herbert. And so, he scrutinized her in return.

She was built like the northern mothers he had heard about from other sailors telling stories—the mothers who could match the men in feats of strength and could cook you dinner after breaking your arm in an arm-wrestling match. He had thought they were jovial jesting meant as a tall tale of boasting, or a jibe when the sailor lost a match but claimed his mother could whup the other sailor handily. Edward now suspected they weren't just stories.

Most striking was her legs, or that which covered her legs. She had on solid copper greaves, which covered her feet, calves, and knees, stopping just short of her thighs. Edward could see small indents and holes in symmetrical vertical lines on either side of the front of the armour, but they didn't look like bullet holes from battle, they looked to be there by design. What design they served, Edward could not even guess.

The medieval armour seemed out of place on a wood-and-rope-and-canvas-laden ship, but not so out of place on her, perhaps. Her hair nearly matched the shade of the greaves, and she walked in them with no sign of hindrance.

He noticed her looking straight at him, and so he ended his inspection and returned her steely gaze.

After a moment, O'Malley nodded appreciatively. "I'll have to test you further, but for now, I think you'd make a good addition to our crew. You've obviously been hardened in battle, and you've got a sailor's calluses." She turned a sidelong look over to Herbert. "You, however, need to leave. We can't have you on our crew."

Just as Edward had predicted, but without the preamble given to him. No inquisitive inspection, no scrutinizing of his features, only a dismissal. Edward had known this would be difficult, but he hadn't thought it would be *this* difficult.

"This man is my brother. Wherever I go, he goes."

"We don't have cripples on our ship," she replied curtly. "They slow us down." She let out a sigh. "Off my ship then, the both of you. No more wasting my time."

With a wave of her hand, some of the crew moved forward, pressing Edward and Herbert back to the gangplank.

"My brother has the best eyes you've seen. He's also the best man at the helm you could ever want."

"I already have a helmsman," the captain replied as she walked away. Then she glanced over her shoulder. "Besides, I don't like the look of him. All I've seen from his eyes are hatred, he's like a cornered dog ready to strike."

Edward flashed Herbert a glance and noticed she was right. Herbert had the same look in his eyes he'd had when they'd faced off against Gregory Dunn, one of Calico Jack's other crewmates, and a crewmate Herbert had personally known.

Thinking on his feet as the crew pressed in on them further, Edward created a convenient excuse. "How can you blame him? Five of your crewmates have had their weapons at the ready from the moment we stepped onto the deck."

This stopped the captain in her tracks for a moment, and, as though they had eyes in the back of their heads, the crewmates pushing them off the ship stopped as well.

"There were six, Ed," Herbert chimed in. "You missed the one with his hand on the hilt of a cutlass hidden by the fife rail." Herbert pointed to a man standing half behind the mainmast.

Edward followed the finger to the man, and with the too-casual, too-slow movement of a man caught in the act, the crewmate moved his hand from where it had rested to the top of the fife rail.

Edward looked over at O'Malley again, and she too had followed Herbert's pointed finger to the crewmate whose hands had been hidden from their view. When she turned her gaze back to Herbert, it was with a bit more scrutiny than before. Just a bit.

This was the opening that Edward needed. If he just pushed a bit more... "If you won't accept my brother as a crewmate, then accept him as a passenger. I'll do the work of two crewmates to make up for it." The words would have come out as pleading from any other man, but coming from Edward, they were a statement of fact.

O'Malley spat. "You'd have to work as hard as three men for all the trouble it'll be worth to bring him along." There was a pause as she glanced at the floorboards of the ship for a moment. Edward let her her peace as she thought it over. The tension in the air lifted as she considered. After another moment passed, she looked straight into Edward's eyes. "If you can pass our tests, you and your brother may join. For the moment."

Edward and Herbert glanced at each other, relief in their eyes but not reflected in their faces. This was just a step back on the plank, a small step to their final goal.

"I'm ready," Edward said, despite not knowing what was going to happen next.

O'Malley eyed Edward skeptically. "Nigel, Tiege, Grant, get yer asses over here."

The man who had first accosted them when they'd tried to board stepped closer, along with two other men of equal stature and similarly weathered faces. All established sailors, all established fighters. All three were not ones Edward wanted to be facing in a fight, especially all at once. Especially in a test he needed to pass.

"Yes, ma'am?" Nigel asked, though to Edward it felt as though they all knew what was coming next.

Edward ignored the next words from the captain of the *Black Blood* and instead chose to take that time to steady his breathing and center himself. He breathed in through his nose the full, unfettered sea air tainted with hints of the vile town and odorous men around him. The smell threatened to break the calm he was forcing onto himself, but he pressed forward, and his heartbeat steadied.

Upon opening his eyes, the three men had surrounded him, the weight of their hard, blood-hungry eyes pressing on him from all sides. Edward focussed his senses on his immediate surroundings, filtering out the noises of gulls squawking above, of the wind rustling the trees and myriad sails along the harbour, of the shouting men and clamour of boots and wood knocking about. He filtered it all out just as he had been trained until it was just him and the three men.

Edward felt a shift behind him, and he stepped aside. One of the crewmates of the *Black Blood* stumbled past him, his balance shattered with a too-confident punch. Edward spun around and punched the staggered man in the back of the neck. The force, multiplied by Edward winding up as well as punching down due to his superior height, sent the man crashing to the floor of the deck. His chin hit the wood with a loud crack, and he lay there slack and unconscious.

Edward faced the other two men, who at first were shocked, then snarled in anger at their crewmate so quickly dispatched. Before they could rush Edward, O'Malley stopped them with a shout. They backed up a pace or two; one man calmed a bit with O'Malley's order, but the other, Nigel, kept the snarl of anger plastered on his face. The more time passed, the angrier he seemed to get.

O'Malley walked over to the unconscious crewmate, her greaves clanking slightly as she nudged the man with her foot. She frowned.

"Impressive," she commented. "I suppose we don't need to see how well you fight if you can do that with one punch." She levelled her gaze at Edward. "Now I want to know how well you follow orders." O'Malley walked back behind Nigel and the other crewmate still conscious. "You're going to let these two fight you, and you will not fight back under any circumstances. I don't even want to see you block any of their punches. Hear me?"

Nigel's snarl turned into a sneer of glee at the prospect. Edward didn't like that look, nor what it meant.

"And what is this to prove, exactly?"

"As I said, it will show that you can take orders," she replied, her Gaelic hints making the words more sinister in their intention. "If I'm to be your captain, I need to know you will do what I say. I can't tell you how many come aboard, wide-eyed and ready to please, only to balk at taking orders from a woman. If I must beat it out of you now, all the better."

O'Malley's smile was even more sinister than Nigel's, and Edward started regretting their leaving the *Queen Anne's Revenge* already. He glanced over to Herbert, who was watching the scene with a mix of horror and coiled rage blanching his face. Edward guessed he was regretting a few things as well.

But they couldn't back down now.

"I won't be much use if I'm dead or have a broken bone," Edward said flatly. He knew there was no way out of this, but he had to try.

O'Malley grinned. "Don't worry yer pretty little head on that, son. The boys'll make sure not to damage the goods. Ain't that right, boys?"

"Yes, ma'am!" the two replied without looking back at their captain.

Edward took a deep breath and prepared for the onslaught.

5. THEY DON'T BOTHER US NONE

The sun was just past high noon when they caught sight of land on the horizon. The small speck of black jutting out on the horizon was still too far off to recognize colours, but was unmistakably a piece of earth in the middle of the vast ocean—too irregular and too small to be a storm, and, should Christina's navigation prove accurate, just in line with their calculations based on their maps and Victoria's approximations of where the island was located.

Anne, through her lookout on the crow's nest, coupled with a spyglass built into the wooden apparatus, was able to see the point of land well before her companions on deck. Unless particularly well endowed with vision above that of a normal man, they wouldn't be able to tell the land was there for some time yet.

"Land spotted," she shouted to Christina below. "Half point to port."

Christina nodded and repeated the order in a carrying voice she had been practicing for days. "Half point to port, aye Captain!"

The loud boom, almost unnatural coming from Christina's mouth, half-woke the wolf, Tala, lying underneath a nearby table. Anne could just make out the coppery-furred muzzle of the creature opening in a yawn as it looked around for a moment, and then, satisfied there was nothing of note occurring, went back to sleep.

Anne watched Christina turn the giant wheel of the helm clockwise, and the unseen rudder shifted with it. Slowly and imperceptibly, the ship drifted to port for a brief few seconds before Christina turned the wheel counterclockwise, and the ship levelled out at the new heading.

Christina, one hand holding the wheel steady, pored over a few instruments to double-check the heading, but Anne already knew her movements were correct. Christina was steadily treating the helm as an extension of herself, intuitively recognizing the shifting of the ship with each bob of the waves. She only needed the instruments for more significant changes or double-checking that the movement she saw and felt was correct.

Anne recalled a time during one of the trials left by the ship's previous owner, Benjamin Hornigold—whom they now knew to be Edward's father—where Christina had been able to navigate an ever-shifting maze. She had somehow managed to find her way through and back from the labyrinth by memorizing the changes and returning the way she had come. At the time, it had seemed nearly impossible, but Christina's mind and memory were unparalleled, and any other crewmate, even Anne herself, probably wouldn't have been able to manage the task.

That memory was a part of her; working out the way the ship moved, how it pitched and rolled, and how her movements of the wheel translated to movements of the ship. As she gained confidence, and provided that the crew followed orders, Anne didn't doubt that Christina could forgo using those instruments except in the direst of circumstances. The ship would become an extension of herself, like a sword to a fighter, until without thought she could wield it as though it were her own arm.

Anne stopped staring at Christina, then took one last look at the approaching land. Their course was righted, and if Victoria's information was correct, they would make landfall on the eastern side of the island farthest from the town Silver Eyes made his base in.

"Relief," Anne called out. William looked up to Anne, then ordered a crewmate up to the crow's nest.

Anne jumped over the side of the railing keeping her secure

in the nest, and with deft hands trained over the years, she climbed down the rope ladders secured in a chaotic pattern from the mast to the deck. Her fingers were no longer the dainty fingers of a cultured woman; they were the rough fingers of a sailor sanded and scoured by handling rough rope, rough work, and the occasional rough rogue.

She landed with a thump on the quarterdeck and walked over to Christina. The noise and jolt brought Anne a glance from Christina and the cautious animal underneath the table nearby. The younger woman's strawberry blond hair fanned out in a great wave across her back despite the tie holding it in at the base of her neck. As Anne came closer, she noticed that the wooden rose Christina typically wore around her neck was what kept her hair in place now.

She touched the rose, gently caressing the beautiful carving of Caribbean pine, the same as the *Queen Anne's Revenge*'s deck. As she did, Christina glanced over her shoulder and smiled, though tinged with sadness.

Christina pivoted on her heels, and the hair fell from Anne's hand. Christina then pulled her unruly hair over her shoulder in front of her, closer to her heart. "It looks nice on you," Anne said, smiling widely.

Christina looked at the rose as best she could as she ran her fingers through the wind-swept strands of her hair. "Thank you." She returned the smile, but it was the same marred smile as before. Then, after a reflective moment, her eyes focused on Anne's hip, and she pointed to the cutlass at Anne's side. "That looks nice on you as well," she said with a more genuine grin curling up at the corners.

Anne followed the finger to the golden cutlass, Edward's cutlass, resting on her hip in its sheath. She appreciated the unique steel at her side. It became a comfort against the anxious energy creeping up from her gut.

"A shame to waste a good weapon by saving it for the fool of a man who left it behind."

The two women chuckled at the barb for a moment, and

Christina seemed back to her usual self. The worry creasing her forehead relaxed a touch, and she let out a large breath. She turned away from Anne and looked back to the horizon. "What do you think we'll find there?" Christina nodded her chin towards the open ocean.

Anne stepped forward and placed one hand on the quarterdeck railing just in front of the wheel, and another on the cutlass at her side. "Victoria said that the island is a major resource for Nassau, providing crops and other supplies to the pirate haven. I can't imagine the relationship is mutually beneficial, so perhaps we can convince the people around the island to join us."

Christina nodded. "And if we can't?"

Anne gave Christina a sidelong glance for a moment and then turned back to the speck of black on the horizon. "Then we burn it and salt the earth."

Christina's jaw went slack for a moment. "Remind me not to become your enemy."

Anne chuckled. "I get it from my parents."

She let out a long sigh, turned around, and leaned against the quarterdeck railing with her arms crossed in front of her chest. "My father, though his station is mostly a formality, wanted to avoid being seen as weak, and pursued an education in war as well as fitness for combat. He doesn't generally take an active role in battles... except in that one instance..."

"Except in that one instance," Christina repeated, no doubt recalling the incident that had seen Edward eventually imprisoned so long ago.

"And," Anne continued, "he ensured that interest was passed on to his children."

Christina's brow raised. "Children? You have siblings?"

"Had," Anne corrected. "They passed from sickness. Some survived longer than others, but I outlived them all." Anne tried her best to keep her composure, but her last few words came out ragged, stilted by remembrance. Childhood images, marred by age and fear, of so many siblings taken by disease, miscarriage, and stillbirth flashed in her mind unbidden. The thought of their rictus bodies scarred by sickness or the simple act of passing the womb already broken sent a shiver down her spine even now.

"I'm sorry," Christina said after a moment of Anne's quiet contemplation. "I shouldn't have asked."

Anne raised her head, noticed tears forming in her eyes, and wiped them away before shaking her head. "No, no, it's fine. I've just not thought about them in... quite some time." Before she went into her contemplation again without thought, Anne got up from the railing and wrapped an arm around Christina. "Besides, I have a new sister right here... I hope."

Christina blushed and looked away from Anne despite leaning closer into her embrace. "You don't need to say it aloud, you know." Her voice was barely a whisper.

"And then how will I see such a cute embarrassed face?" Anne replied, a huge smirk tugging at her cheeks.

Christina pushed her hip against Anne's, forcing her away. "Back to the crow's nest with you!" she shouted angrily, but she couldn't rid herself of the smile on her face.

"All right, all right, I'll leave you alone for now... sister," Anne said over her shoulder as she went down to the weather deck.

Transitioning from the quarterdeck, meant for officers and guests, to the bustle of the main deck would have been jarring to Anne years ago. She had been on ships when she was a child but had stayed sequestered far away from the sweat-soaked, rough, sea-hardy sailors. Now she was one of them, and a pirate no less. She forced herself to acclimate, lest she fall behind.

The men around her, kept busy by William's guidance, were milling about securing rigging, cleaning the deck or weapons, and practicing drills for combat. The wind was favourable, so the work was lax, but still, the signs of labour were there.

The cleaning was hard work, and sweat slicked many a brow and cast shadows on the backs of the rough cotton shirts that stuck to the men's backs. Hot breath over hotter sea air seemed to create its own environment aboard the ship, leaving it muggy and thick, but thankfully the wind cut through it. If Anne were below deck, it would be worse, but it was never as bad as some of the land-based establishments favoured by the same sailors. With no wind to carry the filth away, it would settle until layer after layer made breathing difficult.

At the far end of the ship, around the foremast, Anne could see many crewmates practicing with weapons and some holding contests of strength. Pukuh, the one-armed Mayan warrior prince, was doing push-ups as a crowd cheered him on. Three other crewmates—and maybe a fourth; it was difficult for Anne to see against all the rigging and bundle of bodies in the way—were also doing push-ups with Pukuh, but they all had the advantage of two arms.

One by one, sweat dripping to the deck, the other crewmates collapsed to the sole with a thump and a loud gasp for air, until it was only Pukuh left. The crewmates cheering them on exclaimed loudly for the victor of the contest but cut short as Pukuh kept going. Anne could see him straining, his one arm bulging with the effort and his whole body moving as he worked his way up and down. She knew how difficult it was to do one-arm push-ups, but he was as prideful as he was fierce. As his final act of pride to the astonished onlookers, Pukuh grinned at the top of his stride, then curled four of his fingers in, leaving only one left to hold him up. Through shaking extremities, Pukuh managed that one last push-up and then slumped to the deck.

The few in the crowd, as well as some who had gathered at the last moment by the cheers and the silence, erupted in cries of compliment, congratulations, and disbelief. They picked Pukuh up off the deck, slapping him across the back and pushing him around in displays of revered brotherhood. Through the sweat and exhaustion, Pukuh smiled slyly from the praise, saying words Anne could only guess from where she was. After it was over, the men went back to their drills, while some others continued the contest, though with far fewer onlookers.

Some of the crew were sitting in groups talking with fervour and exclamations with broad gestures, and others were singing along with Jack as he played a tune on his fiddle. It was a good day when he brought out the fiddle. When the man brought out his drum, it meant a storm was approaching, or a battle was close. The fiddle meant lively jigs and jaunty tunes about a sailor and a bar wench, or a sailor and a talking fish, or a sailor and most anything one could think of. Anne didn't know where this well of music came from for Jack to draw from, or if he simply plucked the words from the air as he did the strings of the fiddle, but the man was talented. A fiddle day was a slow day, but an enjoyable one.

Jack noticed Anne watching, and he had another crewmate of less experience take his place playing music. The other crewmates feigned disappointment and the man taking over lightly smacked and kicked the naysayers with a smile on his face before he began playing.

"Mr. Christian," Anne said with a slight bow.

Jack chuckled and pointed at Anne as he approached, then stopped and did a flourish. "Miss Anne," he replied with a posh, mocking drawl so unlike his north-western.

"To what do I owe this pleasure?" she asked.

Jack walked with her over to the port, a bit away from the rest of the crew. "I merely wished to inquire about your wellbeing."

Anne smiled. "I am well and thank you for asking."

Jack nodded, his expression genial, but nonplussed. He leaned in and lowered his volume. "Some in the crew express concern over Edward's sudden departure. You've done well in painting Edward and Herbert as the silent assassins while we create a distraction for them, but I know there is more to this." He looked Anne straight in the eye, his face deadly serious. "The late, sleepless nights, the imbibements when he thinks none are looking, the irritability, and now this?" Jack tilted his head as he frowned. "Edward's been treading water for a spell, and now he disappears? I've been down that road before. I may have even set some of the stones down for its foundation."

Anne looked away from Jack's gaze for a moment, out to sea. She recalled Jack's story about losing his family to a jealous naval admiral, George Rooke, and his struggles with the drink, and the gambling. He had been able to overcome it somehow.

She knew what had been happening to Edward too. She tried to talk with him about it, but he wouldn't open himself to her. And now, he found his father alive and trying to kill him? It would be enough to drive anyone mad.

After a long silence, she asked, "How did you manage it?"

"Aye, there's the rub, miss. I still am." Jack joined Anne in facing the sea and leaned his arms on the railing. "Every day, at some point in the day, I want it. Most times, it's the smell, and you can't avoid that here by any means," Jack said with a dark laugh. "But, some days, it could be nothing and just like that," he said, snapping his finger, "the worm's in you and not letting go." Jack was silent for a moment as he moved around and began gripping the railing. "The only thing that keeps me going is knowing that I have a family here. That I didn't lose mine back then, I just gained a few new members now." Jack glanced at Anne, his eyes shining. "I can't tell you what Edward needs to get by in the day, but I know he needs us, and he needs you."

Anne took a long, measured breath, making sure not to let her emotion show. She wanted to tell him everything at that moment. She wanted to say to him that Edward had run off on his own with no consultation. She wanted to tell him that she's just trying to keep things held together, wanted to scream it, but she couldn't. She needed to be resilient, and they needed to present a unified front to the crew. If they knew the truth, she wasn't sure she could keep the crew together.

She looked at Jack Christian once more. He was as loyal as they came, a faithful friend of Edward's and smarter than his appearance would lead one to believe. He would understand

and could provide a voice of reason to the crew where she could not.

"Mr. Christian, I will not lie to you. We may be heading into a battle soon, and we cannot have the crew worrying over Edward and his decision. I hope you can understand and help the crew to understand, for their morale. If Edward is on this island, then we will laugh about it, and you and I can have a long chat with him together." Anne placed her hand on Jack's.

"And if he's not?"

"Then our chat will have to be delayed, and in the meantime, we'll be the best damn distraction Calico Jack has ever had to deal with."

The longboat landed at the natural shore on the coast of Los Huecos, carrying with it the landing party appointed by William, as well as a few sightseers. *Queen Anne's Revenge* bobbed with the waves just a short distance from the coast. Far enough that they wouldn't hit land, but not too far in case the landing party needed to abscond quickly.

Along with Anne, William, and six other crewmates, Alexandre, the *Queen Anne's Revenge*'s surgeon, and Victoria, his partner in medicine and possibly more, as well as former crewmate of Calico Jack, sought to join in of their own accord. When asked about their wishes for joining, the Frenchman replied with a curt "research" in his usual sly manner. Victoria refrained from answering, but her typically cold eyes were more distant than usual, a well-submerged burg rather than her typical frost.

Anne saw no benefit to leaving them on board and significantly less use to arguing with them, so she let them join. When Victoria emerged from below wearing her leathers and had her buckler strapped to her arm and her short sword at her hip, Anne became suspicious. When Alexandre brought a large satchel that jangled with the tune of the surgeon's instruments, and he too had a pistol and his immaculate rapier at his side, Anne's suspicions turned to an anxious knot in her gut.

What calculations had you come to this conclusion, mon ami?

Anne had already been expecting trouble on the island, but she was hoping they could gather some intel first. The first rule to winning any battle was knowing the other person's strengths, as well as your own; whether to strike fast and hard like a battle axe, whether to whittle the enemy down like a thousand mosquitoes sucking a man dry, or whether to retreat and seek another way all depended on the information. Without such intel, Anne would be lacking.

Anne *hated* to be lacking.

After she landed her feet on the shifting but stable ground of the sandy coast, Anne closed her eyes with her back to the other crewmates. Anxiety would do her no good here, especially when she needed to project absolute and unwavering strength. As a woman attempting to lead hardened men, she could settle for no less. She took the anxious feeling, wrapped it in a flaming hand, and with one last curse to Alexandre for his gift, she snuffed it out with a lengthy but silent exhale.

"Eyes sharp, men. We don't know what to expect out there," she shouted over her shoulder. The men behind her yelled an "Aye" back as she walked up the incline to the rolling hills ahead.

At the top of the first small hill, the sand of the beach met the grass in stark opposition to one another. The sand appeared to be clawing its way forward as the grass and earth fought to stay aloft, causing the grass to curl down and almost touch the sand beneath an overhang. The grass clung to its former solid ground like a climber on the edge of a precipice. One slip and it would crash away, and it too would become the sand.

Across the small beach, Anne could see many such scenes of the eroding coast, exposing years of compacted earth and stone to the air. The soil here was unstable near the beach, and if it held true across the island, then they were unlikely to have any ports aside from the town that Silver Eyes occupied: one major town for trade, which the other villages supplied.

Once at the top of the hill, Anne was able to get a better view of the island, or at least what she could see of it. The rolling hills obstructed much from view, but she noticed the top of a few buildings to the north, one being a large bell tower, as well as a well-travelled dirt road nearby.

William and the other crewmates crested the hills to join Anne, and she directed their attention to the village nearby. "We'll head there first. Stick to the road and keep your weapons hidden as well as you can manage for now. We don't want to alarm the villagers and have them sending scouts to warn Silver Eyes."

Anne looked over her shoulder, and the crewmates who were watching her nodded their understanding while some took in their surroundings. They each had cloaks covering down to their ankles, and each of them adjusted the weapons on them to remain concealed under the heavy fabric.

"Hubert, Lucas, head to that hill over there and keep watch." Anne was pointing to a rather tall hill just west of the town. "You should be able to see the town and the ship from there. If you see anyone leaving town or any ships approaching, find us." The two crewmates gave an "Aye, Captain," before leaving for the hill.

Anne led the others down the dusty dirt road towards town. As they approached, the hills tapered off and turned into fields filled with rows upon rows of farmland. Anne could see wheat prominently, with some just ripening for harvest, as well as large fields of corn, and smaller fields of potatoes, tomatoes, varieties of lettuce, and other greens Anne couldn't distinguish.

Going from the salty air of the sea to the hot sand and earth on the coast, to the freshly tilled soil, manure, and vegetables felt like stepping into another world. Most of the places that Anne had been to, not just while with the *Queen Anne's Revenge*, had been towns of considerable size, large bustling machines composed of men and women working at a pace set to a particular rhythm, the rhythm of people trying to stay alive and make a living in a harsh world. Stepping into this village, which couldn't house more than fifty residents, was like stepping through the gates to a new world. A smaller world, a slower world, one removed from the harsh realities of life on the sea, or life led by the whims and fancies of others.

As they walked into the village, they passed by farmers, old grizzled men with their sons at their side, working the fields. Using hoes, they delicately removed weeds from the budding vegetables or crushed bugs threatening the harvest between rough, dirty, but skilled fingers. They waved and called pleasant hellos to Anne and her company, broad smiles on their faces as though they had no care in the world and were welcoming to any and all visitors.

The joviality forced the knot back into Anne's gut.

This was not the attitude of a village of oppressed men and women under the thumb of a tyrannical pirate regime. It wasn't even reminiscent of a remote village visited by eight strangers who, even with weapons hidden, had the appearance of fighters. No one sounded an alarm, none rushed to tell the other villagers of their arrival, and not a single person gave them a wary look of concern.

Peculiar. Anne could describe it no better than *peculiar* in her mind. If they hadn't been in the heart of enemy territory, it would have been a simple thing, an oddity she could whisk away with the thought that they were a strange group of people. Here, though, it set her mind to a razor's edge.

Without thought she settled a hand on the golden cutlass at her hip. She only came back to her senses when she felt the tip of the metal, guarded in a sheathe, pressing against the fabric of her cloak. She adjusted her weapon and forced her hands to her sides.

When they reached the village proper, where the farmland turned into houses and a few small businesses, she had to force herself to keep her hands still.

There were men working wagons, repairing wheels and

feeding horses, women gossiping near the local general store while a pair of men played a game of chess on the deck near its entrance, and some just walking to another part of the village on an errand. Anne could hear the slow, methodical clang of metal striking metal in a nearby smithy, though she couldn't place the building among those she could see.

In the centre of the hamlet, Anne was able to better see the tall bell tower, and it was by far the most arresting architecture around them. The other buildings looked well worn, old, and humble. The bell tower had all the same trappings, but the bell itself glinted against the late afternoon sun with a brilliance no ordinary metal could produce. The golden light reflected off what appeared to be a pure gold bell of at least a few hundred pounds. That golden bell's metal resembled Edward's cutlass at her side, and a blade owned by his father, Calico Jack—or by his other name, Benjamin 'The Golden Horn' Hornigold.

The sight of that bell smashed away any doubts about this being an island under Calico Jack's purview. There was no chance this hamlet could afford, or even desire, a bell of such opulence. The bell had some significance on the island, per-haps some significance related to the strangeness going on with the citizens. Whatever the meaning, Anne didn't wish to stay long enough to find out, but she had the feeling that to contin-ue, she would have to find out.

Each of the villagers in the centre of the village took note of them, nearly in unison, and each did the same simple wave and hello the farmers and their sons had done on the way in. Two flicks of the wrist, a slight bow of the head, and back to what they were doing before. If not for the consistent banging from the smithy, and the horses chomping, the village would have been silent for the few heartbeats that the wave took.

Alexandre and Victoria walked past Anne, and only then did she notice she had stopped moving. "*Intéressant...*" the Frenchman mumbled on his way past.

"Wait, Alexandre," she called sharply.

Alexandre stopped and turned on his heel. "*Oui*? Yes?"

Though he had stopped, his tone was curt and perfunctory. His eyes wandered with each movement from the villagers, and his tapping foot alluded to his impatience more than anything about his manner. It seemed his foot was the most spirited thing at that moment, a stark contrast to the people around them who seemed to be merely going about the motions of activity. If this were a play, the villagers were the atmosphere, and he the principal.

Anne leaned forward and spoke for Alexandre's ears only. "There's something… odd about all this. We need to stay together."

Alexandre smiled, though the smile was as devoid of life as the hamlet around them. "Then you may stay together. I wish to learn more of this… *étrangeté*… my own way."

As though the matter were settled, he turned back around and walked away. It was then that Anne noticed Victoria already talking with some of the citizens, a sheaf of paper in one hand and a piece of graphite in the other. She had her shield and short sword exposed, and she and the people she was talking with paid them no heed from what Anne could tell.

Anne shook her head and rubbed her temples. After a moment, she composed herself and headed towards the general store to see if she could gather some information. Before heading up the steps to enter the store, she instructed the crew, save William, to stay outside, but within sight.

Anne and William both stepped up the well-worn wooden steps and into the general store. The cracked paint on the wood and the groans and creaks as they stepped spoke to the age of the building, and if that hadn't been enough, the scuffs and indents that warped the wood over the years was a reasonable testament.

Inside the store, a small establishment that could fit no more than thirty in the room standing shoulder to shoulder, the walls were lined with an assortment of miscellaneous items. Glass display cases separating the standing area from the owner also contained all manner of trinkets for sale.

On the left, there were bags and tins of spices, dried meat and other fresh produce from the farms outside, next to what appeared to be a second-hand set of pots, a dark iron fire poker and tongs made by the local smith, and some tools Anne wasn't familiar with. At the back, Anne saw other, heftier tools for maintaining livestock and axes and pistols and muskets with ammo and cleaning instruments in the glass cases. On the right, there were homespun fabrics and clothing made in town, from what Anne could tell, and separated on its own were well-made clothes and dresses that must have been imported. In the glass cases in front of the clothes, there were glasses of assorted sizes, ladies' gloves, and toys for children.

Because of the size of the village, Anne surmised the general store was the sole source of any of the items found inside and thus probably sold liquor stored in the back as well. That made the general store the hub of information and trade, and their best chance at getting information.

That was if this were any ordinary hamlet with ordinary citizens. And, so far, this had been anything but ordinary.

The owner of the general store stepped out from the back and into the main room when he heard Anne and William enter. He gave the two the same wave and hello the others had and then walked over closer to them while still staying behind the glass cases so that he was handy to any of the items for sale.

"Hello, good sir, we're—" Anne bit her tongue.

She had been going to explain that they were sailors seeking supplies due to a storm forcing them off course when they happened upon the island, but she had doubts about her own cover story. The way these villagers were acting, however, could be part of the manner they were *supposed* to act around Silver Eyes' men. Perhaps the strangeness was synchronized through practice, and perhaps the relationship was a healthy one for both parties and explained why they were given a warm welcome. Maybe it was all in her head, and maybe not.

Anne decided to err on the side of caution and do her best

to act as though she belonged there. She straightened her back, her eyes cast down with a slight air of hostility and authority.

"We're here for the next shipment," she continued. "But this is a new assignment for us, so we don't know who's in charge."

The older gentleman behind the counter smiled widely, his greying moustache curling as his plump cheeks rose. "Understood, ma'am. No trouble at all, I will see to the shipment personally. The name's Jules, and you're in the right place." His voice was upbeat and amicable, as though he were talking with a wealthy patron and trying to make a sale. Anne gave her name as Sofia Stewart, and though she loathed using that last name, it provided her protection now. "Any change to the supplies?"

"None," Anne replied. "But I will need a manifest for inspection. How long until the cargo is ready for shipment?"

Jules' face scrunched as he looked outside the window to the hamlet. Anne followed his gaze over her shoulder. She could see the crewmen milling about within view of the general store, and Victoria was talking with the women who were gossiping out front while Alexandre observed the gentlemen on the step playing their game of chess.

"Given the time, we could have it ready before nightfall. The road's a bit treacherous at night, are you sure you want to be heading back tonight?"

"No, I suppose not." Anne took a few seconds to assess the situation. If they indeed were from inland and part of the pirate's crew, they would not be arriving by ship. No roads were leading to the coast for cargo, and there had been no harbour that they could see for the stretch of land they'd been able to observe when sailing in. That meant mentioning the ship would be out of the question. "Would you have some lodging for my men and me for the night, so we may head back on the morrow?"

"Most certainly," Jules replied. "You can sleep upstairs. There are a few beds and some cots."

"Thank you," Anne said.

The interaction was pleasant enough to set Anne's mind at ease. The owner of the general store and the others in town simply thought they were part of Silver Eyes' men, and they acted accordingly, and seemingly not out of fear, either. If nothing else had happened, Anne would have thought that it must have been because the relationship between the two groups was mutually beneficial.

Then, Anne saw a fly crawling around on Jules' hand. He didn't seem to notice the fly, and because he was standing stock still, the fly was comfortable staying where it was. The fly soon moved up his arm, onto his neck, across his cheek, and settled on his nose. And he never moved, nor did he even twitch with the recognition that something unpleasant was there.

Anne glanced over to William, and by the look on William's face, cutting through the man's usual stoniness, he had noticed the oddity too. He looked as confused and disgusted as she felt.

"Jules, there's a fly… on your nose," Anne said, pointing to the insect.

Jules chuckled and waved a hand in front of his face. "So there is," he replied. Then with a shrug he said, "They don't bother us none."

"Right," Anne said, drawing the word out at the end. "I suppose they don't."

"You there," Alexandre called from outside the door of the general store, "Princess, Captain, Missus Thatch, whichever it is these days. Come."

Anne shot Alexandre a look of annoyance and was about to lay into him about his liberal use of titles in front of people they couldn't trust, but he had already stepped away from the entrance by the time she turned.

Anne left the shop to follow Alexandre, just in front of the two men playing the game of chess on a small table between two benches at the side of the store's deck.

"What is—?" Anne began, but Alexandre held up his finger.

"Observe," he said, as his finger pointed towards the men.

Anne looked at each man sitting at the table, a young man and an older gentleman who appeared to be in his fifties. The state of the game looked typical, but suggested an amateurish nature. Anne felt that if played correctly, the younger man, playing black, could win with checkmate in ten moves, or played poorly reach check within eight. Nothing appeared out of the ordinary.

"How is the game, gentlemen?" Alexandre asked.

"Terrible, just terrible," the older man replied. "Rotten. You teach the young everything they need to know, and then they use it against you."

Alexandre lifted a piece of paper he had been holding to his chest a moment before, and Anne noticed the same words, exactly as the old man had said to them, written on the paper. And there was more.

"Now, now, George," the young man said. "You can't expect your mind to remain as sharp as it ever was. I have to win a few games here and there."

"Nonsense," the old man cut in. "Respecting your elders means letting them win, young man."

The young one laughed, and then looked up at Alexandre, Anne, and William. "We shouldn't be much longer with our game, and then you can have a go if you'd like."

"Not if I have anything to say about it," the old man said finally, and then the two went back to their game.

Each word, verbatim, was written on Alexandre's page. No variation in the words whatsoever, and unless Alexandre was psychic or a seer, the two had said the exact thing to him while Anne and William were inside the store.

Before Anne could wrap her head around the implications, or even begin to formulate a question, Alexandre pocketed the papers and stepped closer to the two men playing.

He knelt closer to the table, placed his hands on the chessboard, and glanced over his shoulder at Anne to see if she was watching. After a moment, to ensure neither of the men play-ing had their hands on the pieces, Alexandre pushed the chess-board to the other side of the table, away from the men, and then backed away.

The men didn't react. They both stared in the same spot on the table where the chessboard used to be, as though it were still there. After a moment, the older man made the motion of picking up a piece, a rook by Anne's estimation, and moved the imaginary piece across the non-existent board.

"How about that?" he said triumphantly.

"Not bad, old man, not bad."

The older gentleman scoffed, taken aback. "I oughta have you switched for that. Make your move. Not bad, he says."

Alexandre turned to Anne, looking at her for a moment as though what he'd showed her were enough. Anne stared at the two men for a moment longer, pondering the problem.

She spun on her heel and walked back into the general store. After she and William had exited, he had gone back to some busywork about the store. Upon hearing them enter again, he gave the same hello and wave in that practiced way the others in the hamlet had all done.

"I'm rather hungry, and I'd like to purchase some of the dried meat you have."

"Why, certainly," Jules replied.

He walked around the perimeter of the store to the left side with all the food and pulled down a glass jar filled with the dried and spiced meat within. He placed the jar down on the glass cabinet in front of him and took off the top. The long strips of what appeared to be beef wafted a gentle fragrance of pepper, cloves, and the unmistakable iron-like smell of dried blood towards Anne.

"How much?" Anne asked.

Jules scrunched his face in thought as he has done a few moments before, then pulled out his ledger from behind the counter. He rifled through the pages, his finger skimming down the lines of the ledger as he searched for his product.

"Hmm, let's see... For one strip of dried beef, it would be... doo-doo-doo... Zero pieces of eight."

Anne had been fixated on the ledger and almost didn't hear what Jules had said. She was sure she had heard him wrong and looked up from the ledger, her brow cocked, and head turned slightly to hear better. "Pardon?"

Jules briefly glanced down at the ledger again, then repeated, "Zero pieces of eight."

Anne couldn't help but pause for a few seconds, incredulous, shocked, disturbed, or some combination of the three halting her natural ability to react quickly. "I'll take two," she finally said.

Jules held out his hand, waiting for the 'payment.' Anne mimicked the act of reaching into her cloak for some coins and dropped the imaginary pieces into Jules' outstretched hand. He accepted the mock coins and then tilted the jar towards Anne, allowing her to take some of the beef.

Anne, channelling the Frenchman and wishing to test things a bit further, reached inside and took all the strips of dried beef out of the jar in one bundle, leaving the container empty. "Oh! It seems you're all out."

Jules looked back into the jar, not noticing, or perhaps *unable* to notice, that Anne had taken well more than two pieces. "Oh my, terribly sorry about that, miss. I'm sure I have some more in the back, just give me a moment." Jules put the jar down and walked to the back of his store through an open doorway.

Anne turned around to Alexandre and William. "Something's not right with these people," she said, her fist clenched in a death grip on the dried strips of meat.

Alexandre smirked. "Astute observation."

Anne's anger flared, but she tempered the rage with a clench of her jaw. "Do you know what's wrong with them?" Anne gestured with the strips of beef, and after she realized she was still holding the batch, she handed some to William, some to Alexandre—despite him clearly not wanting any—and placed the rest on the counter.

Alexandre's brow raised. "My dear *princesse*, you of all people should know better." He crossed his arms in front of him, his face uncharacteristically serious. "Knowing a thing means you have an intimate awareness of the surrounding circumstances of a thing. This is no simple illness defined by a large *rouge* spot on an appendage. I have many theories, but not enough facts to say with any certainty what ails these people. They could be infected with *un parasite*, they could be acting, as unlikely as it may be, or they could be beings from the sky with no concept of our culture beyond a set of pre-described functions and phrases."

Anne's anger turned to a sour exasperation. Alexandre may be exhausting and withheld information at times, but he was proud and revelled in lording his superior intellect over others. If he didn't know a thing, and he said as much, then he didn't know it.

There was something they were missing, a crucial piece of information that would tie it all together. Anne took a bite from the beef and stared at the worn floorboards of the general store as she thought over the matter. She went deep, digging to every nugget of information Victoria, Christina, and, most importantly, Herbert had given about Silver Eyes over the years, searching for something that Alexandre didn't know that could turn one of his hypotheses into the most likely scenario.

"Three things come to mind that may narrow our focus," Anne said before looking up at Alexandre again. "One is the golden bell. It would be no coincidence were it to be the same metal as Edward's cutlass"—Anne touched the cutlass for emphasis—"and the same as Benjamin Hornigold's horn and his own cutlass. When he blew that horn the night we tried to kill him, it was as though the people around him went into a trance. Not all in the tavern, but most." Anne paused a moment, and after Alexandre nodded, she continued. "The second and third are things Herbert has said about Silver Eyes that you may not know."

"Yes, that could be valuable information," Alexandre agreed.

"He's said before that his crew never loses their morale, and when I questioned him about this further, he meant that in the most literal sense. They don't stop fighting, even if they lose their men, even if they lose their limbs."

Alexandre stroked his chin as he looked off to the side, tabulating the additional variables. After a moment, he looked at Anne again. "And the third?"

"Herbert also mentioned once that Silver Eyes has a unique method of persuasion. Whenever there were disputes with him among the crew, he could turn them around with a few pats on the shoulder, and some whispered words. Any would-be enemies, no matter how upset they were with him, turned jovial in mere moments. I don't care how silvery his eyes or his tongue are, no one's that good at persuasion, at least not with one hundred percent effectiveness."

Alexandre nodded as he took a moment to absorb the information. Then Anne saw something she never thought she would or could ever see from the Frenchman: his eyes flew open in shock for the briefest moment, and then he was angry. No, not angry; enraged. His eyes smouldered with volcanic activity, a stark contrast with his relaxed body. That look was the look of a man ready to kill.

"These people are under a forced trance." Alexandre said the words as though he were making a comment about the weather, but Anne could tell he was disgusted.

"Are you sure?" As soon as Anne asked, she felt the fool for asking. One did not doubt Alexandre's diagnosis.

"Of course."

Alexandre was now looking at the back of the shop, in the direction of the storage room where Jules was rummaging around unseen but heard.

"Can you help them out of the trance?" William asked, his first comment in some time.

"I don't know."

Alexandre was not his usual self. Anger showed in his typically passive eyes, but it went deeper than that. During times when he was short with people, as he was now, it was with an exasperation of not wanting to be a part of a dull conversation and a desire to end it as soon as possible. Now... Now Alexandre's short replies felt as though he were holding back, like he could explode at any moment, or as though he were distracted, not by something interesting to him, but by something upsetting.

"To be this far gone... " Alexandre closed his eyes and shook his head in a mournful expression and muttered a French expletive under his breath. "They must be under several layers of their own mind. Months of work went into this."

Anne suddenly realized what that would have meant and why Alexandre was so disgusted by the event to actually show it, and it made her sick. The people were docile because they had no choice. In their fugue, they probably weren't even aware of what was happening.

"Whatever you're thinking, it is far worse than that," Alexandre said, his eyes still smouldering, but Anne could see his profound pity for these people. "Putting one in a trance is a useful tool for the willing, something that can help ease pain or strengthen the mind. The trick is that you can't be put into a trance for long unless you let yourself. And, there are tricks to bring one out of a light trance as well. To do this," Alexandre gestured to the hamlet, "one would have had to start small. Perhaps one would begin with promising to ease the mind of the ailing or exhausted, then with a sense of letting go of worries. Deeper and deeper in the mind one goes, the easier it becomes to say yes. Soon, one wants to say yes without knowing why. Then, he could have made them question everything. Why do you toil for a worthless coin? It is just a burden. Give it for free. Released from your worldly possessions, you will have no more to worry about. Why live with worry?"

The anger made Alexandre's accent thicken, but he didn't

lapse back to French, his mind caught between the two in a more perfect balance. His hands were a wild flurry of gestures with each statement, the kind only seen from those raised on the impoverished streets of Paris. He was more animated than he had been in years, and Anne was beginning to understand why.

"After this, consent is meaningless. The trance is so deep and penetrating that a sense of self can be overwritten. You may think it impossible, but with enough time and a few key steps, one can break a mind. I could convince you that you were not of royal lineage, I could convince William that he committed atrocities that had never happened."

"And this is just one of several villages on this island," William said, breaking into Alexandre's abyss of atrocities.

Alexandre sighed and resigned his arms across his chest once more. "*Exactement.*"

Alexandre's explanation and William's observation sent an icy chill down Anne's spine. How many people had Silver Eyes entranced? How many were doing things against their will and being taken advantage of? Worst of it all, how many of the women were being victimized by this? Anne, though her time aboard was brief, had been on Calico Jack's ship before. His men were savage monsters that wouldn't hesitate to commit heinous acts against women, she knew that for a fact. Victoria was also living proof of it.

"This is abhorrent, and an affront to *le médecine* and *les science.*" Alexandre looked deep into Anne's eyes. "Whatever happens on this island, Silver Eyes dies by my hand."

Another wave of shivers crawled across Anne's body. She nodded, knowing it wasn't a request, but a proclamation.

"Without knowledge of the trigger, of which there could be several, I may not be able to help these people. If I knew it, I might be able to reverse it, but there is no way to know."

Anne cocked her head and brow, confused. "What about the bell? Isn't that the trigger?"

"Perhaps, and perhaps not. We do not know if it is meant

to trigger a deeper state of trance, if it is some type of control should the citizens not comply, or if it serves some other purpose." Alexandre glanced over his shoulder in the direction of the bell tower, though the bell itself was shrouded by the walls of the general store. "It would be dangerous to ring the bell not knowing what it does."

Anne nodded. "Agreed. We leave the bell alone for now." She turned to William. "Send a few crewmates back to the ship and let them know we'll be staying the night here. Perhaps with that time, we may be able to reclaim one of the citizens." Anne eyed Alexandre, then glanced over her shoulder at Jules, who was just returning from the storage room.

"Terribly sorry, miss, no more in the back. Here, your money," he said while holding out his hand.

"My thanks," Anne replied, following the act.

With her newfound knowledge, instead of the same unease she had been feeling before, she felt a profound sense of pity for the men and women of this island. Pity, and a wave of rising anger boiling up.

"You must have your rest, Captain," Alexandre chided. "If we are to have you leading our troops, you must be of sound mind."

Anne stifled a yawn, cursing the Frenchman for talking of rest at the late hour it was. Alexandre, Victoria, Anne, and William had huddled themselves in the storage room of the general store. Soft lamplight illuminated the windowless room, casting shifting shadows and bounding bands of light against the barrels, boxes, and bags of supplies in the crowded room.

Their charge, Jules the shopkeeper, sat slumped in a chair in the middle of the four. If an onlooker caught a glimpse of the half-shadowed face of the man between them all, they might think he was asleep, but he was not. He was under a trance, this time of Alexandre's doing.

Anne knew nothing of the practice and had thought not long ago it was superstitious nonsense, and so thought it equally odd that to remove one from a trance, they must again force them into the same experience. That lack of knowledge, and thus an inability to truly help, and the stifling yawn, made Alexandre's words sound like honey. The only thing keeping her awake now was a vague sense of duty and curiosity over the entire strange matter.

"And what of you?" she eventually asked.

Alexandre smiled in his usual, civil way, and though Anne couldn't be sure, it seemed warmer to her somehow. "I rarely sleep, and Victoria, for entirely different circumstances, is plagued by a similar affliction as I. We will see you in the morning, and perhaps you will then be able to talk with the real Jules."

Anne didn't need much convincing, and with a dull nod and heavy eyes, she headed up the stairs in the storage room to the second floor of the general store.

There, a few crewmates who weren't out on watch were sleeping on cots, leaving two beds on the left side of the room for William and Anne. With a few words, Anne ordered William to rest as well and refused to lie down until she saw him do so first. He was reluctant, but he too had had a long and tiring day from the early morning sailing until now, and she could tell that he fell asleep soon after his head hit the pillow.

Anne laid her head down to rest, tossing and turning as she ran through the events of the day in her head once more until eventually sleep took her. Her sleep was short-lived when a sound forced her from her bed to full alertness.

It was the cutting crack of a pistol fired outside.

6. BY THESE COPPER LEGS O' MINE

Edward's whole body ached in a painful expression of his own stupidity. Bruises blotched his face, back, arms, and legs from the beating Grace's crewmates had given him. True to their captain's word, they'd managed not to break any bones, but Edward wasn't sure how much better off he was for it.

The worst was his back, as they had opened the wound given by his father, which had been only a week old at the time. Edward did his best to protect the injury without making it seem as though he were guarding it as per the rules of the engagement, but it had been unavoidable. After that point, he focussed simply on not crying out in pain over the ordeal.

And after it all, he had to man a ship that was not his own, taking orders from a captain he had to act amicably towards.

As his arms shook, he secured coarse rigging; as his legs wobbled, he ran the length of the ship to perform increasingly menial tasks, tasks meant to break him and have him regret his decision. And as he bled on the deck from his forehead and back, he kept going. Despite the pain, the weakness, and the not-so-subtle slights from the crewmates tripping him up, he did the work of three men—just as he had been told to do, just as he had agreed he would.

To Edward's dismay, this only served to infuriate several members of the crew. The more he pushed on despite his injuries, the more contempt he could feel in their gazes; the heat against the back of his neck told him those gazes were measuring him and finding him wanting no matter how well he performed.

The primary source of the contempt came from the first man they had spoken to before boarding the *Black Blood*: the pock-marked, sour crewmate named Nigel. He had an inner circle of other crewmates Edward learned about over the day's work, and they were the ones trying to trip or knock him over at each corner when the captain wasn't looking.

Despite this, some in the crew seemed to warm up to Edward after his stubborn refusal to submit to his injuries. As the day progressed and his sweat and blood poured out of him, he noticed a few go out of their way to aid him. When he fumbled with a knot his numb fingers just couldn't manage, one man finished the loop for him. When he snuck in a few laboured breaths behind the mast and away from prying eyes, another crewmate secretly handed him a tin full of water. It wasn't much, but it helped.

"I've been where you were before," the man with the cup said. "It'll get easier as soon as Grace trusts you're capable."

Edward took the cup with a shaking hand and downed the water in one enormous gulp. "If I don't die before then," he sputtered through his laboured breaths. He glanced over his shoulder and around the foremast towards where Nigel and his friends were talking amongst themselves.

The crewmate who gave him the water followed Edward's gaze. "Just ignore Nigel. He'll tire of you eventually. This is just his way." The man turned back to face Edward, and he smiled. "I'm John, by the way."

The name made Edward's eyes widen, and his pounding heart skipped a beat. John was a common name, but nonetheless, it still brought to mind the old crewmate Edward had had aboard his ship before he had become a pirate and stayed on afterwards. The same crewmate whose neck had been sliced open right in front of him by the same man who had tortured Edward for days before leaving him for dead. The thought brought with it the same unpleasant ache of a different kind.

His throat seized, and he couldn't move. He breathed deep through his nose, desperately trying to quell the raging squall in his mind. He reached for his flask, popped off the stopper, and tried to drink, but it was empty.

"Anything stronger than that swill?" Edward eked out, referring to the lightly rum-laced water he had been given. The rum kept the water from forming a scum on a long voyage with little fresh water but did little else for one looking to ease a particular pain.

John smiled and took the cup from Edward before filling it from a secret flask of his own. After getting it back, Edward downed it in one gulp just as he had the water before it. Edward knew and was hoping that with all the activity, the blood loss, and the sweat, it would hit him harder than it usually did. He wanted the numbness of a different kind.

"My thanks," he said after a moment.

The thought of Edward's former crewmate brought old memories of the man. The way he'd looked with his salt-and-pepper hair, his typically nervous disposition outside of battle, and his relationship with his father. Before John had been killed, when his tired eyes had showed Edward the look of an old man's soul stretched thin as smoke and ready to let the wind take it off, he had confirmed that Edward's father was still alive. Had John been aware of what Edward's father had become? Had he been aware of the things his father had done to him, or would do to him, or had he merely been trying to tighten Edward's resolve to live by telling him a sweet lie he'd had no way of knowing was accurate?

Edward's eyes shot up as the flood of memories came back to him. *No*, he thought, *John knew. He was given the keys to my ship before I received it. He met Benjamin Hornigold, he said as much himself. He met my father and kept the lie to take me to the trials where I nearly died. How much did he know? How deep did this plot run?*

Edward pondered the question for another moment, but it only served to heat his cheeks and his core with fresh anger over the lies he had been fed and embarrassment over his falling for them. He shook his head to cast away the demons he called the past and looked over the young man in front of him right now.

The John in front of him had little in common with Edward's old John. He was younger than Edward by quite the degree, in his early twenties if he wasn't in his teens still, and it was clear that he was new to the crew, or new to battle. He had a few small scars, one on his face and another few Edward could see snaking their way out of his shirt towards his neck, but he was far from the battle-hardened sailors aboard the *Black Blood*. His black hair was cropped short, too short for the youth's narrow features. In his mind, it was easy to separate this John from his John, but far harder for his body to.

"Strange for one on a crew such as this to show me a kindness," Edward commented as he turned his gaze to the horizon.

Being at the front of the ship meant getting the full force of each smash against the waves. Each time the ship lurched below the line of the ocean in front of them, seawater misted Edward and John. The mist was refreshing on Edward's hot, tired, aching body.

"You know much of Calico Jack's crew, I see," John said, his mouth a line. "Perhaps if this were Calico Jack or Lance Nhil's ships, your words may ring a bit truer. Grace doesn't use fear or magic to control the crew as they do. She just follows a simple rule: her word is law. Break that law, you're off at the next port if you even make it that far."

Edward took stock of the young man's choice of words, specifically the bit about magic. Did he mean Nhil? Silver Eyes? Or was his father implicated here as well? Edward had seen inexplicable things over the years—metal unlike any other, islands that would take far too long for human hands to construct—not to mention the visions his crew had seen in the Devil's Triangle.

Edward suddenly had a sickening feeling that he and Herbert were in over their heads. If his father had some unknown magic, how could they defend against it?

He noticed John looking at him, and he remembered where he was. Now was all that mattered. He would have to worry about the future when it was on them.

"Doesn't sound much different from intimidation to me."

John shook his head and placed a hand on Edward's shoulder. "Trust me," he said, his eyes serious, "I know."

This first kind hand, after so many seeking to trip Edward up or to stab him in the back, served as a calm wind to his sails, a buoyant driftwood in a treacherous ocean on all sides.

The elation he felt turned to bile in his mouth. How many times must his father's minions betray Edward until he learned his lesson? This John may look nothing like the John that had been his crewmate and confidant for years, but Edward could trust this one no more than he should have trusted the first.

Nigel didn't strike Edward as bright, but it didn't take a bright man to recognize that a gentle hand can lure one closer to a hidden knife. It is especially so when the gentle hand comes after so many harsh ones. John might be in league with Nigel in secret.

He could no more trust John than he could Nigel, or any of the crew aboard the *Black Blood*. Edward decided he would always have to keep one hand near a blade and sleep with one eye open. Thankfully for him, Edward thought as he eyed Herbert on the quarterdeck, he had a second pair he could rely on.

"That was foolish," Herbert said from behind Edward as he did his best to close the stab wound in Edward's back.

Edward winced as the needle passed through his skin for the third time. After so much pain over so many years, the pain of the needle came to him like an old friend whispering jibes and slapping him on the back. If he were mad, he might even say he enjoyed the delicate pain the needle provided, but he wasn't mad, and he jerked as the needle pierced his skin again.

"We're here, aren't we?" Edward said, peering over his shoulder at Herbert's face buried in the task of sewing him up.

Edward was sitting on a box in the hold of the *Black Blood*, surrounded by shoulder-high stacks of watertight barrels and other boxes of pungent spices. On the side of every barrel and box, Edward noticed the label of a shipping company that operated in the West Indies. He wasn't sure exactly which company it belonged to, but he knew it was one of the larger ones. It spoke to how prolific Calico Jack and the crew aboard this ship were, given the audacity to target one of the companies able to defend against pirates.

"Sit still," Herbert ordered, his tone harsh. As soon as Edward readjusted and complied, he finished the stitch in his back and covered it with a cloth before wrapping a strip around it. "It won't be nearly as good as Alexandre would have done, but it'll hold if you keep the weight off."

"My thanks," Edward said, trying to crane his neck to see the wound and stitching.

"You're lucky it had healed a bit before that incident. It could have been worse. If I didn't know any better, I'd say your father knew what he was doing. The wound was meant to bleed you, and the cut was clean and precise."

Edward spat. "If he wanted to kill me, he could have, easily. That's the point. I think he means for me, for us, to bleed." Edward shook his head. "He had so many chances to make things so bad for us we couldn't recover. When he attacked Bodden Town, he could have stayed behind and attacked again after we anchored. In the tavern, everyone was under his control, but they let us go."

Herbert's mouth was a line, as straight as the horizon at dusk, betraying no curve of emotion. "Any ideas as to why?"

"None," Edward replied.

For a moment, the two sat in silence as Edward donned his blood-stained shirt and coat. He thought it over, recalling everything that they knew about his father.

With his recent remembrance that John had been part of the plot, it wasn't unreasonable to think that John had been sending letters to his father. He'd had the means. He had been the person in charge of selling cargo; he could easily have sent a letter here or there. From there, it was reasonable to think that his father knew his pirate name of Blackbeard and more.

It made sense now why Calico Jack had never retaliated for the killing of one of his commanders, Gregory Dunn, until Edward had finished the task of unlocking the ship. His father was the one who'd given him the ship, and had wanted him to face those trials first.

The thoughts and the rumination itched Edward to the point that he needed to move. He couldn't sit still for a moment longer. He rose to his feet but had to remain bent slightly due to the low ceiling of the hold.

Edward kept his voice low despite being in the hold farthest from where crewmates in the deck above would most likely be. "My father gave me the ship as Benjamin Hornigold with the intent to go about unlocking pieces of it. If I survive, then I become stronger as the ship itself becomes mine. Once that happens, why attack and provoke us? Would he have done it even if we hadn't killed Gregory Dunn? I don't see the purpose."

Herbert shrugged and gestured towards Edward. "Perhaps this is the final test then? Perhaps this would have happened regardless of us attacking Gregory Dunn. I loathe to take advice from *him*, but Alexandre once said to me, 'People always tell more than they wish to. You need but to listen.'" Herbert tried a French accent but butchered it in the best way possible.

Edward laughed at Herbert for a moment before addressing the quote. "And what am I to listen to, exactly?"

"What did your father say to you in that tavern?"

Edward only needed a few seconds to recall it. "'Try again when you grow a spine.'"

Herbert cocked his brow. His eyes and the crook of his neck as he stared at Edward was the look of a man who didn't want to say something out loud that should have been obvious at that point.

Edward sighed. "So, you're saying that my father planned all this from the beginning, and he wants me to kill him?"

Herbert's brow lowered, then he spread his hands as though he were unveiling a bountiful feast, a feast of evidence towards the conclusion Edward had spelled out.

Edward's earlier frustration and itch faded away and left a hole so deep it could take the very light of the sun with it. He fell to the box he had been sitting on before, sinking into it like the light into the emptiness inside him.

"My father wants me to kill him."

Edward and Herbert headed back to the deck above the hold where the crew's quarters were. All that separated the hold from the crew's quarters were the maze of barrels and boxes on one end of the ship, thinning out near the other, and a short ladder.

The narrow space between the cargo was barely enough for Edward to walk through, let alone Herbert in his wooden wheelchair, but he managed with only a few snags. Edward had his own issues with his height in the cramped part of the ship. He had to remain bent over as they walked through the hold towards the ladder.

Edward climbed up the ladder, one hand carrying Herbert's wheelchair and the other gripping the rungs. Each step was a labour in balance and delicacy, and Edward needed to take his time. After a few heaves, and a tenuous leverage over the lip of the other deck's edge, the wheelchair was up, and Edward himself wasn't far behind.

"Next time," Edward said to Herbert over the side to the hold through a few laboured breaths, "we leave the chair."

Herbert chuckled as he began his climb. "Aye, Ca… Aye, Ed," Herbert amended quickly. This was the *Black Blood*, and Edward was not his captain.

Herbert's journey up the ladder was nearly as laborious as Edward's, as Herbert could only rely on his hands for stability, leaving his legs dangling beneath him and swinging with each advance up the rungs. Once on the other deck, Edward held Herbert's chair steady for him as he climbed into in and got comfortable again, placing a small blanket over his emaciated limbs to hide them from sight.

Edward recalled that Herbert had once said the act was meant more for others than himself, as he had already come to terms with his circumstances. Hiding his legs did nothing for him—they were a part of him—but for others, it stopped the staring and the shrinking that came after they realized they were staring.

After Herbert settled, they went the short distance to the crew's quarters, now adjusted for dining. The hammocks, usually stacked three high in rows along the hull with a mere inch or two of clearance for each row's swinging arc, had been put away. The accessible area was now filled with crewmates in clusters sitting flush on the deck as they ate from large soup bowls.

This ship, unlike the *Queen Anne's Revenge*, had no designated dining area, no tables, no benches, no segregation between living and eating space. And no privacy. By the time each man had their bowls, Edward could tell that the dining space would be shoulder-to-shoulder with bodies. The thought of having to sit shoulder to bloody shoulder with these men in an already oppressively humid environment rankled Edward more than the rigorous work above deck had.

Close to the stern, near the cut-off to the hold but centred between port and starboard, was a large iron stove in the middle of a pit of sand held in by sturdy wooden planks covered in more iron. The stove was an older design than in Edward's ship and had far less utility. The meals it could supply were limited to the standard stews common on long voyages made in pots as big and broad as Edward was.

Near the stove, hanging from the rafters of the ship in twine, were a variety of dried spices swaying with the bobbing of the waves. From a distance Edward couldn't recognize many of the spices, save basil and parsley. They still looked fresh from what Edward could see; given that they were just in port they may have been bought the day before, or they could have been stolen from a merchant ship before that for all Edward knew.

Mixed in with the heavy and thick air of sweat, shit, and salt from the sea, Edward could smell the distinct aroma of boiling potatoes, but that was about it. None of the spices hanging in the air, nor those in the stew, made it to his nose. All else was lost in the pot, but Edward surmised it was some meat salted heavily enough to dry the throat, and some other vegetables that fared well over long voyages, hearty vegetables that on their own could be tasty and healthful, if only one joined it with complementary foods. The problem was that most complementary foods were impossible to keep aboard a ship.

And after months on board, that was when the scurvy came in. Edward was fortunate enough to never have been that far from shore when he was younger, and after Alexandre joined, he claimed to have knowledge of a concoction that helped in prevention over long voyages, though Edward wasn't privy to the ingredients. It helped his crew avoid the bleeding gums, the loss of teeth, and the bone weariness and pain that came before the fever, the tremors, and the death.

Thinking about the sickness, Edward thought back to the crewmates he'd had the displeasure of meeting over the day. Many had lost teeth, but not one man had the signs of the disease, or if they had, it seemed it was long behind them. He wondered what was their secret, as they certainly couldn't have another Alexandre aboard.

As Edward took in the surroundings of the ship and how small it was, it felt as though the *Queen Anne's Revenge* were a castle in comparison. The economy of space in the *Black Blood* seemed to be taken to an extreme, and the best way to describe it would be with one word: cramped.

Edward felt cramped in the small quarters and the mass of controlled clutter around the ship. Each deck, and each section of each deck, was more compact and efficiently used. Even on

Bartholomew Roberts' small ship, it felt more open, as though he could move and breathe freely. Here, the confined spaces boxed him in, the weight on his chest bending him inward like wood bowed from stress. Edward was trapped in a tinderbox with over one hundred enemies in the middle of the sea, and he was on the edge of sparking.

But not all was dire. As Edward had been taking stock of the scene before him, he noticed John, the same John with the cup of water, walking towards Edward and Herbert with three bowls cradled precariously in the crook of his arms. John carried the food, as important as a child in this exhausting work aboard a ship, with the same delicacy and mannerism of carrying his own baby.

Edward stepped forward and took two of the bowls from John's arms and handed one to Herbert. Before Edward or Herbert could give their thanks, John spoke up.

"If you men would enjoy a bit of privacy, I happen to know just such a location," he said with a genial smile bordering on a youth's naïveté.

Edward glanced at Herbert for a moment. "Lead the way."

John took them away from the crew's quarters and towards the bow of the ship. They passed by some other men late in getting below deck for their share of food, drawing long, covetous stares at the bowls in the three men's hands.

Midships Edward noticed the surgeon's room, slightly off-centre with the rest of the ship, thick walls of hard timber on all sides save for the open doorway with no door running down the middle on both ends. It looked hardly big enough for two men to lie out on a table, and as they approached, Edward could see just that: two cots side by side with two men lying in them and a third empty one happening to be poking out on the starboard side, while on the port side, Edward could just make out closed shelves and storage for a surgeon's instruments.

On the starboard side there was a small space just barely wide enough to walk through that John was leading Edward and Herbert towards. It had evidently been a design flaw in the construction of the ship, as the surgeon's room could have been centred to allow ample room on both sides for any and all types of cargo to head towards the hold. As it stood, the port side was open enough for three to walk shoulder to shoulder, but the starboard could barely fit Herbert's chair, if that.

For that reason, it seemed, the walkway had been blocked with a barrel and a makeshift curtain. John placed his bowl on top of the barrel and gently slid the wooden keg over, allowing access to the alcove beside the surgeon's room. He moved the curtain aside and motioned Edward and Herbert inside.

"I don't think I'm going to fit," Herbert said, with a slight frown quickly forced into a smile when John looked over at him. Before John was able to respond, Herbert spoke again. "I'll manage, you two go on."

Edward took the lead and entered the alcove without another word on the subject. He didn't want John to dwell and mutter useless platitudes on the subject, as he knew Herbert wouldn't want that either.

Edward and John entered the alcove and sat down, Edward on top of a barrel at the other end of the cramped space, and John leaning into the bowed shape of the ship's starboard planks. Herbert positioned himself where the barrel had been previously, side-faced to the opening with his legs touching the corner of the surgeon's room. Herbert locked himself into place and then turned in his chair to better see the other men.

"There," Herbert said, a small smile on his face, "this should do."

John handed out two cloth sacks to Edward and Herbert, holding biscuits, four each, for the day's rations. The ship's biscuits were hard as rocks and would break the teeth if eaten as they were, but they were necessary after the hard day's work.

As though on some stage cue, the three men took a biscuit each from their bags, knocked them on a plank of the ship once, and dropped them into their stew. The ritual was so common amongst sailors, none typically gave it a second thought as the biscuit soaked and softened in the thick broth.

Edward did give it a second thought, as the memory of where and when he'd learned of the ritual came to mind. It was his father who had taught him, as it was his father who had taught him most everything he knew about ships.

He was brought back to his younger years, brought on by a now tainted nostalgia, to a time when his father had brought him on a short fishing trip with his friends. The small boat had had only one sail, and a single deck to store provisions and their haul.

"Salt pork again, is it?" Edward's father said with a wry smile.

Edward remembered looking up at his father; so enormous and imposing was his frame in those days he could think of nothing but awe at the form he wished he could attain someday.

"Er'y day is salt pork," one of the shipmates said. Edward couldn't remember his face or name, but he remembered those words. "Afternoon, salt pork, evening, salt pork, 'morrow'll be salt pork, and the day affer that too. Every bloody day salt pork."

"Now, now, gents," the cook said, "that's just not true. We've got salted beef too."

The group of them laughed at the comment as ship's biscuits were handed out. The men got four each, but Edward's father only handed him two. Edward remembered wanting to object and ask for more, but he didn't want to make a fuss in front of his father's men.

Edward's father took a biscuit in hand, held it up and gave his son a glance to see if he was following along. Edward had already been mimicking his father and looked more towards him than at the bowl or biscuit, despite his hunger.

His father smacked the biscuit against the wood of the ship at his feet, then dropped it into the stew. A half step behind, Edward did the same. His father smiled at him, and Edward smiled back.

The Voyages of Queen Anne's Revenge

The memory was a curious but arresting look back at the father of his younger years. It was so far removed from the father he'd met just a few moons back, the one who now called himself Calico Jack, that it felt like a different person. His father had never been cold to him, had never scolded him without reason, and had only been hard when he'd needed to be. Edward had never known his father to do vile things to both women and men, let alone all the other horrible stories he had heard told about Calico Jack over the years.

Edward would be lying to himself if he thought it didn't make what they were about to do easier. Calico Jack wasn't his father now, not really, and the more he thought it over, the more Edward thought there was no way to avoid giving his father exactly what he seemed to want.

Edward pushed aside the dark thoughts and focussed on the hunger in his belly. The other two were already well into their stew, and Edward needed to catch up.

As Edward had suspected, the stew had been saturated in an ungodly amount of salt, the results of curing and storing aboard a ship. There was almost no way to rinse the salt away, and so it ended up in the stew. This was on a whole other level from what he experienced aboard the *Queen Anne's Revenge*, and it made Edward's toes curl.

Sensing another cue, John produced three cups from his own cloth holding his biscuits and filled them with the laced water from a waterskin.

The three men, so focussed on their food, neglected each other's company until they had halved their stews and thrown another biscuit into the mix. Edward was first to take pause and speak.

"How does your crew manage the scurvy? I notice few have the signs."

John smiled. "See the red bits in the stew?"

Edward took closer note of the broth, leaning to catch the light coming from grated rafters above them. Just as John had said, there were bits of some red vegetables in the stew. Edward isolated the vegetable and chewed on it. After a moment, his tongue felt as though it were on fire.

"Hoo, I think I've had this before. Some type of pepper, is it not?" Edward managed through painful breaths. He took a drink of water, but it only made the pain worse.

John chuckled. "Yes, it helps ward off the disease, and if it's properly dried, it can last quite some time. And the rats don't seem to like 'em, so we have no fear of losing them on a long voyage."

"Clever," Edward said as he held his hand over his mouth. The heat was dissipating slowly, but at that moment it was nearly unbearable.

"Interesting that it becomes so masked in the stew," Herbert commented as he stirred his spoon and peered into his bowl.

"Not much is needed, from what I'm told."

"I'll have to remember this, though I don't know if I want to," Edward sputtered, the heat now starting to simmer down.

The three men chuckled at Edward's misfortune and continued eating for a bit in their small private space on the ship.

A noise at Edward's back sent pricks down his neck and arms. He got up and turned around, some combination of his senses telling him he should be on alert.

Sure enough, a hand pulled away the curtain on Edward's side of the secluded spot. The hand belonged to Edward's chief tormentor and his reason for staying so wary despite their making it aboard the *Black Blood*. Nigel's pock-marked face came into view, a broad, wicked grin pulling at his cheeks.

"What 'ave we here?" he said. "Couple'a babes ready for the slaughter?"

Edward heard footsteps behind him, and one of Nigel's friends was on Herbert, a knife at his throat. It was the man whom Edward had knocked down during his trial to join the crew, though Edward could not recall his name.

Herbert's eyes were wide. Edward saw his hands inching to the secret compartment of weapons in his wheelchair, and it made him painfully aware of his own lack of arms.

Edward turned back when the sound of wood scraping across floorboards sounded from Nigel's direction. He'd moved the barrel aside during Edward's distraction, and held a long knife in his hands. Behind Nigel was another man, blocking any chance of escape.

"Let's finish wut we started earlier."

Edward raised his hands in a defensive position, his years of training and conditioning working without thought. He assessed the length of the knife, his distance from Nigel, and Nigel's reach. Edward generally had the advantage in height, but it meant nothing in the confined, trapped space beside the surgeon's room.

At least they can patch me up quickly, Edward mused, a soft, dark chuckle escaping under his breath.

"Nigel, stop this madness!" John shouted, but he hadn't moved from his near supine position against the starboard wall.

"I'm jus' giving the greenhorn what's coming to him."

"What should he have done? Laid down and died? The captain told him to fight you, and so he did."

Nigel gritted his teeth and glanced over at John. "He shouldn'a tried to join in the first—"

Edward sprang, his hand darting down and then up towards Nigel's wrist. Nigel's eyes—anyone's eyes, for that matter—were too slow for the smooth and efficient motion. Like a viper, Edward snapped at Nigel's wrist, striking it smartly. The swiftness took Nigel by surprise, and the knife flew from his grip and lodged itself into the wooden wall of the surgeon's room with a thunk and a twang.

Behind him, Edward heard a scuffle that he hoped Herbert was in control of. Edward couldn't afford to look away from Nigel now, even if it meant getting stabbed in the back again.

A voice broke through the small din of the fight, taking the wind out of everyone's sails. "By these copper legs o' mine, if you all don't stop yer fighting, I'll dump the lot of you overboard." The words came from behind Nigel, a simple, almost soft, declaration that carried with it a queer kind of weight.

The tension was cut at once, a sharp contrast to the still swaying blade in the plank of the surgeon's room.

"Get out here, all of ye."

Nigel gave Edward and John a harsh look before turning around and exiting the alcove. Edward gave himself a moment to glance over his shoulder at Herbert, who had gotten the better of his opponent and looked unharmed. He gestured to Edward, signalling everything was all right before he headed the long way around the surgeon's room along with Nigel's friend. Edward and John were the last to leave the small space.

Nigel and his friends all lined up in front of Grace and the other men, while Herbert stayed off to the side away from Edward. John pulled Edward back, and the two stayed a few paces from the three who had just attacked them.

"Want ta try and explain just what you were about to do?" Grace asked.

"Jus' a little welcoming party for the new recruits, ma'am," Nigel responded, with a bit too much cockiness by Edward's estimation.

Grace grinned as though she enjoyed the joke Nigel made, then kneed him in his nether regions more swiftly than Edward had knocked the knife from his hands.

Too much cockiness by far.

Nigel doubled over in pain, grabbing his ballocks in both hands. He fell to his knees with a gasp of pain.

Grace bent down slowly to Nigel's pain-postured level. "You would'a killed him if I hadn't come along. Just admit it, for both our sakes." Her words were soft, but they carried the same measured, even, and cold words of command. This was not the kind of tone that could be taught, only the kind learned over a lifetime of experience.

Nigel, still whimpering, protested at first, before lapsing into begging. Edward understood the protesting, but not the begging. Why was he begging?

Grace rose to her feet in that same measured, even, and slow way she had moved when she'd knelt. "I don't permit liars on my ship," she said, "nor those who kill a crewmate."

In one motion, Grace pulled a pistol from her belt and fired it at the back of Nigel's head, his last supplication brought short by a lead ball through the brain. His pulpy mass exploded onto the deck below as the loud crack rang across the ship and took all other noises with it if but for a brief moment.

When the other noises returned, although stunted by the crew recognizing the sound of gunfire, Edward was able to process what had just happened.

Edward felt pressure on his sleeve and noticed John had gripped his shoulder and a part of his clothes. When Edward looked over, he let go.

"Ugh, got blood on me boots!" Grace lamented. "Get this mess off my ship," she commanded. The senior officers leapt into action and dragged the bloody body of Nigel away.

Grace looked into the eyes of the two remaining attackers, followed by Edward, John, and Herbert, one by one. "Let this be a lesson to each of you. I'm the captain here, and I don't take kindly with my crew trying to kill each other. Or being a cunt. Don't be like Nigel," she said, waving a hand at the splayed viscera on the deck and over her copper greaves.

Satisfied with the looks of shock plastered on the faces of her audience, she gave a curt nod before she turned and walked away from the scene. The slamming of her copper boots echoed down the deck, cutting through the growing crowd's animated questions about what had happened.

The whole event was so quick, the only remnant left of the fight and of Nigel was his knife still lodged in the wood beside the surgeon's room.

7. FOR WHOM THE GOLDEN BELL TOLLS

The crack of the pistol awoke not just Anne, but most of the men on the upper floor of the general store. That sharp, whip-like sound touched at the inner parts of the mind that controlled urgency like no other, and for those with the sense, it stripped away all tiredness in an instant. Those without the sense were not long for this world that Anne and company found themselves in.

Anne glanced at William, who also awoke just as she did, and then she jumped from her bed and over to the window overlooking the hamlet. William was but a half-step behind her, and the rest of the men a few steps behind him.

Anne scanned the small crossroads of the hamlet below for signs of the fight. She only allowed herself a few seconds before she began to turn around and head outside, but William stopped her with a point of his finger.

She looked back to see two of the crewmates who were out on watch retreating to the general store as they loaded pistols. Another crack sounded, and a puff of dirt shot into the air a few feet from one of the crewmates.

Anne had seen all she needed to see. "To arms," she declared.

Before the last syllable left her lips, the crew were on the move. William wasted no time in procuring his sword and slinging a musket over his shoulder. Anticipating her need, he tossed her golden cutlass and a rifle to her. Anne caught the two as she rushed to the stairs to the main level of the general store.

She jumped down the steps two at a time and passed

through the storage room with a tied-up Jules sitting in the chair where she had left him earlier that night. Alexandre and Victoria were at the front of the store, observing the crew-mates losing ground outside as they prepared muskets for an offensive.

Anne slowed her pace for a moment as she took the rifle off her shoulder and handed it to Alexandre in exchange for the loaded musket. With a practiced hand and a bit of black powder from Alexandre, she readied the musket with a few flicks of her thumb. Walking sideways with the musket aimed towards the unknown assailants, she exited the store, found her mark, and shot.

After the shot was away and the acrid smoke surrounded her, she ducked back into the store, confident she had hit her mark, and not wanting to risk getting shot in return.

William was next out the door with a loaded musket in hand. He fired, sending more smoke into the small space, with no wind to take it away. He moved outside the store to a near-by pillar keeping the roof of the store's deck aloft.

Alexandre handed Anne her rifle, now loaded, and took back the spent musket. She bent down below the window of the general store for a moment and closed her eyes. She count-ed the shots and where they were coming from.

Only two men remained by her estimation, and they were staggering their shots to keep Anne, William, and the others at bay. They were skilled in battle. Three bangs. A thud. Only one man left.

Anne counted down the seconds. She knew the approxi-mate time the last man took to reload based on the time be-tween previous shots. There would also be a momentary hesitation when he moved out of cover to take aim. She aimed for that hesitation.

Anne sprang from her cover like a snake from between two rocks. She flew through the smoke, forcing her eyes open de-spite the burn and the watering. When the smoke broke, she saw movement to her right. She aimed down the centre of her rifle at the movement and pulled the trigger. The bullet, more accurate than the musket she'd shot before, hit the target right through the neck. The man, just in the middle of aiming, reared back, firing wildly into the air. The last crack sent a wave of smoke in front of the man. Spurts of blood from his neck broke through the grey cloud and splattered on the dirt road.

Anne relaxed but remained on alert. "Any others?" She didn't look away from the direction the enemy had come from but said the words loud enough for her crewmates to hear.

"Two more, headed to the bell tower," one of the crewmates said.

The bell tower. The unknown element. The trigger for something unknown. *An alert to others?*

Anne's mind raced with questions, but a single thought rose above them all: *Stop them.*

She dropped her spent rifle and stole William's loaded musket before gliding into a sprint towards the bell tower. She caught a glimpse of the other crewmates coming out of the general store, armed to the teeth, before everything turned into a blur.

Anne was faster than the rest of the crew. Lighter in step, lithe, and catlike, she ran like the wind of a storm beating close to the ground as it swelled up a narrow street. Her feet were a flurry on the dirt road, the sound of a mad dance on the cobbles.

She passed the silent houses with the dead-still villagers resting inside. She fought the silence of that stillness with her beating feet and pounding heart in her ears. She would stomp away that silence any way she had. Until she finished the job, she would not brook any silence.

Figures in the night cut moonlight shadows onto the ground forty paces in front of her, and twenty from the bell tower entrance. The figures, cloaked in brown, ran toward the bell tower at a quick pace, but Anne was quicker.

She slowed a step to aim the musket and fired at the closest figure. Her aim was true, and it hit the man in the back. The man staggered, turned around, and drew a pistol. She ducked, and the bullet rushed over her head. She ran, pulling her cutlass from the sheathe. The man pulled out his own blade, but he was too slow. She sliced his gut open in passing. She moved forward, not looking back and not losing stride, her golden weapon outstretched and gleaming in the moonlight as she ran.

The second man busted through the door of the bell tower and tried to close it behind him. Anne leapt, her legs thrusting at the door just before it closed. The planks splintered and the door burst open, the cloaked man behind it staggering back into the bell tower.

The man fell, grasping for purchase. He found it on the bell's thick rope. His gaze shot up as he realized what his hands gripped. Anne rose from her jumping kick and thrust her blade at him before he had the chance to gain his wits. The man jumped into the air. Her cutlass pierced his chest with a soft thunk. He held tight to the rope, despite the wound, with a preternatural strength for a man soon to be dead. He pushed his full weight back down to complete the pull on the rope. Anne, holding fast to her blade in his chest, couldn't hold his weight.

The rope came down with his desperate pull, and the golden bell sounded overhead, its tone unlike anything Anne had ever heard before, and she was in the centre of it.

The chime was low and reverberating, and louder than all other sounds. It overpowered her heavy, frenzied breaths for air, and it seized the beating of her heart in her ears. She felt as though she were a sail held taut.

The low reverberation echoed in her bones, rattling her chest and legs and arms as though she had whacked a heavy stick with all her might against a metal beam. She let go of her sword, still stuck in the chest of the man who rang the bell, and staggered back from the pain of that noise.

As the bell rang, the low unnatural tone shifted and changed into a high pitch. The slow change could have been beautiful, as though she were present in the most compelling and evocative opera she had ever had the privilege of attending. Instead, the high pitch split her skull in twain with its crescendo. The noise became Anne's world. There was nothing but her and the noise.

The instinct to stop the noise subdued all other thoughts and overpowered her self-preservation. It compelled her to cover her ears, fall to her knees, and close her eyes to quell the melody of that bell.

After a moment, after an eternal, painful moment, the din subsided, and Anne opened her eyes and unclamped her ears, the world returning to her.

Silence had fallen in her absence from the world. Silence of the dead, or the soon to be.

The man Anne had killed inside the tower held fast to the rope with his death's rigour, keeping the striker of the bell at bay. Her golden cutlass still protruded from his chest, drops of blood pattering to the wooden floor. She eased him up gently to allow the striker to stay at rest before she cut him down so the bell could not sound again.

She stepped outside to see William and some of the other crewmates scattered about on the road leading back to the general store, eyes flickering back and forth. From the looks on their faces, even William's, the bell had rattled them just as much as her.

In that confusion in the wake of the bells cresting, Anne needed to be the rock that held the crew together. She took a deep breath, held in her frustrations, anger, and questions, and snuffed them out.

Just as she was about to issue orders to scout for more of the enemy crew, she swallowed her words when a tone similar to the golden bell rang out from the interior of the island. Though far off, it was clear and just as strange and ominous. Thankfully the volume of the ringing was low and didn't have the same effect as it had earlier.

A signal then, Anne thought. Some of the tension left her shoulders as she understood the reason behind the bells. It didn't change the fact that they had been found out by the enemy, but knowing what the bell was for eased some worry in her mind.

A few more tones sounded from different places on the island, one after the other. From what Anne could tell, there were four distinct rings, which meant there were at least four other bells. After another moment, the sounds faded, and silence returned.

The second element that robbed Anne of her speech was something altogether different. A door of a nearby home opened, and one of the residents of the hamlet stepped out. His slow, shuffling feet broke through the silence once more.

Anne moved to meet him. "You should head back inside," she said, and then she remembered the strange way they had been acting earlier. She gripped her cutlass tighter. "It's late, sir, you should be in bed."

He took another shuffling step forward. His face was pale in the moonlight. The shadows of some trees overhead shaded his eyes.

Another door creaked, splitting the silence again. Anne saw motion at another home down the dirt road.

She gripped her cutlass tighter still. Something wasn't right. "Back to the general store, now!" she ordered.

The man came closer, and Anne saw his eyes. They were hollow and lifeless, and there was no recognition of a spirit within them. Anne had only seen something similar in the eyes of men and women broken in one way or another through trauma, left in the world like husks, their bodies and minds forever torn.

The crew were stuck in place, watching the man as he came closer and closer to them, as though caught in the trance of those dead eyes. They couldn't tear themselves away from the spectacle, invisible tethers holding their feet in place.

The hollow man sprang into action, sprinting towards Anne, William, and crew. He moved quicker than Anne would have thought possible. He burst through the wooden fence between his house and the road, sending wooden chunks flying away with force.

The crew were too slow to react, and before they could move, the man hit a crewmate in the chest with a punch. The sailor toppled backwards as though hit with a cannonball, and Anne heard the distinct pop of bones breaking. The crewmate rolled back onto his side, clutching his chest and gasping for breath.

Anne's mind reeled with sudden realization. The golden bell was a trigger, a trigger for an even deeper trance, one that washed away all reason in the brain, perhaps washed away even the reason that kept one from utilizing the full power of their own muscles to avoid injury. And on top of that, these people with untold strength, stamina, and speed were hostile.

"William, help James back to the store," she ordered. "Everyone, run! Run, you fools!"

The crew, back in their right minds after seeing their mate attacked, followed orders and dashed back to the store. The hollow man, drawn to the movement, ran after the first who went into action. He leapt onto another crewmate and ravaged him with blow after horrifying blow.

The crewmates ahead kept running, but those behind stopped and levelled their muskets. They each unloaded their shots at the hollow man, careful not to hit their now bloody crewmate. With each shot, the hollow man recoiled, but he didn't stop his assault. *Crackcrackcrack, crack, crack.* Fifteen shots later the man fell over, his body as dead as his mind.

Anne pulled the hollow man off the crewmate, but it was too late. His skull had been bashed in with such force, it appeared as though he were the victim of a horse trampling.

"He's dead," she said curtly. "Back to the store!"

Anne took one look back to William to see that he was making along well and then hurried back to the store herself.

Against the myriad of stomping boots, Anne heard more creaking as doors were opening across the hamlet. She didn't let up in her stride, taking note of the noises but not letting it draw her attention. She passed the crewmates who had gone ahead of her. She needed to get to the store first.

On approaching the store, Anne noticed a few crewmates who had stayed behind, as well as Alexandre and Victoria. All were on alert from the activity they had heard and stood watch with weapons drawn.

"Barricade!" Anne yelled when she saw them. "We need to barricade the store, we're under attack."

Anne's words, urgency, and the crewmates just behind her flying towards them lit a fire under the crew's feet, and they ran into the store. Alexandre and Victoria seized the table holding the chessboard and the chairs from the deck, scattering the board and pieces across the dirt.

Anne jumped up to the deck, sliding across the wooden boards as she stopped in front of the entrance. She took a moment to breathe as she entered the store, once more taking stock of the thousand items and sorting them for their usefulness in her mind.

The crew brought boxes from the storage room, dense and filled with food or other items, into the central part of the store and began stacking them haphazardly.

"Bring them to the front, cover the windows. Make sure there are no gaps. Put the barrels in front to secure them in place." The crew, with a sound mind directing the action, put more focus into their work. "And someone bring me rope."

Just as someone brought her rope to work with, the crewmates who had joined her at the bell tower were making their way into the store again. She put the new men to work at once, forming a line from the storeroom to the side windows to bring the boxes forward.

Anne put the rope over her shoulder and closed one of the store's double doors, sealing the locking latch at the top and bottom of the door. William and the injured crewmate had yet to return, so she left the other door open.

Anne exited the store and peered down the road leading to the bell tower. William and the injured crewmate were slowly coming to the store, but behind them, the awakened townsfolk were gaining ground. Further to that, down each road leading to the store came more of the hollow people.

"Hurry," she yelled to them, though she knew they understood the urgency all too well.

The injured crewmate looked over his shoulder at the people gaining on them, but it didn't seem to give him renewed purpose. Instead, in his eyes, even at that distance, Anne could tell he had resigned himself to his fate. William pushed harder, taking on more of the weight, but his strength alone wasn't enough to make it in time.

The injured crewmate pushed William away before he pulled out his pistol. "Go," he muttered. There was an absolute strength in his soft declaration. William faltered but for a moment, then thanked the man for his bravery, and ran at full speed to the store.

The crewmate fired his pistol into the crowd as he did his best to back away, drawing the attention of the hollow people towards him instead of William and the general store. He tumbled over a nearby fence, lumbered to his feet, and pulled out a cutlass. He sliced wildly at the men and women approaching, a valiant effort against the storm, but they overwhelmed him. The hollow citizens tore the crewmate apart.

William reached the store, and pulled Anne back inside, not sparing a look back to the crewmate who had sacrificed himself to buy them time. Anne snapped back to the moment, resolving, no doubt as William had, not to waste those precious moments given them.

They closed the other door and latched it shut, but Anne knew it wouldn't be enough against the incredible strength that these entranced people were capable of.

"Bring the heaviest barrels over here in front of the doors."

The crew brought over three barrels so heavy they had to roll them across the floor rather than carry them. They placed all three directly in front of the two doors, flush against them.

Anne took the rope from over her shoulder and wrapped it

around the three barrels, pulling them tightly together. After the rope was secure, she tied both ends around the handles of the doors in a reef knot. The crew brought three more barrels and worked in pairs to place the new ones on top of the first, completely covering the door. With more rope, the six were secured into place as a unit and would be nearly impossible to topple.

Nearly impossible for normal humans.

"It's not enough," Anne muttered. "Is there more rope?"

"More?" one of the crewmates replied as he looked at the massive wooden fortification they had made.

"There is some left, though *le patron* is holding onto it at the moment," Alexandre said, though he trailed off as he seemed to realize something in his statement, and his gaze travelled to the doorway to the storage room.

Anne followed his gaze, and understood the problem at once. She drew her cutlass, the ringing of the foreign steel mimicking the cry of the bell in a way that made Anne wince.

As the sound of the blade waned and Anne focussed her attention on the back room, she could hear a vile frothing as if of some beast coming from the depths of the storage.

"Step away from the storage room!" she shouted.

A half a heartbeat passed before a loud snapping came from the storage room, followed by stomping boots across wooden floorboards. Jules barreled into the main room of the store, knocking against the walls.

His eyes, both aware and not, both alive and not, trained on Anne in a strange half-focus as though he were only taking in the shape of her and the cutlass in her hand.

Anne tried to act first and stepped forward, planning to strike, but Jules moved more quickly than she did. He darted forward, moving like a trained fighter, and lashed out at her as he dodged her strike. Anne pulled back her shoulder and twisted away from the blazing-fast fist, avoiding the blow and repositioning.

Though his strength and speed were extraordinary, it was

no replacement for proper training. He was a simple general store owner, not a fighter, and Anne had the training and the wherewithal to react to him.

Jules was wild, but hammered with a strength unparalleled. As each blow came Anne's way, and as she dodged just out of the way, she felt the force of each one. If any one of them made contact, bones would break.

William struck in the chaos, a fierce punch to the head knocking Jules back, but only slightly. Jules snarled, beast-like and feral, and turned his attention to William. Anne reared back and thrust her cutlass into Jules' stomach, gutting the portly man.

Were he a normal man, Jules would have doubled over in pain, but he kept fighting even as his intestines spilled out in front of him.

William faltered in the face of the walking dead man. Jules shot his fist forward. William pulled back, but too late. Jules' fist caught William in the left shoulder. A successive snap of several bones cracking broke through the tense air around them. William stifled a cry of shock and sliced his sword down and across Jules' head. The blade slammed halfway through Jules' skull and caught in the man's brain.

Finally, mercifully, Jules fell to the floor of the store. William held onto his blade as it fell with the dead man, stuck in the hard bone of the skull. He wiggled it free and backed away from the body, breathing hard. For a moment, William and Anne stared at the body together, along with several of the crewmates.

A noise outside drew their attention. The citizens of the hamlet were approaching the storefront en masse.

The din began as a small rap on the front doors but grew to a thunder of slamming bodies, breaking glass, and cracking wood. The six tall barrels at the front jolted forward with each second, teetering as though precariously perched on a precipice edge.

Instinctually, the crew rushed to reinforce the lifeless

wooden barricade keeping them from the horde of hollow men and women on the other side. They pressed their large sailor's bodies against the curved planks, adding weight to them.

On the sides of the general store, the citizens attacked the glass windows and less secure wooden boxes covering them.

Anne, pushing with her might against the barrels in front of the door, could see through a small gap as they broke through the glass and grabbed at the boxes in their way.

Though the townsfolk had obviously lost their wits, there was some intelligence still working the gears in their minds. The men slamming against the doors were ramming in unison, and the others took down the ramshackle wall to access the interior. Blood stained the hands of those prying at the boxes through the broken glass, shards sticking out from long slashes running up their arms.

"Gunners forward!" she shouted through the synchronized slams. "Aim for the head or the heart!"

The brave souls who heard the call jumped up to the ledge holding the boxes and barrels against the windows. Victoria was one such soul, and she fired into the thick of the men and women coming at them. First, she aimed at those taking down their protection, and then she took aim at the men attacking the front doors.

With each shot, smoke filled the room and settled in the small space. It wasn't long before the air was thick with the remnants of the black powder. The smell was bad enough, but the worst of it was the choking and seizing it brought to the lungs, and the effect on one's vision.

Anne could manage her breathing better than some, but the thick grey mist overtook her eyes and made them water.

"Cease—" Anne coughed as the smoke entered her throat proper. It arrested her voice as her body forced it out. "Cease fire!" she managed after a laboured moment.

The gunfire stopped after a few more shots into the thick mass of bodies in front of the store, and though the crew stopped firing, it only stopped more smoke from accumulating.

With no breeze, it lingered in the spaces between the crew's bodies, shifting and swirling with the small movements in a dance of air rarely seen.

A loud splintering noise split through the grunting on both sides of the store as one of the barrels burst open in the front. Its contents—potatoes buried in sand—spilled out in front of the double doors.

Suddenly, the synchronized slamming against the doors stopped, and there was a brief silence, a stillness of the air. At that moment, the silence closed in on Anne's heart and fixed it in place with an icy hand.

Just as suddenly as the silence came, it left again. The slamming didn't return, and instead, the wave of the hollow people outside the store rushed at the broken barrier. They punched and pulled at the weak spot, the chink in the armour, all hands and fingers prying and tearing at splinters and sand and potatoes. They smashed the wood to pieces inch by inch, creating an opening for the raging pile of people on the other side.

Anne knew it wouldn't be long for them if they stayed. "To the roof!" she shouted above the clamour, another cough of smoke choking the volume of her words. "Retreat!" she yelled as she led the charge up to the second floor of the store. Along the way, Anne grabbed an axe from the shelf.

The second floor of the store opened like an attic, with a hatch at the top of steep ladder stairs not unlike their ship. Anne climbed first and held the door open for the crew to climb in more quickly.

The crewmates who had made it inside the store were uninjured, aside from the smoke lingering in the lungs. A few of the men coughed and took long and laboured breaths as they entered the storage room and climbed the stairs up to the second floor.

The only one injured was William, who was last up the stairs. He couldn't move his injured shoulder, but one could hardly tell if it slowed him any as he climbed the stairs like any other.

As soon as William was on the other side of the horizontal door, Anne planted her feet square as she held the hatch open with her hip. She lifted the axe she had pilfered from the storefront in both hands and slammed it down on the top of the stairs. The axe cut through the wooden beam a quarter way, revealing it to have an old, blunted edge.

Anne cursed under her breath and wrenched the axe free before tossing it aside. She pulled out the golden cutlass, the strange, ever-sharp metal made of the same ore as the bell, and it rang into the frigid night once more with its peculiar song.

Just as she pulled it out, the first of the citizens who had made it through the front of the store ran into the back room and began climbing the stairs.

Anne sliced the blade downwards at one of the hinges bolting the stairs to the top floor, and it cracked in half. The stairs went slightly uneven but still stood.

The man who was climbing only faltered a bit when his weight shifted beneath him, but continued his ascent.

Anne had no time to rear back for another strike; if she did, the hollow man would be on her. She pulled back and threw the hatch closed. The man's hand crashed upwards through the hatch, and he clawed at the boards.

William, who had stayed by her side, locked the hatch in place before the man could push it open. It wouldn't do much against that abnormal strength, but each second counted.

Anne didn't waste a breath for thanks and ran to the second floor sleeping quarters. "To the roof!" she said as she pointed to two windows overlooking the front of the store. Her voice was almost back to normal without the smoke choking her throat.

The crewmates used their muskets to break the glass of the windows and clear the debris before jumping through. Anne turned around to watch the doorway to the second floor, her cutlass poised in front of her.

Slam! The hatch pulsed up with a loud thud and clank of

the metal lock. Anne tensed and bent her knees. *Slam!* Another crack against the wood from below. Anne backed up, feeling the crewmates behind her thinning as they went to the roof. *Slam!* The pounding came with a creak as the wood strained to stay together. She gritted her teeth and shifted to holding the cutlass in both hands.

Slam! The wood broke open in two, one plank still attached to the lock as the other side flew open. The side that opened hit the wall and came back down on the head of the man at the top of the stairs, but he climbed through unabated.

"Anne!" Victoria called out to her.

Anne turned around and jumped out the nearest window in one motion. The shards of glass still attached to the frame cut through her clothes and sliced into her skin before she landed on the small roof on top of the deck. A musket shot rang out behind her just as she fell, the crack of the black powder coinciding with the crack of her shoulder against the wood.

Alexandre helped Anne to her feet, his typically placid eyes burning with that same volcanic rage she'd seen before but mixed with a pitying expression on his face. He felt sorry for the men and women attacking them at that moment, for the reason behind their unreasonableness.

Anne gripped his arm. "If you have time for pity, you have time to think a way out for us."

Alexandre glanced at her and then doubled back as her words hit him. He smiled, but there was none of the small warmth in it she had felt before she had gone to sleep. "Is it not obvious?" he said. "We must kill them all."

"How can we kill them when we can't even hold them here?" Victoria yelled over her shoulder at Alexandre as she shot into the window again.

"We won't have to hold them for long," William said at the side of the roof.

Anne joined him at the side of the roof and looked in the direction he was pointing. In the distance, she could see the shapes of twenty people advancing in the waning moonlight towards the town. They came in the direction of where they first landed, so chances were they were crewmates from the *Queen Anne's Revenge*.

And, if that weren't enough of an indication, Anne could make out another figure ahead of the pack running at blazing speeds towards them. The figure had a spear in one hand, and he was missing an arm.

As though challenging William's assertion, one of the entranced jumped through the window at Victoria. Victoria fell backwards, her musket braced between her and the crazed man on top of her. Victoria kept rolling back and kicked the man off the roof with her momentum. Anne watched as the man fell headfirst to the ground, his neck snapping violently to the side in a deathly contortion.

Before Victoria fell off the roof with the man, Alexandre caught her hand and pulled her to safety.

"Back away from the windows," Anne commanded. "There's too many of them. Kill them as they come onto the roof."

The musketeers moved away from the open windows and stepped back as much as the small space allowed. Another citizen climbed through the windowpane a moment later, and an iron ball met his temple. With the musket spent, the crewmate moved out of the way to allow another a better vantage point.

Anne glanced back to the road and saw Pukuh nearly at the centre of the hamlet. Anne called to him, and he looked up to their perch, losing a half step. Anne pointed to the front of the store.

"Fight them one on one. Aim for the head or heart."

Pukuh motioned with his spear in her direction and slowed his gait even further as he approached the corner of the general store's front deck. He lowered his stance as he glided towards the remaining enemies.

The twenty crewmates on his tail approached, weapons drawn. Noticing Pukuh's caution, they slowed to join him. Anne repeated her message to the newcomers before turning around to the rooftop battle.

The change in vantage point proved effective at managing the numbers, and before long the sounds of raging, entranced people dissipated, and the battle with them. When no more enemies jumped through to attack them, the crew risked looking inside.

After confirming it was safe and all the villagers were dead, Anne and the rest of the crew on the roof re-entered the second floor. They went down to the first floor where the other crewmates, along with dozens of dead bodies, awaited them.

The smoke of the earlier musket fire had abated, and Anne could see and breathe more freely. Blood splattered every wall and covered much of the items in the store. Twenty to thirty bodies lay in piles in each corner and out to the deck, blood and guts and brains pooling and oozing out of their now truly lifeless bodies.

The crewmates who had come to their rescue, including Pukuh, appeared winded, wounded, and confused as they looked over the bodies of what, to them, were ordinary farmers and housewives.

Before anyone could ask, Anne spoke up. "Everything will be explained in time. For now, I want to be back on the ship to rest. Questions can wait for dawn."

Anne awoke in the middle of her sleep for the second time that night, but this time it was not with the cracking sound of a pistol ringing into the night. It was with the warning of more to come on the horizon.

"Ship approaching off the port bow. To quarters!" she heard William shouting outside her door.

Before the inevitable knock came, she was out of bed and opening it to his startled face. Behind him, men were clamouring to ready the cannons and muskets for a ship battle.

Anne and William went to the weather deck, where Anne

traced across the horizon towards the approaching ship. She pulled out a spyglass and saw a sloop heading for them. Dawn had broken, and she would have overslept if she had gotten enough sleep the first time. As it stood, she was burning the candle on both ends, twice over.

Anne wiped away the tired from her eyes, took a deep breath, and prepared herself for a battle of a different sort.

Amidst final preparations for battle, something strange happened as the sloop approached. It slowed to a full stop just out of range of the cannons, just close enough for her to see the name *Whydah Gally* on the side, and Anne could see its crew lowering a longboat into the water.

What sort of trickery is this? "Muskets to port! Hold steady," she commanded.

She watched the longboat as it slowly came closer and closer to the *Queen Anne's Revenge*. Before long, she could make out those in the boat, as well as the one at the head, standing tall and lean with a familiar pretty face and jet-black eyes.

Anne gasped and shook her head in disbelief. "Sam?"

8. PIRATES AND THIEVES

Edward went to stroke his beard absentmindedly before he remembered he had shaved it off not a few days prior. His hands shook. The haunting feeling he so desperately wanted to suppress had returned. He took another drink from his flask.

"May I?" Herbert beckoned with his hand outstretched.

Edward, Herbert, and John all sat just outside of the alcove near the surgeon's room. Edward was sitting directly on the deck, his arms resting on his bent knees and his back against the wall of the room. Herbert was in front of him, leaning forward in his wheelchair, and John was to his left sitting on a tall box of cargo.

Edward took another swig and reluctantly handed it to Herbert, who took a generous portion for himself.

The crewmates who had gathered before at the sound of the gunfire had dispersed back to their eating or work above deck. Very few crewmates seemed surprised or even upset over the news that their captain had just executed Nigel, and the few that were didn't hold the feeling for long.

"You said she didn't rule this ship through intimidation," Edward mumbled. The words blurted out without his meaning to say them, and he regretted them at once. It was a childish accusation of a lie and felt more lash than a question.

John looked at Edward, knowing the words were meant for him. His face was stone, but his youthful eyes showed the pain of that lash. "And I stand by it," he said simply. "She saved your life, probably all our lives, by doing what she did to Nigel."

"And then she threatened us," Herbert chimed in.

"She told you the rules. I already told you that her word is law, that's the difference."

"And where exactly are these laws written?" Edward levelled John with a forceful gaze he hoped had the intended effect. After John was silent for a moment, Edward continued. "She rules on whims only she can know. Had he done something else that displeased her, she could have come up with some other law of hers to justify the act. How are we to know when we step on her toes?"

John rose to his feet and balled his fists. "Nigel was told to leave you be. He disobeyed that order. Or did you forget that?" John stared daggers at Edward in defence of his captain. He seemed almost a bit too invested. "Would you have done any differently were you captain and someone nearly killed a crewmate over a petty dispute?"

Edward glanced over at Herbert, remembering how he had punished him for disobeying orders. Had Herbert been more like Nigel, would he have killed him over it? He'd left Kenneth Locke stranded on an island to die, doing everything but pull the trigger—and he'd later regretted it when Kenneth came back as Cache-Hand. He'd also admonished Bartholomew Roberts for sparing Walter Kennedy.

John seemed to hit hard at Edward's sensibilities. He hadn't been as consistent upon reflection as he had hoped he had been in practice. In some ways, he had become harsher, and in others, more lax in his responsibilities.

Edward let out a sigh as he looked away from Herbert and stared at the deck. "I don't know what I would have done had I been in her position," he said. "Perhaps you are right, and perhaps I would have done the same."

John's hand and face relaxed in tandem as Edward backtracked. "So, what does this mean?"

Edward shook his head. The rum was beginning to make him hot, or perhaps it was the slight twinge of embarrassment. "I suppose it means I owe you an apology for my outburst." John appeared taken aback at the comment but accepted the apology. "And it means we need to be more cautious around our new captain." This time Edward glanced over towards Herbert, the words meaning more for him than what he was letting on in front of John. Herbert understood the message and gave Edward a nod.

There was another moment of silence as the group reflected on what had just happened, as well as the tense conversation. Each of them seemed shaken by how close they had come to be a splatter of gore on the deck of the ship.

John looked at Edward, a small smirk on his face now that he had calmed down. "If nothing else, this will make quite the story. First day on board and you got someone killed. That must be an accomplishment somewhere."

It was Edward's turn to be taken aback this time, and he was shocked into a different kind of silence for a moment. He glanced over at Herbert, who had what felt like the same dumbfounded expression on his face as well. Then the two burst out laughing, and John joined in.

"I suppose that is true," Edward said through the laughter. "On a pirate ship perhaps less so, but I shall see it as an accomplishment nonetheless." Edward, for the first time in a long while, laughed sincerely and with genuine mirth. It forced him to rise to his feet and clap John on the shoulder.

After another moment of laughter, and a sharing of Edward's flask, the three compatriots, now in better spirits, headed back to the crew quarters.

Now that supper had officially ended for the first shift, and the evening shift had broken their fast, the crew slung hammocks in the cramped space. With the numbers they had, as well as the small size of the quarters, each row of hammocks was stacked three high. The bottom one would have one's posterior scraping the sole of the deck, the middle gave no room to move without touching the mate above, and the top ran the risk of smacking one's head on the overhead.

Herbert chose the middle as it allowed him ease of sliding

into and out of his chair. John went to the top as he was smaller than Edward, and it forced Edward to the bottom. His bigger frame and heavier build meant that he was touching the floor more than the average crewmate. Instead of just a light scraping with the sway of the ship that could be ignored, his hip struck the sole hard with each swing. He tried to tighten the hammock, and it provided some relief in exchange for more rigidity, and so instead of no sleep, he was left with little sleep.

Not that his dreams would allow him much more regardless. The rum mitigated the deeper sleep that brings with it images both pleasant or harrowing familiar to most folk, but it couldn't stop them completely.

Two times in the night, Edward awoke with a start, stopping himself just shy of hitting Herbert's backside with his face. As with most dreams, whether joyful or distressful, he lost all knowledge of it upon his waking. All he had was a fog of dread arresting his thoughts and a tremble of the fingers that wasn't from a cool breeze. He had no way to know for sure, but from the way his sleeping mind and body reacted, the dreams couldn't have been pleasant ones.

Edward had been paralyzed by similar dreams for nights on end, long enough that he couldn't remember the last time he'd had a full night's sleep.

After a few hours of fitful slumber, the beat of a drum and a young man shouting orders to wake and relieve the other crewmates forced Edward awake.

Edward's body ached more than it had before he'd tried to sleep. His tired limbs were slow to act, and pressure in his head pushed from the back, increasing the fog and exhaustion he felt. He resorted to rubbing his eyes and slapping his face to wake himself, and taking another drink from his ever-emptying flask to stave off the pain.

Herbert, though forced to journey as a passenger, also rose and entered his chair to join Edward on the weather deck. He looked a touch more refreshed than Edward did, but it was clear that he too had trouble sleeping on the foreign ship.

John jumped down to the sole of the deck, fresh and ready to go with energy only youth could muster. Even with only a few hours of sleep, he seemed to not need any more. Though if Edward could place a wager, he had a feeling that before long, John would lag behind the more experienced crewmates.

The three headed towards the ladder leading to the weather deck, and Herbert and Edward went into motion with a practiced efficiency of long years together. Herbert jumped off his chair and climbed up the ladder as swift as a snake. Edward, after a few breaths and repositioning to not reopen his wounds, and declining help from John, lifted the chair overhead. Balancing it with one hand, and with the other holding to a rope leading up the steep ladder, he climbed to the weather deck. After another moment's respite to catch his breath, he took the chair further up some steps to the quarterdeck where guests were meant to stay.

After gingerly placing the chair down, Herbert climbed in. "Are you well?" he asked Edward, keeping his voice low.

Edward nodded, though he knew his breathing would say otherwise. He also caught himself leaning on the handle of Herbert's chair for support and stopped himself.

"You haven't been sleeping well, I notice." Herbert left a second question unuttered.

Edward decided to sidestep Herbert's undertone with a retort. "Neither have you," he said, not looking at Herbert directly.

Herbert frowned. "Come now, we're in…" Herbert's gaze flitted to the other crewmates already on watch, and the closest few near the helm. He lowered his volume again. "We're alone here. We need to be together here more than ever. If you need help, you need to tell me."

Edward's everything itched at the conversation. He wanted to be away from it more than anything. He clenched his fist and levelled a steely gaze at Herbert. "And how exactly can you help me here?" he snarled. "How can you when you can't even rig a ship in that chair of yours?" Edward rose to his full height as Herbert's expression turned from brows raised to furrowed, with a side of clenched jaw.

"That was unnecessary," Herbert replied with bared teeth.

Edward knew that what he'd said was wrong, but he was too tired for remorse. "I'm sorry," he said hastily, too hastily for sincerity, "but I can handle myself, and it would behoove you not to place more of a burden on me with your incessant questions." Edward rubbed the sleep from his eyes, hoping to catch some of the frustration in between his thumb and fore-finger at the same time. "I've got work to do," he said as he walked away.

Throughout the night, Edward was tasked with securing rigging, keeping watch and relaying navigational information to the helmsman, making minor repairs to the spare sails in the quarterdeck cabin, and when that was exhausted, he had to swab the deck.

All the while, the crew were taking every opportunity to make his job harder than it had to be. From outstretched feet trying to send him tumbling to 'accidental' drops of tools to the sole of the deck, to creating the messes they forced him to clean, the crew united in a passive-aggressive battle to break him.

And, to make it just that much worse, when Edward had a chance to look up from his work and wipe the sweat from his brow, he took notice of the other crewmates on night watch lounging and not even working a third as hard as he.

If this were any other ship, he would have taken issue with the disparity, and at that moment, as irritable as he was, he felt such rage over it he could have slit someone's throat. On this ship, and with the smirks the other crewmates were giving him, his hardship was by design, the silent architects of his misfor-tune being the captain's declaration that he does the work of several men to make up for Herbert's presence, and upheld by the mate in charge and the crew.

At the end of several hours of that backbreaking work, and the leering crew watching, it was finally time for a change of crew on deck. Herbert told Edward he would stay on deck to observe for the rest of the night, so Edward headed towards the ladder below deck.

The mate in charge stopped him. "Hold there," he said. "You're to stay working."

Edward's hand twitched, the itch to grab the man by the throat almost overpowering his reason. He said nothing, just stared down at the man while breathing hard from the exertion.

Something about Edward's silence, his towering height above the mate, and his crazed look seemed to give the man pause, and he backed up half a step. "Captain's orders," he stammered.

Edward felt too exhausted to even speak a response. He simply grunted as he pushed past the mate and went to the quarterdeck, all the way to the stern behind some rigging and storage, to rest before the new crewmates arrived to start working again.

John was on Edward's heels just as he turned around to flop onto the deck. "What happened?"

Edward took several deep breaths before answering. "It seems," he paused for another breath, "I am to do the work of several men in the most literal of senses. Not only am I working while others gawk like some beggar freak in the street, but I cannot even rest as a normal crewmate would." John didn't know how to respond and stammered a few words, which Edward paid little attention to. The stammering reminded Edward of his dead crewmate with the same name. "Get out of here before I take out my frustration on you."

John looked like he had been slapped in the face. He took a few steps back, turned about, and was quickly out of sight.

Edward closed his eyes and draped his forearm over them to rest as much as he could, but through all the layers, he could still feel Herbert's gaze on him. "If you've some witty comment to say, just be done with it so I can rest what little amount possible."

"Hmph," Herbert scoffed. "You know you're quite skilled at pushing allies away? Does it come naturally, or is it from your father?"

Edward's hand clenched, and his breathing caught in his throat, but he didn't move his arm away nor open his eyes. After a moment, he could hear Herbert's wheelchair scraping against the wood of the ship as he turned around and let Edward be.

Edward lay there motionless as the rocking of the ship swayed him in all directions. The frigid night breeze pulled away his heat, both from exertion and anger, and when he had calmed, he opened his eyes to the pale waxing sliver of the moon.

A gift from my father? I wonder.

Edward rose to his shaky feet and gave himself another moment to muster the strength he needed to continue. After that tenuous moment, he went back to work with the new set of crewmates who looked much more full of vigour than he.

That extra vigour didn't change their attitude towards him, and the new mate in charge continued the work of the last. They conspired in pushing Edward beyond his limits while letting the other crewmates be. Since Nigel's untimely end, those meagre few who had seemed to be of a better calibre, who had helped him in the morning, were either gone or no longer sympathetic to his plight.

The thought only served to irritate Edward further, and incidentally bestowed him with a bit more wind in his sails.

Edward worked, and pushed, and pulled, and ripped every last ounce of strength he had. He had been going with practically no rest for nearly a whole day, and he felt it in his bones.

The sounds of the mate shouting orders, the wind whipping

the sails, the waves lapping against the ship, and even the creaking of the vessel itself washed away. He only felt his heart beating up around his ears and the breath in his chest.

The cool sea air felt crisp and alive as he took it in and made it a part of him over and over. It made him feel strange at that moment, though. Coupled with the exhaustion, he felt as though he were floating in that wind surrounding his body. He was no longer himself, but he was the sea and the air.

Before, it had always been in battle, but now the only battle was against himself and his own body. He told himself to take stock of this feeling, whatever it may be, and hold it within. Through the fog of his mind at that moment, he knew this was important.

Edward looked around the ship with new eyes, as though seeing it for the first time. The crew around him were inconsequential, just statues atop a beautiful piece of craftsmanship.

After a moment to take in all he felt and memorize it, he noticed the statues moving on the quarterdeck in a peculiar pattern.

The crew had bunched up on the quarterdeck, several of them surrounding Herbert. They had trapped Herbert between them all, and he couldn't get away.

Edward kept hold of his state of mind, the floating feeling between the sky and sea, where he could see everything clearly. He glided over to the statues, the crewmates who were not his crew, the many faces he cared not to take stock of.

On the quarterdeck, two of the statues moved to stop him, and Edward understood better then why they reminded him of statues. Their movements looked unnaturally slow and stiff at that moment.

Using the lessons Anne, William, Pukuh, and countless battles had taught him, he grabbed the men and used their own momentum and limbs against them. With the most minimal effort on his part, Edward pushed one of the men over the side of the railing of the quarterdeck, where he fell to the deck below, and the other tripped and dashed down the ladder behind Edward.

The other men surrounding Herbert took notice of Edward approaching and said words to him, but he couldn't hear them. He was floating too far above everyone for the words to reach him. The sea air would not carry the words to him across its sweet notes.

He walked forward on legs so far beyond numb that it felt as though he were gliding across the deck. Judging by the faces of the men in front of him, he must have looked like a spectre coming towards them. They pulled back at his gaze and moved out of his way without a touch, each of them turning pale when they looked up at him.

Next to Herbert, two of the men, stouter or stupider than the others, it would be hard to say, stayed put. They made threatening gestures and appeared to shout obscenities, a possible plea for him to stop his advance.

Edward stopped, but not because of anything they said. He bore his gaze down on the first man who had the gall to take a step forward and before long, the man's threatening words caught in his throat. He coughed and stepped aside.

The other man had hands on Herbert, and though he looked confusedly back and forth from his comrades to Edward, his brow was slick with sweat, and his lips trembled.

Edward stared into the man's eyes and then recalled a saying that the eyes were the window to the soul. He pictured himself bashing the man's head into the fife rail of the nearby mast and the man's body twitching before it went limp. As he imagined it in his own mind's eye, he slowly pulled his massive fist into a ball.

The final crewmate received the message in his core. The tremble in his lips extended to the rest of his body as he let go of Herbert and backed away. His body involuntarily hunched in deference as Edward's gaze followed him to the fife rail, where the wooden railing appearing behind him caused him to jump.

Edward took the last step towards Herbert and looked him in the eyes next. He didn't conjure any image in his mind, nor did he think he looked at him with any malice, but in Herbert's eyes, Edward could tell he looked crazed.

He felt of two minds at that moment. On one side, he was free from all his exhaustion and pain over the last hours, and it also gave him the respite from the arresting thoughts that plagued him of late. On the other, he felt a different pain from the look in Herbert's eyes: the look of fear mixed with the look one would give a stranger together told Edward he wasn't himself.

His mind split into the two thoughts broke the spell he was under, and he could once more hear the whispers and movement of the men surrounding them.

"We're done for the night," he said as he looked at Herbert, but loudly enough for those around him to hear. He turned around and faced the night crew. "Any objections?"

"So, what were they on about up there?" Edward asked when they were below deck.

Herbert paused for a moment, not looking at Edward as he pushed his chair forward towards the crew quarters. "They took issue with some notes I had taken."

"Notes?"

Herbert stopped his advance and reached into his jacket pocket, then passed a small booklet to Edward. He didn't explain any further, and Edward expected he was to find the answer himself.

Edward flipped through the pages of the booklet, taking note of small drawn charts and numbers he was able to recognize as calculations of wind speed and orders issued by a helmsman. As he went further, he took notice of names and designs relating to the brigantine they found themselves on. At the front few pages were a list of corrections and errors on the part of the helmsman and lower-ranking officers in charge of the *Black Blood*. He also noticed a few attributed to the captain, Grace O'Malley herself.

Edward chuckled as he closed the booklet and handed it back to Herbert. "Well, pray they've learned their lesson today."

Herbert cocked his brow. "To tell it true, I didn't know what to expect, but that's not how I thought you would react."

"Just keep that thing hidden. It may prove useful." Edward leaned closer to Herbert to whisper. "And perhaps with your eyes, you can make a list of those who are loyal to Grace O'Malley and keep a tally of their faults. That, too, could prove useful should we lose favour with our dear captain even more."

Herbert nodded, and instead of returning the booklet to his pocket, he placed it in the hidden compartment in his wheelchair.

Edward and Herbert returned to the crew quarters and back to their hammocks. John was fast asleep, swaying overhead. Edward was last in his hammock, and he lumbered in as the pain began coming back to his conscious mind. He fell into the hammock and closed his eyes and mercifully fell into a deep sleep reserved for the genuinely spent.

Just as instantly as he had fallen asleep, Edward awoke from John slapping his arm. Edward looked about in a half-dazed state. He rolled out of the hammock and rose slowly to his feet.

The slight pain he'd experienced just before falling into his dead sleep hit him in full, and across every inch of his body. He was slower now, and there was little he could do about it save push past. He recalled the floating feeling he had experienced before and tried to channel it, but it was just beyond his grasp. If he had been flying on the weather deck before, now he was simply jumping a few inches off the ground. He could hold it for the briefest moment before it turned to sand between his fingers.

John, Herbert, and he all ate a hearty meal and were given a brief rest before they returned to the weather deck. John had informed Edward that he managed to sleep through another shift, and given that they had returned early due to the previous incident, Edward estimated he had gotten a full five or six hours of sleep. It was the most uninterrupted sleep he had had in some time, and though he hoped for more, he feared it would be the last for another great while.

Edward and Herbert continued taking double shifts while getting only the barest amount of sleep as the crew pushed Edward to the brink of collapse each time.

After the second full four hours, Edward's nausea from the constant work took over, and he vomited over the side of the ship. He managed to keep silent and out of sight as he tilted his head over the side by making it look as though he was on his knees swabbing the deck near the starboard rails.

He cursed himself for his weakness. His body felt hollow and leaden at the same time, and his throat and temples throbbed continuously with each beat of his pounding heart.

That momentary weakness, hidden from the crew's eyes, was the lowest point for him. After that, the situation aboard improved, and not merely because he no longer felt nauseated.

The mood aboard the ship seemed to shift with each passing hour, and with each change of the crew. Perhaps due to pity, respect, or perhaps the words of warning from the crew involved in the earlier incident—Edward could not know which—the crew of the *Black Blood* stopped their attempts to break him. The feet trying to trip him, the 'accidents' meant to make his job harder, as well as the other crewmates not working as he broke his back slowly trickled away until none in the crew seemed to go out of their way to make his life more difficult.

After three days of the routine, the crewmates were treating him with a mild indifference rather than the overt contempt they had been expressing earlier.

And, to Edward's surprise, he had gotten used to the extra labour. His body began healing and growing stronger from the effort, and after his nausea had lessened, he worked with John to acquire more foodstuff so he could maintain his energy and not run himself ragged.

Afternoon on the third day, the *Black Blood* landed at the harbour of an island unfamiliar to him and to John. Edward felt it useless to ask others in the crew where they were as they too may not know the answer or would refuse to answer.

After they secured the ship, Grace gathered a landing party and issued orders to keep the ship ready to sail. After a moment of searching, Grace's eyes met Edward's, and she motioned for him to join her, her hands rock-solid against her hips, and her straight back and stern eyes brooking no argument—not that Edward wished to arouse her ire by attempting refusal.

Edward, his body still stiff and his muscles radiating heat, casually walked over to Grace and the two senior officers making up her landing party.

"I want ya with me. Be good ta see how we do things on this crew."

"And what exactly is it we're about to do?"

Grace scrutinized Edward like she had when they first met, but this time it was less an appraisal of his worth and more a search of his person. She leaned to the side to look beyond Edward's massive body. "Did none of you bastards give him any weapons? Someone bring him a sword and pistol before I start asking more questions."

A mate nearby rushed to a reserve of weapons and brought Edward what Grace asked as he avoided her gaze. Edward put the cutlass at his side and hid the pistol under the front of his shirt, secured in the loop of his belt.

"Does that answer yer question, or do ye have any more?"

Judging Grace's tone to be annoyance, Edward didn't reply.

"Hmph," she scoffed, to which Edward thought he had made an error in not standing up to her. "To shore, you lot."

Grace led the way, followed by her senior officers, and Edward trailed behind them, trying to match their pace.

The town they had landed in seemed an unlikely locale for brigands and pirates, being barely big enough to call for a harbour for docking ships. The most wealth it appeared to have were its farmland Edward could see off in the distance.

So, that means it's a hiding place? But for whom?

Edward placed his hand on the cutlass at his side, and he thought the answer to his question was meaningless. Whoever was hiding here wouldn't be hiding for much longer, he supposed.

As Edward, Grace, and the two crewmates strode forward, Edward could feel the air growing thick as eyes followed them. Everyone in that small town was watching them. The hair on Edward's arm prickled under the gazes of the unseen men and women behind closed curtains and shuttered windows.

"Don't mind 'em," Grace said over her shoulder. "We're about ta do this town a favour."

The excitement coming from Grace made Edward uneasy. For the first time since Edward's moment of pure exhaustion three days prior, he felt a creeping turmoil bubbling up in his gut.

Edward reached for the flask but stopped himself short. Instead, he tried to grab hold of the feeling of floating from before. He tried to still his mind and push down the hollow gravity just beneath his ribs.

For a moment, a meagre few ticks of a clock's second hand, Edward held fast to that feeling and then lost it to the ether. Edward imbibed once more to still the trembling.

The four of them entered a local tavern and inn, and to Edward's astonishment the establishment was filled to the brim with merriment, a stark contrast to the rest of the quiet town.

With each slam of Grace's copper greaves, the room fell quieter until there was a hush in which one could hear a pin drop. She took a seat out from a table and sat down with that same casual nature she'd had just before she killed Nigel.

"Bring him ta me." In that hush, Grace's voice filled the room just as boisterously as the din that had preceded it.

There was a moment of stillness where none made a move, and all eyes stared at Grace. The brigands whom Edward supposed they were here for all seemed to know who Grace was and, judging by the terror in their eyes, the knowledge momentarily locked them in place.

The townsfolk, the owner and the tavern wenches who all looked injured in some way or another, didn't seem sure what to make of the newcomers. They, too, had a look of terror in their eyes, but there was a bit of relief in their faces, as though they hoped the newcomers would soon relieve their town of the brigands occupying it.

Grace turned her gaze to one of the men and then pointed to him before snapping her fingers. The man interpreted the message, and he ran up to the second storey to one of the rooms of the inn.

"Blackstad, sit down. Those idle hands of yers are gonna get ya killed."

It took a moment for Edward to remember the name they were using aboard the *Black Blood*, and then another moment to realize he was gripping his cutlass as though he were about to unsheathe it. He relaxed his hand and took a seat on the other side of the small table, leaving enough room for whoever was about to join them.

After another moment, the door of one of the rooms upstairs burst open, and a tall, lanky man with a greasy mess of a beard and equally messy long hair came out. He was pulling up his trousers as he took note of where Grace was. A few seconds later, after the man who had gone to get his comrade exited, a half-naked woman ran out and into another room.

Edward noticed that the woman was bloody and bruised, and he thought he could see tears streaming down her face as she ran by.

The man lazily fixed his trousers and strutted down to the first floor, his casual and cocksure attitude on full display. He didn't match his comrades' moods in the slightest, and by the time he stepped to the first floor and took a chair, sitting backwards on it with his arms resting on the back, his men relaxed a bit.

For every bit that the other men relaxed, Edward tensed. It felt as though he was the only sane person of the lot and the only one who was sure of what was about to happen. He had to restrain himself from pulling out his pistol and cutlass right then to put an end to it all.

The man glanced from Grace to Edward, to her men, and then to his own men, and back. He grinned. "It's been a long while, Grace."

"Cut it, you know what we're here for."

"Aww, Grace, you wound me," the man said, his words dripping with sarcasm. "We're old friends, ain't we? What happened to civility? Is there no honour amongst us thieves?"

"We're pirates." Grace tilted her head. "*You're* the thief."

The man appeared taken aback. "Some would say we're the same, you and I."

"Enough. Save me some trouble and return what ye stole."

Though Grace was doing her best, her commanding tone had little effect on this man. Whatever relationship they had had, the man underestimated her. Or, for all Edward knew, it was plain stupidity. Whatever the case, it was not going to end well, of that Edward was sure.

The man adopted a confused, amused expression. "If a pirate claims ownership of something and a thief steals it, is it still a crime?" He held his palm open as though he were pondering the question. "I suppose a few lawyers could settle the matter, given enough time."

Grace ignored the fool's ruminations. "I've asked ye nicely, I'll not ask again."

The man cocked his brow. "Oh, threats now? You're outgunned, Grace. And I've got a stable full of horses rested and ready to take us to the opposite shore before the men on your ship know what's happened." The man leaned forward. "So why not just pack up and leave before my men and I pump your pretty face full of lead?"

Upon the escalation of events, the thieves became emboldened once more. They joined in with their leader's declaration, and some even pulled out their weapons to bolster the intimidation.

Grace simply sat there, staring down the leader with her cold, calm expression. Her officers didn't seem intimidated by the thieves' threats either, and they stood there with arms folded, staring at the other men in the room.

Grace waited for a full minute until the thieves' words died away and there was minimal murmur of activity and threatening gestures. As soon as it was quiet enough, she spoke again. "You know what the difference between a pirate and a thief is?"

The sudden change in subject brought him and his compatriots up short. He turned to them and flashed a wry smile before gazing back at Grace. "No, what?"

Grace leaned forward, and Edward's hair stood on end for the second time that night. "Thieves are weak."

Grace slammed her boots to the floor, grabbed hold of a hidden apparatus and pulled a string. The sound of several shots of gunfire rang out. Lead shots burst into the leader of the thieves' chest. He was dead in an instant, blood pouring from several wounds.

Grace's copper greaves for which she was famous held some mechanism inside them to fire bullets. It was seemingly a well-kept secret to those not in her crew, as the thieves had no idea what had happened or from where Grace had shot their leader.

Grace's senior officers, before she had even fired her secret weapon, drew their own weapons and attacked the rest of the thieves. The other men failed to react in time, and three of their comrades were dead almost instantly.

The thieves still living reached for their weapons, and Edward pulled out his cutlass and stabbed one of them. This drew the attention of more than a few of those remaining. Edward pulled his loaded pistol from his belt and fired. The bullet hit the last enemy in the head.

The leader of the men, so bold previously, lay there bleeding out. Grace's secret attack had made a gory mess of his chest and legs.

Grace hadn't moved from her seat since her secret weapon's firing that had started the conflict. She glanced from side to side, looked Edward up and down, then got to her feet as smoke still rose from the holes in her copper greaves.

She searched the dead man's pockets and found the item they had come for, but Edward couldn't see what it was. Grace pocketed the thing as quickly as she snatched it.

"We're done here. Back to the ship."

9. SMOKE

"You thought I wus dead?" Sam Bellamy bellowed before bursting out in his old hyena's laugh that was equal parts nostalgic and unsettling.

Anne had taken Sam into the captain's quarters, partially to show him the room he had never seen before owing to his departure prior to it being opened, and also to speak with him privately.

Anne shrugged. "We had no way to confirm Cache-Hand's claim, but we hadn't heard about your recent promotions."

"Can't say I blames ye. I thought I killed ol' Ed." Sam's face grew dark as he looked to the floorboards of that once familiar ship. "Cache-Hand beat 'im bloody, then cut him to ribbons before they poisoned 'is food and tossed him in that Irish lake. I tried to keep him safe, tried to get him out, but there was no way." Sam looked up at Anne, pain in his eyes. "Ye got ta believe me, I tried."

Anne tried her best to smile back at Sam. The memory of that time, how thin and ragged and… *broken* Edward had looked made it difficult. "No one blames you, Sam," she said before reaching across the table to squeeze his hand. "You did what you had to to survive. And, besides, he survived. I'm sure you played a part in that."

Sam seemed genuinely relieved by Anne's absolution. After a moment, his eyes went down to the golden ring on Anne's hand. He pointed at it, at first bemused, and after a moment, amused.

"Yes, it was done after we opened this room, and the ship was renamed."

Sam leaned back and let out a sigh. "Too bad I missed that.

Musta been an event. A bloody princess marrying a pirate? Never thought I'd see the day, though I suppose I still didn't."

"I am a princess no longer. However, perhaps when this is all over, I shall be a Pirate Queen given how most speak of Calico Jack."

"Then when we reunite," Sam began, affecting a mocking posh English accent, "I suppose I must give a toast to my new Queen." He gave a brief bow in his seat before grinning up at Anne.

She smiled and then laughed, a real moment of levity with an old friend. After that, she poured them both a drink from a nearby cabinet, and they sipped on the spirits.

"Speakin' of that. You mentioned he and Herbert went off somewhere. What's gotten into them?"

"Well, the fools went off to kill Calico Jack on their own. Some sense of duty which they alone can fix."

"What's Edward got duty in all this? Herbert I can square away, but Edward?"

Anne leaned back as she recalled. "I suppose you wouldn't be privy to that bit of information," she muttered softly. "Have you *met* Calico Jack? Have you seen him in the flesh?"

Sam nodded and then looked off to the side as he took to remembering. "Aye, I met him once."

"Did he look at all… familiar to you?"

Sam looked impatient. "What're ye on about here? I never took you fer a dancin lady."

Anne paused another moment before shaking her head and falling back to her blunt nature. "Calico Jack is Edward's father, and formerly he was Benjamin Hornigold, the one who gave Edward this ship."

Sam sat stunned for a moment, his mouth slack. "You must be mad. There's no…" Sam's expression changed, and he looked away in thought once again. "The eyes…" he muttered to himself. "But that would mean…" Sam held a hand to his mouth as he ran through it all in his head. Then when he looked up at Anne, she simply nodded her head, and he took a big gulp of the drink in front of him.

"Needless to say, that is why Edward wishes to do this alone," Anne said before taking a drink herself. "So, you haven't said much about yourself. Tell me how you came to be the captain of such a fine sloop?"

Sam nodded in the direction of his ship through the window of the captain's quarters off the stern. It listed lazily behind them, as though it were aimless without their captain aboard. "Aye, she's a fine ship, you speak it true. Made some friends in Cache-Hand's crew, convinced them to take it for ourselves. Left Cache-Hand with half his crew and none of his spoils the night after capturing it."

Anne chuckled. "How long ago was that?"

"Not three quarters of a year after leaving the captain for dead."

Anne shook her head. "What poor timing. That would not have been long before we met with him, and Edward killed him." She waved her hand. "No matter. Tell me more. How did you come to be in Calico Jack's crew?"

"Ran a few ships aground in his territory and had a little fun redistributing the wealth back to the common folk. Musta caught his eye after the pups started calling me Robin Hood."

"You still breathe, so it was a positive encounter, I presume?"

Sam snorted. "Not if ye call owing him all the money spent a boon."

Anne nodded. "Yes, I see. So, it won't take much convincing to have your crew switching sides, I have it?"

Sam shook his head. "Nah, they see 'em as another Cache-Hand, just one that we can't run from. Havin' you here and Edward there changes things. Might just be able to convince 'em if we have some support." Sam fell silent for a moment, uncharacteristically contemplative.

Anne smiled. "Less than two years and already being a captain has changed you."

Sam's mouth opened, an instinct to chime back with some

witty remark, but instead he leaned back in his chair. "My last captain commanded me to live. Fool captains die quick on these seas." Another moment of silence took hold as Anne and Sam let the weight of his words settle in the air. Sam broke that silence. "So, what's the plan to save our fool?" he said, smirking like the old Sam she knew.

"Perhaps you can help with that," Anne replied. "What are the defences like for Silver Eyes' village?"

Sam's brow cocked strangely, and he shook his head as though he couldn't comprehend what he had just heard. "What are you on about? Ed ain't here. That means he's headed to Nassau. We should be going there now as soon as I convince me men."

Anne stifled a sigh and shoved away the weakness that beckoned it forward. "I would agree with you, save the circumstances we've found ourselves in. We must stay here and save this island from Silver Eyes. These people need us."

"Like hell they do!" Sam shouted, bursting from his seat. "This place can burn. *Edward* needs us. Ye can try ta convince yerself it's fer those people, but yer not so soft ta risk yer life for a bunch'a farmers."

Anne locked her fingers together and rested her elbows on the arms of the chair in a movement of practiced authority. "You're right," she said. "Edward needs to keep his plan secret. We don't know the details, but we know he needs surprise on his side. The enemy knows our ship, and being in Nassau would risk a battle at sea." She gave the briefest pause for her words to sink in. "And beyond that, these people, with your help, can provide a distraction."

"Aye? And how's that?" Sam asked, placing one hand on his chair as he looked down at Anne, trying to match her presence.

"We make a show of power, and you tell Silver Eyes they need reinforcements to fight us. You convince Silver Eyes you should be the one to head to Nassau and instead back Edward up when he arrives. You and your ship being in Nassau will not raise alarm." Anne took a long breath and a drink, her half-formed plan coming together in her mind. "If Edward's father and his subordinates are as smart as they think they are, then I imagine the main village is a fortress with battlements. A single ship, no matter the size, would pose little threat, but if we choke the food supply on land and at sea, we can starve them. And as no one will be coming to their rescue, we'll eventually take the island for ourselves."

Sam scoffed. "Ye make it sound so easy." Sam began pacing the room as he drank from his cup. After a moment he let out a frustrated grunt, pulled something from his belt wrapped in cloth, and placed it on the table. "If yer gonna stay, you'll need this."

Anne glanced at the mystery wrapped in cloth, then back at Sam. He simply nodded towards it before taking another drink. She took the object and unwrapped it to find a small golden handbell.

"That'll work on the crazed on the island, but not that bastard's men."

Anne did a double take on the small, unassuming bell in her hands as the weight of the ringer took root. "So, this will reverse the trance?"

"The what?"

"The spell that the citizens here are under."

Sam nodded. "Aye, that'll do it," he affirmed. "His men don't have the same spell, though. Whatever they got, it makes 'em tough bastards, but they still got all the goods upstairs," he said, tapping on the side of his head. "The farmers and such're just distractions."

It was Anne's turn to scoff. "We almost died to those distractions."

"That's what that's for," Sam said, pointing at the handbell. "Otherwise, they'll attack everyone."

Anne looked at the handbell with new eyes as the wheels began turning in her head. "Is that so?" she muttered.

She gave the handbell a small ring, and a sharp tone filled

their room. It was so wholly unlike its larger brother she had head not a few hours before, but it struck a chord in the centre of her just the same. She felt as though the ring of that bell was pulling her soul forward, the same as when your body moves to join the swell of the wave and the inclination of a ship. Judging by the vacant stare in Sam's eyes and the bulge of his jaw, he felt it too.

After the tone fell away to nothing, Anne's and Sam's wits returned. "This may be useful to ye too." Sam pulled out a silver key from his pocket and placed it in front of Anne. "It's a tight squeeze, but there's a passage on the east of the fort near the waterline. It's there for a flanking attack should the fort be breached, and that key will let you past the gate. Don't think about bringing any cannons, the reef'll kill 'em."

Anne rose from her seat, dropping with it her all the authority and bluster she had previously mustered, and embraced Sam. "Thank you, Sam. With these, we'll surely win."

Sam's generally cool facade blew over, and he looked flushed. "I ain't done nothin' but what a man ought. Don't go givin' me a big 'ead over it."

Anne smiled. "Happy to see you alive nonetheless. After all this is over, we'll have a feast, and you can tell us all about your adventures with your merry men, Mr. Hood."

Sam chuckled. "Aye, that we will, my Queen."

After another brief embrace, Sam walked towards the door of the captain's quarters before looking over his shoulder. "Prepare yer men. After I convince me crew, we'll need to make a show of it."

It was Anne's turn to be confused. "What do you mean?" she asked as she joined him.

"Can't go on back to Silver Eyes ta convince him we need reinforcements without a bit'a damage, now can we?" he replied. "A short skirmish oughta be just the ticket. We can damage the ship ourselves, but without some live fire for 'em ta hear, it won't seem real. Jus' a little smoke, s'all."

"Just a little smoke? Happy to oblige." Anne held out her

hand, and Sam shook it. "Oh, and take this with you." Anne removed the scabbard and golden cutlass from her hip and handed it to Sam.

Sam took the cutlass in hand, lifting it slightly out of its scabbard to see the golden hue of the mysterious metal before returning it to its resting place. "It'll soon be in its owner's hands."

The two left the captain's quarters and assembled the crew on the deck. It took some time for the men to settle and for Sam to talk with a few of his old friends, but eventually, they were able to explain the plan. Sam's crewmates who joined him appeared to already have his approval, and after they went back and convinced the rest to join in, they would signal the *Queen Anne's Revenge* by raising the black. Once the *Queen Anne's Revenge* was prepared, they too would raise the black, and their 'battle' would commence.

With all the details decided, Sam and his crewmates went back to their ship, and Anne and the crew waited. And waited. And waited still.

"It's taking too long," Christina said as she petted her wolf Tala. The two were leaning against the quarterdeck railing and watching the bobbing of the *Whydah* off the stern.

Anne had her spyglass trained on the other ship. Sam and the other crewmates were talking on the weather deck, but she couldn't make out the details. "They're just talking."

"Maybe some in the crew don't like the thought of betraying Calico Jack," Christina commented.

"Or Benjamin Hornigold," Pukuh added as he came up beside Anne to observe the other ship.

Anne took her attention away from the spyglass and glanced over at Pukuh. Pukuh looked gravely serious as he turned his gaze back to Sam's ship.

"You may be right," Anne replied.

An unmistakable crack met Anne's ears, sending an alert down her spine. She reached for the cutlass at her side as she looked over her shoulder. The other crewmates, the lot of them, even Tala, had their ears perked and brows furrowed from the noise.

Anne went back to the spyglass and found the source of the noise. She could just barely make out the figure of Sam with his jet-black hair and a smoking pistol in his hand. He was standing stock still, and Anne thought she could see his other hand holding a sword at his side.

"What happened?" Christina asked.

"Sam executed a crewmate." *You said you were no fool, Sam. I hope you know what you're doing.*

"Let us hope that man lacked mates," Pukuh said.

Anne didn't reply. She tensed her jaw as she watched the scene on the other ship unfolding.

Sam put his pistol away and brandished his sword, gesturing with it as he spoke. After a moment or two, the crew went into action. Some took the body of the dead crewmate and tossed him overboard, as others raised the anchor and prepared the ship for sailing.

Sam, still holding fast to his sword, walked up to his own quarterdeck. Halfway up the steps, he turned and looked over at *Queen Anne's Revenge*. Sensing or seeing all the eyes on him, he openly shrugged his shoulders and shook his head. Anne couldn't see through the spyglass, but she felt he was grinning.

Anne chuckled despite herself. "You dammed fool," she muttered.

After a time, and a flurry of activity, the *Whydah* raised the black flag on its tallest mast. The simple skull of death with crossed bones, similar but different enough from Calico Jack's crossed cutlasses, waved in the wind at them.

Anne put away her spyglass and turned around to the crew, who had gathered around when the gunfire sounded. "Let fly the black. Load starboard, men! We've some smoke to make."

10. WARNING SIGNS

"What happened out there?" Herbert asked.

Edward had returned from the excursion onshore with Grace and was now below deck with Herbert and John. They were huddled in a corner near the ladder leading up to the weather deck, Edward sitting on the lip of a barrel and John standing next to him with Herbert in his chair holding tight to the nearby cargo.

"Grace killed a bunch of thieves who had stolen something from her, or someone else. I wasn't privy to the details."

Edward still felt tense from the encounter. Aside from the few minor altercations aboard the *Black Blood,* it had been some time since he had been involved in a real battle. He closed his eyes and took a few deep breaths. Thankfully, Herbert and John both let him alone for that moment he needed to channel that feeling of floating. It came more naturally this time, and he was able to hold it for longer than any other time save the first time when he had been near fainting from exhaustion.

"Does everyone aboard know about the captain's greaves?" Edward asked John.

John's eyes widened. "She used *them*?" He seemed shocked at the notion, but soon let out a low whistle. "Whoever it was must have irked her something fierce. She rarely uses them."

Edward laughed. "The man was irksome, that much is sure. And whatever it was that he stole, it's been returned."

John let out a sigh. "That's a relief, but it also means you two are about to meet *him*."

137

Edward took a moment to register John's meaning. "Calico Jack?" he asked to be sure.

John nodded. "We were tasked with retrieving something stolen from him, but don't ask me what it was. All I know is it was important, and when Mad Jack Rackham tells you to sail, all you ask is how far." John's tone was light, but Edward could tell there was a hint of anger in his voice. That hint spoke to a feeling he dared not utter on a ship full of men in Calico Jack's employ.

Perhaps… "You've met the man?" Edward asked, his attempt to pry open that shaded window subtle.

Herbert understood the game, leaning forward to whisper. "I've heard that he's… well." He paused to flash a concerned look to Edward and John. "Well… that he's not to be trifled with."

John's mouth became a line. "Yes, well, I will say that you are right. And as you're new to the crew, you'll have to meet with him before you're truly considered a mate. If there's one piece of advice I can give you: don't question him, but don't simply bow to him either. He likes to have men he can trust, but who also have a backbone." John rolled his shoulders and glanced at his sides to ensure there were no ears nearby. "Whatever happens, if he tries to play his hunting horn, just run. Run as far as you can and escape the island by any means."

Edward knew the horn John was referring to, but the sudden nature of his dire warning took him aback. His mouth went slack as he searched for words a person who shouldn't know of the horn would say, but it didn't seem to matter, as John took it differently.

John shook his head. "No questions, not here. It's not safe. Just remember to run."

Before Edward or Herbert could say another word, John was already walking away and beckoning them to join him.

Could there be more to the horn than just a signal? Those men and women in the tavern… Anne said they seemed in a trance. Was it the horn's doing?

Before Edward could ruminate on his questions too long, Herbert was nudging him forward and out of his thoughts. Edward glanced at Herbert, who motioned with his chin towards John's backside. Edward nodded, and the two went to the crew's quarters to eat.

The meal, as it had been the time before and the time before that, was a stew of salted beef with various vegetables and the spiced pepper that burned Edward's tongue. Edward threw all his ship's biscuits into the stew at once to soak up the spice, and it seemed to work. Either that or he had become used to the heat of that foreign pepper after so many times.

After the meal, Edward and Herbert were about to make their way above deck for the next shift of the crew, but a mate stopped them.

"Captain's orders," he said as he stopped Edward with a hand on his chest. "Get yer rest, yer useless to her if yer dead on yer feet."

Edward glanced at Herbert and John, who were both as shocked as he. "Truly?"

The mate nodded. "Aye." The mate glanced back and forth all the way over his shoulder and then leaned forward to whisper as best as he could in Edward's ear. "She's taken a shine to ye, so be sure and not refuse her… if ye catch my meanin'." The man winked before taking the crewmates above for the next watch.

"What do you suppose he meant by that?" Herbert asked.

Edward's gaze went from Herbert and fell on John, but John shrugged and seemed as dumbfounded by the exchange as the others.

It didn't take long for Edward and Herbert to stop worrying over the mystery and sleep in their hammocks. The gentle rocking of the ship and normal noises of a bustling machine of wood and men lulled Edward to sleep surprisingly quickly.

Edward awoke in what felt like an instant, the ache of his muscles and bones hitting his whole body immediate and with a fury. After a few stretches as he awoke and readied for work, the pain was mostly gone.

Edward and John's work and rest schedules were now aligned and, together with Herbert, the men went above deck to tend to the ship in the dead cold of the night.

The other crewmates working nights with them were a more amicable sort than Edward had dealt with for most of his time aboard the *Black Blood*, and so the work was lax and the conversation genial. Edward, Herbert, and John learned more about John and his time aboard the ship, but the conversation steered clear from any mention of Calico Jack's mysterious horn.

John told some fantastical stories of battles against the Spanish off the coast of Honduras, where they were secretly paid by the British for each ship sunk. They performed so well that the British couldn't pay and agreed to turn a blind eye to the pirates' other activities.

During one such battle, Grace's pistols jammed, and she was forced to use her greaves where she single-handedly killed five Spaniards at once. After that, so it was told, the Spanish began calling her *Gracia de la Muerte*, or Death's Grace.

He also told of the time where a third of the crew swore they had seen a ghostly ship on a foggy night, which they pursued despite the danger. They eventually came upon an empty vessel, full sail and cargo, drifting at sea, no crew anywhere to be seen. Even Grace, not one to be superstitious, was rattled and ordered the ship burned, cargo and all.

One thing missing from each of John's stories was the man himself. His version of events seemed to not have a place for him, save as an observer, as though he were inconsequential.

When pressed to hear a story about him, John reluctantly obliged. He told a story about when he helped an orphaned girl being accosted by bandits in a town the crew had stopped in. The girl fled with the crew aboard the ship, for fear that the bandits would just come back against her after they had left.

"What happened then?" Herbert asked.

John's mouth parted for a moment before his lips twisted

into a sad smile. "Her ending was something I would not wish to revisit."

Edward and Herbert shared a look after John's comment and changed the subject.

The two shared their own stories, taking care to not let slip anything too detailed to allow John, or any eavesdroppers, to glean who they were. When those stories seemed exhausted, Herbert weaved a few tales plucked from the sea air itself that involved the Blackstad brothers in their prime. The tale he told was so full of bravado and wild fancy it beggared belief, but after the ghost ship story, it may not have mattered much.

Over three days, it was the same routine. Edward could rest and work as a normal crewmate instead of working for two as he had before, and he, Herbert, and John all shared their time together aboard. When they weren't working hard on the ship, they shared their stories, talked about life aboard a ship, tips for managing the needs of their wooden estate, and sometimes just a relaxing silence.

Edward also noticed that his sleep came easier each time he lay down, and he awoke less and less in the middle of his slumber. The feeling of overwhelming dread left him, and he often found his flask full at the end of the day.

On the third day, before Edward went to work again, he was called to the captain's quarters by one of the mates.

"Why does Grace want to speak with me?" he asked.

"That's for her to know," the mate replied. "Don't keep her waitin'."

Edward glanced over his shoulder at Herbert and John, and they both had stern looks on their faces though Edward suspected it was for different reasons. Edward steeled himself as he followed the mate past the surgeon's room, past the ladder to the weather deck, and over to a small cabin at the bow of the ship.

As he made the walk, he quickly ran through their backstory, what little they had come up with, in his head. He also checked the weapons at his side, cutlass and knife, should he need them. If it came to that, though, they were already dead. He couldn't kill everyone aboard a ship eighty strong. He was confident in his abilities, but that was impossible.

The mate knocked on Grace's door, and when she gave the word, he opened the door for Edward. "Blackstad here to see you, ma'am."

"Thanks, Richard," she said before she waved him away.

Edward watched as the mate closed the door behind him, noticing a broad grin on his face as he did so. He didn't like that grin. As tense as he was in enemy territory, if the mate were expressionless as William, he would have felt the same. The grin just made it more explicit.

"Sit," Grace commanded, pointing to a chair across from the table.

As Edward stepped forward to take a seat, he glanced around the room. It was small and spartan, as it had to be aboard a brigantine, but it was larger than it would be in a sloop. The only light in the room came from a few hanging lanterns and two windows at the back.

One corner held a bed big enough for two, and beside it, a few sets of clothes hung on hooks fastened to the wall. In the opposite corner stood a bookshelf teeming to the brim with sailing books, charts, and other instruments, and next to it a table with various tools, disassembled weapons, and copper. Some of the tools and items had fallen to the deck from the swaying of the ship. Edward saw the same scene on the table in front of them, with sailing charts, books, and weapons and tools from edge to edge.

Edward sat and locked his fingers together, mimicking Grace—a trick Anne and Alexandre had taught him when trying to endear someone to you, mimicking another person's body language to put them at ease.

However, Grace's gaze seemed immediately drawn to Edward's hands, and she instantly changed her posture. She leaned back and folded her arms in front of her and stared at him for a moment.

Edward didn't dare move. He realized Grace was too smart for such tactics, and if he folded his arms, it would be much too obvious. He decided to take the offensive. "What did you need, Captain?"

She didn't respond for a moment, staring at Edward as she waited. Then she relaxed, if only slightly, and reached into a drawer on her side of the table. She pulled out two glasses and a decanter filled with brown liquor. After filling both glasses generously, she passed one of the drinks to Edward.

"I wanted ta welcome ye to our crew," she finally said.

Edward held back his surprise with the motion of taking the cup in hand and took a drink to think up a response. He needed another moment to let the burn of the whiskey subside. "I suppose I passed some test?"

Grace grinned and raised her glass to him after she took a drink herself. "That's right. Ye handled yerself well out there, if a bit slowly for my taste. Next time, try to keep up if ye don' want ta be shot."

"Now that I know about those legs of yours, I'll be more aware."

Grace leaned back and placed her feet up on the table. Dried mud flaked off the bottom of the copper boots onto the papers below, and Edward couldn't help but think Herbert would be appalled that the charts were being soiled. Grace ran her fingers over the copper greaves.

"They're quite a pair, thas' for sure. Pain to reload, though."

Edward nodded. He could tell that she was relaxing around him; perhaps the drink was helping, but maybe this was an advantageous direction to take the conversation. "You must have made them yourself judging by the tools you have there." Edward nodded his head towards Grace's workshop over his shoulder.

"Aye, that I did. These legs've got a few other tricks. Play yer cards right, and maybe I'll show them to you." Grace slid her hands down her legs to her thighs and looked at him with an unmistakable expression of lust.

Edward was in the middle of a drink and had to hold back a cough and sputter. *Bollocks! That's what that crewmate meant by not refusing her. I must change the subject.* "Your name," he blurted out.

"What about it?" Grace replied, annoyance clear.

"I'm not too learned when it comes to history, but was there not a famous Grace O'Malley whom some would say was also a pirate from a couple of hundred years ago?"

Edward thought he could hear Grace let out a small sigh as she moved her feet off the table. "Aye, that there was." She took another drink of her whiskey. "O'Malley ain't me last name. Had no need of me last one affer..." Grace trailed off but shook her head and moved on. "Probably good fer you to do the same if ye want to go back to yer home someday." Grace pointed with one finger at Edward's ring, sloshing some of the whiskey on the table as she did so.

Edward looked down at the golden wedding ring on his left hand, and he could feel his cheeks flush. Grace took his redness as embarrassment and chuckled, but he was far from embarrassed.

Wrapped around his finger was that familiar gold that was not gold, and he hadn't spared it a second thought. He and Anne had been married for so long it had become a part of him, and it was made of the same material that his father, perhaps more so under the alias Benjamin Hornigold, was known for. He was so worried about letting something slip in what he said that he forgot about the smallest piece that could almost immediately give him away.

As it dawned on him, he became painfully aware of how quiet he had been. "I'll keep that in mind, thank you." *Keep the conversation going. Don't draw attention to the ring anymore. Names. Keep talking names.* "I had a friend who was named after a rather famous pirate as well. Though I doubt his parents had known about the man when they named their son. I don't think he was aware of it either as I only learned of it recently myself."

Grace burst out laughing, the whiskey hitting her now. "Ain't that somethin'? Named after a killer and not even knowin' it."

Edward let out a sigh as he switched the whiskey to his right hand to lower his ring from sight. He would have to remove it later, but what he would do with it after that he didn't know.

It was then that he realized what he had said exactly. He talked about his friend, Henry Morgan, the one he had killed, and he didn't get the same feeling he had in the past. His hands weren't shaking, and the sense that the world narrowing in on him was gone as well. And, though he was thinking of it now, the flashes of those who had died because of him, including his old quartermaster John, never came unbidden to his mind's eye.

Perhaps the whisky is hitting me as well, Edward thought as he took another drink.

When he looked up, Grace was there beside him, sitting on the edge of the table with her legs spread and her back arched. She wore a smile that was unmistakable save to the simple or the blind.

"So," Edward said, drawing out the word as he did his best to lean away from her, "I'm curious as to what it was that we were there to retrieve during my test?"

She reached into her pocket and pulled out the item she'd taken from the thief's corpse and handed it to Edward.

It was an ordinary necklace made of what Edward thought was driftwood in the shape of a spiral seashell, half as big as Edward's palm. He turned the necklace over in his palm a few times as he examined the unique shape. He couldn't place it, but he felt he had seen the necklace before. Could it have been when Grace was picking it up? No, the angle was wrong. It had been somewhere else, a long time ago.

Then it hit him.

This was his mother's necklace.

"So, you figured it out, did ye?"

Cold sweat trickled down Edward's face, and his body seized. "What?" he managed to get out.

"Knew you was a smart one." She playfully stroked his hand. "Ye worked it out that that's the boss man's property, didn't ye?"

Edward couldn't say a word. All he could manage was a nod of his head as he placed his late mother's necklace on the table. This was too much for him to digest, and he felt sick to his stomach. He got up to leave, but Grace pushed him back down to the chair.

Grace leapt on top of him, straddling him and pinning him to the chair. She pulled his face up and kissed him. The surging pressure of her lips against his kept him pinned like a surging wave. The smell of gunpowder and whiskey—and, strangely enough, cinnamon—broke through his other senses as she forced her tongue into his mouth.

Edward gained his senses and pushed her off. It was then that he noticed just how petite she was compared to him. She certainly had more muscle than the average woman, including Anne, but she almost looked dainty compared to his large form. She was an attractive woman, with curves like a crested sail in the wind and a face that could belong in a painting. Though it was short, with her red hair she could be mistaken for Anne's older sister in the right light.

What am I thinking right now? Edward's better judgement came back to him, and when Grace tried to force herself back on him, he pushed her off again as he rose to his feet.

"Ah, ye like it rough, do ye?" she said, not losing her smile as she loosened one hand from Edward's grip before grabbing his groin. "Aye, seems ye do," she purred.

"No," he bellowed. The force of his single word took her aback, and she pulled herself away from him.

Before she could gain her wits about her, and before Edward could move for the door again, there was a knock from outside.

Grace regained her composure and folded her arms as she took a few steps away from Edward. "What is it? I told ye not ta disturb me."

"Aye ma'am, it's urgent. Ship off the starboard bow."

Grace cursed under her breath and stalked to the door to her cabin, her stride rushed and heavy.

Edward followed a few steps behind, and Grace left the room without looking back at him. He closed the door to her cabin as he chased her and the mate up the ladder to the weather deck, where some other crewmates were rushing up to see the commotion.

As Edward emerged to the humid brine of the sea air, he could see almost the entirety of the crew watching the seas. Many held spyglasses to their eyes, and those who had none held their hands up to their eyes to look through the pinhole of their palms, and others tried their best with their naked eye.

Herbert and John were both on the quarterdeck where Grace headed. One of her senior mates handed her a spyglass, and she peered through it. As Edward climbed the ladder up, he turned his gaze starboard. Even without aid, he could see the distinct dark shape approaching on the horizon. Whoever was aboard the ship, and whatever allegiances they held, would be unknown until they were much closer, but one thing was clear: they didn't fear to pass another ship on their route. That meant much more than a flag could ever tell them.

"Change course. Head west," Grace commanded her helmsman. "We'll take the scenic route to Nassau."

The helmsman shouted orders to the milling crew, who swiftly went to work changing the sails and rigging, and working with the helm to move the ship further to port.

Grace, feeling her job was finished, handed the spyglass back to her mate and headed to the quarterdeck ladder. Edward decided he would not join her and instead stayed put where he was.

"Wait, Captain," Herbert's voice called.

For a moment, Edward thought Herbert was talking to him, and he stifled his normal response when he remembered who he was. He looked over to see Herbert glancing through his own spyglass west, their new destination.

"What?" Grace's tone had shifted from annoyance to anger.

"I suggest we head east. We will be heading into a storm if we sail west."

Grace's brows furrowed as she glanced over her shoulder towards their destination. After a moment, she looked at her helmsman, who frantically sought his own spyglass.

"I see nothing," he said after nary a glance west. "The boy lies."

Judging the matter settled, Grace once more turned around to head back to her quarters.

"Are you daft?" Herbert shouted. "There's a halo around the sun, and the pressure of air has been decreasing as we've been heading north-west. If we go further west, it'll drop even further, and those clouds I see will be right on us if we head that direction." Herbert was pointing due west as he spoke. Edward looked to the sun, and he too could see the hazy ring around it, a visible marker of increased moisture in the air. He couldn't see anything wrong with the clouds, but Herbert's eyes were better than his. "Are your senses dulled along with your wits? Can you not smell the air? It's saltier than the stew we eat!"

If it were not for every eye being on them, hot and grim, Edward would have laughed at Herbert's comment. As it stood, the ire in the air overpowered the air pressure Herbert was trying to point out.

"Enough," Grace said, her words barely rising above the din of the ship, but still bubbling with anger. "Yer not the helmsman on this ship. I suggest ye hold yer tongue unless ye want it cut out."

"Captain," Edward interjected, "my brother has better eyes than most, and knows the sk—"

"Not another word from you either, ye pissant." If Grace had been angry with Herbert, she was spitting fire at Edward. Her glare could melt a glacier.

Edward pressed forward, not caring about the flames. "Your crew will die," he said calmly.

Grace gritted her teeth, her usual calm completely broken. "Below deck, both of you. Before I throw you overboard."

Edward held back his own frustration. This was partially his fault for drawing Grace's ire by refusing her. He took a deep breath before he motioned for Herbert to join him. The eyes of the crew followed them as they headed into the dark, but Edward was sure Grace would call them back when the storm hit. And he hoped it was sooner rather than later.

11. A BELL TO FILL THE HOLLOWS

"Why do we wait and sit around like kittens?"

Pukuh, hunched down on all fours as he peered over a ridge at a nearby hamlet, looked nothing like a kitten. Despite his native garb making him look like a large eagle, there was no mistaking the hunter beneath the outfit ready to strike.

"We're not here to kill them," Anne admonished, "we're here to help them so that they in turn may help us."

"And this bell is to fill the life into their eyes?" Pukuh said, touching the bell wrapped around Anne's waist.

"That is the hope," Anne replied.

Anne, Pukuh, William, and a handful of crewmates stood on the outskirts of a hamlet, waiting and watching for an opportunity. As they had feared, and as their old crewmate Sam Bellamy had confirmed, the sounds of the bells across the island had triggered the men and women going about their lives. They, like the ones who had attacked them, were now mindless husks wandering about without purpose save to fight any who approached.

"That hope will be as hollow as those people unless we act on it."

Anne grinned at the one-armed warrior itching for a battle. She gripped his shoulder to gain his attention. "Patience."

Pukuh let out the tense breath he seemed to be holding and nodded as he showed her a small smile. After that, he relaxed a bit.

Anne turned her attention back to the hamlet, watching the people milling about. She, like Pukuh and William, was watching and waiting for an opportunity where they could use the bell.

They had learned that the people were drawn to sounds, but

only when they couldn't see what produced it. Though Sam denied it, the hollow people did seem to retain some of their faculties, and they were able to judge what was human and what wasn't.

Communicating with each other was beyond them. Despite their having worked together to ram the general store's door, they worked independently. If several had heard a noise, they all had to see the source. None told the others what it was to save labour.

That knowledge would be to Anne and the crew's advantage.

Anne noticed one man splitting off from the rest and walking down one of the side roads leading out of the square. She motioned for one of the crewmates behind her to bring her a stone as they had discussed.

She waited a bit longer before tossing the stone over the ridge where she and the crew were waiting. The stone fell with a thud down the road, kicking up a small cloud of dust with it. The man was looking the other way when it fell, and it must not have been loud enough, because there was no reaction.

Anne lobbed another, larger stone down the road, this time using a bit more force. It went a few feet farther than the last one.

The man turned towards the noise and moved closer, looking around for any sign of the source of the sound as he did.

Anne threw another stone, this time much closer, and the man took the bait. He moved faster, whatever intelligence left driving him towards the ridge where he knew the rocks were coming from.

Anne, as they had planned, slunk back further down the ridge with the other crewmates waiting in the wings. They were a bit farther from William and Pukuh, who would be in the thick of it once the hollow man approached, but not too far away should the need arise.

William and Pukuh rose from their hiding spot just enough for the approaching man to see them, and he gained even more speed when his eyes fell upon them.

Anne pulled out the handbell from around her belt and held it ready.

The man bounded over to the other side of the ridge and lashed out wildly, striking at the two in front of him.

William kept his distance and positioned his right shoulder towards the attacker so that his injured shoulder was out of harm's way. Pukuh was behind the man, waiting to ensure the fight didn't go sour.

Anne rang the bell softly, the small ding of the golden metal striking her ears and pulling on the hairs on the back of her neck. Pukuh raised his spear in the air, a signal that he heard the sound, but the man remained unchanged.

The crewmates around her were tense at the sight of the hollow man in front of them, fighting with no regard for his own preservation. Anne couldn't escape the influence of that tense atmosphere, and she too felt stiff in her movements.

She struck the bell once more in a natural up and down stride. The ringer hit at the top of the arc closest to her ear, and she felt its strange pull once more in the deep of her chest.

The man continued his assault. Anne cursed under her breath. It meant she had to get closer for it to work, or it wasn't working at all.

Step by step, she advanced while ringing the bell in the same rhythmic motion. If they were to find an accurate distance, she would need to be consistent.

The hollow man, however, had other plans. As Anne approached, and William fended him off with precision strikes and manipulation, she caught the hollow man's eye. He changed targets and ran straight for her.

Anne gritted her teeth and held the bell out in front of her as though it were a pistol. With the flick of her wrist, she tossed the bell into the air just after it struck its tone when the man was not ten feet from her. She changed her stance, ready to jump out of the way and try the trick Alexandre had told them about, but something changed.

The man slowed gradually to a complete stop in front of her. She watched as the life and intelligence entered his eyes once more, and he suddenly looked confused.

He glanced about him, all eyes and several weapons pointed in his direction, but he didn't seem alarmed by the threat to his life, simply confused.

"My apologies, ma'am," he said after a moment. "I seem to be lost. Could you point me towards the main road?"

Anne let out a sigh, partially from the relief of tension, partly from what was two steps forward and one step back in their plans. There was only one way to make sure.

"Sir, are you well?" she asked, throwing as much sincerity into her words as she could muster. "We were just talking about the price of some of your town's produce when you suddenly went stark white, and now you appear confused."

The man now appeared shocked and recoiled. "Oh my! Perhaps I've come down with a fever. Well, no matter, I have my wits about me now." Anne couldn't help but scoff at the remark, but the man seemed not to acknowledge it. "Now let me think, for a ten-pound sack of potatoes that would be zero pieces of eight, we have some fresh zucchini you might like for zero pieces of eight, and…"

The man rattled on down a list of different vegetables and fruit, giving the same price for each as though it were a standard amount.

Anne once more cursed under her breath. "Alexandre," she called. "See what you can do."

Alexandre and Victoria came over, and Alexandre began his own hypnosis to lull the man into a waking slumber. Anne walked over to William and Pukuh nearby.

"I am at fault for not keeping the man's attention, my captain," William said as he bowed his head. Old habits from the days he was in service to the crown were hard to break even now.

"It is no one's fault save Silver Eyes and his abhorrent treatment of these people. And whatever madness drove him to create this hellish island is our misfortune. We must change our plans as we know now we cannot ask these people for help."

"So, we will leave them here, yes?" Pukuh asked.

"No, we can't risk leaving them at our backs like this when we don't know exactly what drives them. Silver Eyes could have instilled a fail-safe whereupon if none come to take them out of the trance, they come inland." Anne looked over her shoulder at Alexandre and Victoria tending to the man as the other crewmates watched them with a mix of fascination and horror on their faces. "Perhaps with a bit more time, Alexandre will find a means for them to join us in the fight."

"So, what do you propose, my captain?"

"I'll need more time. For now, we proceed as planned in freeing the people and dismantling the bell towers. We know that there's a limited range even with the bell towers, otherwise they would only need one, so we can take the people with us at a distance."

"Aye, Captain," the two said in unison.

Throughout the next hours, they continued luring the men and women from the hamlet to them and using the bell to free them from the hollow trance they were in. Some required more than one strike of the handbell, which Alexandre thought possible, but they didn't have to use the last resort technique he had taught everyone.

As a test, Anne used it on one of the children as they were the easiest to control, but it didn't have an effect. Alexandre believed that they were too deep in a trance at that time for it to work. Anne hoped that Sam was right that Silver Eyes' crew were not in as deep a trance, as that technique could be their secret weapon.

None of the men and women seemed to revert to their original state, however. All, even the children, were still in that strange trance that robbed them of their right minds and agency. The only beneficial part of it was that they were compliant and didn't protest even when there was no good reasoning behind a request. Anne simply had to ask them to stay where they were, and they did as told.

"Is that everyone?" Anne asked. All told, they had gotten almost sixty people before the sun was at its peak.

William, peering through a spyglass over every inch of the small hamlet, replied without taking his attention away. "I cannot see any left, though this is not the best vantage point."

"Then we proceed with caution," Anne said, loudly enough for the crew to hear. "Begin by taking down that bell tower, but be sure not to let it ring. If you see anyone still in a trance, keep your distance and call out to me, understood?"

In unison, the crew responded affirmatively, then went to work. Some remained behind to secure the men and women in case the worst happened and the bell was struck again, and the rest left to secure the bell.

"One down, three to go."

12. YOU KNOW WHAT THEY SAY ABOUT DEAD MEN?

Edward refused to talk with Herbert after they were forced to go below deck. He had too much on his mind and needed time to think.

The foremost thought on his mind was that of the driftwood seashell-shaped necklace that Grace had retrieved. His mother's necklace. He had forgotten all about it, and almost all about her until that moment.

Edward had never actually known his mother—she had died during his tender years, and he only ever learned of her through rosy retellings from his father.

He couldn't picture her face; his only real memory of her was her hair, black and glossy like onyx, just as his own, rolling over her shoulders with waves like the summer sea.

Outside of that, the only memory that stuck with him was after she was gone, when it had been just Edward and his father. His father trying his best to keep it together in the aftermath, then throwing himself into his work before leaving Edward behind. Leaving him behind with the Hughes, a family that loathed him. Leaving him behind to become a pirate.

What made the memory of the necklace worse was that, according to his father, he had been the one to pick up the driftwood and give it to his mother. His father had carved it into the seashell shape, and it had been hers before it became his.

A thief stole it, and he must have known its value given it was simple driftwood, and Edward's father had sent Grace to retrieve it for him. Did his father value it as a memento of his lover, his son, or both?

As Edward ruminated, a few hours must have passed. He

156

felt the ship beginning to sway harder and harder with the increasing swell of waves crashing against it. As Herbert had predicted, they were heading into a storm. It was only a matter of time until the rain began, and then there would be no way out but through.

"Edward, we need to talk. Enough sulking."

Edward gritted his teeth and bit his tongue lest he say something he regretted. Instead, he rose from his hammock and joined Herbert. They passed by a few other crewmates avoiding work and headed towards the cargo hold.

Herbert left his wheelchair on the gun deck, strapping it to a full barrel with a rope, and descended a ladder to the cargo hold below. Edward followed soon after, grabbing a lantern along the way, then the two went into the maze of barrels, boxes, and bags haphazardly left in the hold. When they felt certain their voices wouldn't carry to the deck above them, they made themselves comfortable.

Herbert levelled a glare at Edward. "So, what did you do?"

Edward scoffed. "What did I do? You're the one who insulted Grace's helmsman, and by extension herself as well." He did his best not to think about what had happened in Grace's cabin and to deflect blame, but he could feel the heat of shame filling his cheeks. The little stubble he had grown back did little to hide it.

Herbert folded his arms, and his mouth was a line. If Edward didn't know any better, he had been practicing to look as emotionless as William.

Edward rubbed his face before letting out an exasperated grunt. "She tried to lay with me, and I said no. What was I supposed to do?"

Herbert's mouth went agape for a moment, unable to formulate words, but he recovered after a moment. "Sleep with her, that should be obvious." His arms were still folded, but his voice rose a touch.

Now, Edward was at a loss for words. "I won't do that to Anne," he said as he looked away from Herbert's gaze.

Herbert paused for a moment, and his tone softened. "We're in enemy territory. She would understand."

"Yes, you're probably right," Edward conceded. "But it would cause her pain nonetheless. I refuse to put her through that."

Edward looked at his left hand and the ring that adorned it. He touched the strange metal as he thought about the ceremony that had preceded his donning it. The sea air, the feeling of the sun on his neck, the grains of his ship's deck underfoot, even Jack's pleasant tune from his violin from that day felt somehow different than any time before or after. It was as though the strange pull of nostalgia had lifted that day's most mundane things and elevated them in his mind.

Anne's dress, her hair, the taste of her lips; even at that moment, in the hold of the *Black Blood*, he could picture them, feel them, as though he were in that moment.

He ached for Anne. His heart pulled at his core, begging for her embrace, for the touch of her lips pressed against his. He felt hollow without her near. How could he, even for a second, think of another woman's features as pleasing to his eyes?

"I don't mean to interrupt... whatever it is you're thinking about right now, but if you were going to refuse her, you could have let her down easy."

Edward came out of his mental anguish over his shortcomings to scoff. "I don't think easy is in Grace's vocabulary," Edward said, which Herbert laughed at and nodded. "Besides, I had a lot on my mind at the time."

"What happened?"

Edward scratched his head, debating whether to share with Herbert the most recent revelation, and the subtle implications that came with it.

"Ed, we're in this together, remember? We are brothers, after all, and I don't just mean because of our fake names."

Edward chuckled and then nodded. "You are right, brother." He readjusted himself on the box he was sitting on, thinking of how to go about telling Herbert. "The day we went on that island and fought those men, Grace was there to retrieve a necklace." Herbert looked confused but said nothing. "The necklace belonged to my mother. My father sent her there to retrieve it."

Herbert whistled low and long. "No wonder you weren't in the mood."

Edward clenched his teeth. "This is no time for jesting."

"Sorry, sorry," he replied swiftly. "So, your mother…"

"Dead," Edward replied. "When I was just a lad. I barely remember her, but she was a light in my father's life. I do know that. Whenever he would tell stories about her, his face would glow."

Edward's gaze dropped to the bottom of the deck of the dark hold. He wished that he had been able to remember her, to know her beyond the stories, to share in her laughter he had been told could put a smile on the sourest, to hear her voice that could quell the storm in the most raging of hearts.

"What was her name?"

Edward looked up at Herbert for a moment before he returned to his gloom. "Areia. Areia Thatch."

Herbert's brow rose, and he scratched his chin. "Is that Greek? I'm not much for languages."

"I'm not sure. My father wasn't forthcoming with my mother's family line. I think the closest he ever came was when he told me that my mother was never meant for this world, whatever that means."

Herbert nodded, and after a moment said, "He must have loved her."

"More than anything else in this world," Edward replied. "Maybe that's why after she died, he… he became Calico Jack."

"Having second thoughts?"

Edward looked up at Herbert. In his eyes, he couldn't see any emotion, except maybe pity. "No, it doesn't change anything. I still want to talk to him, ask him why, but if he wants me to kill him, then I'll give him what he wants. It's the only way to end this."

A sudden noise came from behind them—a box shifting and the unmistakable thump of a boot. Someone was there, someone had snuck up on them, someone had been listening. Edward leapt from his seat and pounced on the person. He threw him over towards Herbert and into the light of the lantern.

It was John. He scrambled to right himself after Edward's toss and held his arms up in front of him. "Please, please wait, Edward," he cried.

"What are you doing here? What did you hear?" Edward rose as high as he could above John, but the low ceiling of the hold didn't allow much vantage. Thankfully John was still on his back, so Edward was able to tower over him.

"I came to get you. The captain is calling you two back above," John sputtered, and the words came in a jumble. He was trembling with fear and backing away from Edward as much as he could in the confined space. "I heard what you were saying about Calico Jack, about him being your father, about how you're going to kill him. Edward, I'm your—"

Edward had already pulled out a knife from his belt. He thrust it into John's neck, silencing him at once. Blood poured from the wound even before Edward pulled out the knife, and afterwards, it flowed like water from a burst dam.

John clutched his neck, desperate to stop the torrent. He reached out towards Edward as he writhed in pain, tears streaking his face and mixing with the blood on the sole. He tried to call out for help, but he could only mouth the words as a limp, weak, gurgled noise escaped his lips before he sputtered blood. His movements became sluggish, his hands fell to the deck, and his eyes fell and opened to the rhythm of a fading heartbeat. Another few twitches and John's life left him.

The kind young man who had shared with Edward his cup and his bread was no more. The one person aboard the ship who had been kind to Edward and Herbert was dead. If only he hadn't snuck up on them to listen, he would have lived another day.

Whatever it was John was about to say to try and gain back their trust after spying on them, Edward couldn't take the chance of him telling Grace of their plan. Or at least that was the justification Edward used for lashing out on instinct born of fear. Instinct born of dozens of battles, a year in prison, and weeks of torture. It did little to quell his shaking hands, or from wondering if he made the right decision, or the bubbling bile in his stomach.

"We need to throw his body overboard," Herbert said after some time.

"Through the portholes on the gun deck. The waves and the storm will cover the noise."

The two nodded and went to work. Edward took John's shirt and tied it around the open wound to limit the blood dripping before he picked up the body. Herbert did his best to soak up the blood using some nearby rags. Their only bit of fortune was the darkness of the hold, and the usual rankness of the bilge just beneath them that would cover the smell. Herbert moved some of the cargo overtop of what remained of the blood and joined Edward near the ladder.

"You head up first and check for any remaining crewmates."

Herbert nodded and climbed up to the next deck. After a moment, Herbert called Edward up. Edward flung John's body over his shoulder and climbed the ladder. He trusted Herbert, but before coming all the way up, he glanced over the deck before he finished the climb.

Herbert went over to the nearest porthole with a cannon nearby at the ready. He pulled on a rope to the side, which opened the port. The noise of the frantic crew above was able to filter in, and it sent a wave of urgency into Edward's mind. The sound could draw attention, and it wasn't what they needed right now.

Edward lifted John's body to the small hole. Water from the crashing waves and the fresh beginnings of rain flew into the ship and splashed Edward as he pushed the young man's lifeless body through the hole. Inch by inch, he shoved and twisted and moved the body through. Herbert also did his best to help while he kept a lookout.

"Hurry, Ed."

"I'm going as fast as I can. These weren't meant for bodies."

Edward felt sweat dripping from his brow, and with each shove, he glanced over his shoulder towards the bow of the ship.

"Almost there," Herbert called, forcing Edward's attention back to the task.

With one final push, the body fell out of the porthole. Herbert tossed out the bloody rags he'd taken with him from the hold, then Edward and Herbert both craned their necks to listen for the splash of the body, but heard none. Edward poked his head out, but couldn't see the body, which meant he was gone, lost in the waves of the storm.

Edward pulled himself in, let out a sigh, and sat down with his back against the wall of the deck. Herbert closed the porthole, and he too let out a sigh as he wiped the sweat off his brow.

After a moment to catch his breath, Edward tensed up again, and he checked his surroundings.

"What?" Herbert asked, anxious.

Edward saw no one nearby, and no eyes on them. "Nothing, just checking. It's over."

"No… it's not," Herbert said, his expression serious. Edward looked at him, still catching his breath. "We need to get above deck, and we can't leave it like this. No one else is below deck anymore. If we head above deck but Grace doesn't see John with us and then he's missing after the storm what do you think Grace will believe happened? Remember what happened to Nigel when he only *attempted* to kill us?"

"What do we do about it then?" Edward asked, but he had a sinking feeling he knew the answer already.

Herbert leaned over, his head underneath the tip of the

cannon. "You need to kill some of the other crewmates during the storm. Otherwise, we'll be the ones joining Davey Jones."

Edward looked away from Herbert. He'd barely had enough time to process how he'd just killed John over a presumption that the young man would tell their tale to Grace. He hadn't even thought about it before the blade had been in his hands. Now, he had to kill again.

The storm outside had already begun, but there was another storm brewing inside, and despite the warning signs, there was no changing course to avoid it.

13. STRIKING DOWN THE BELL OF DEATH

"There it is," Victoria said as she peered through the spyglass.

Anne took out her own spyglass. On the other end of that magnified view, she could see the main town where Silver Eyes waited. It was like a small fort with wooden walls stretching the length to form a stockade and battlements on the top where she could see cannons as well as soldiers manning them. The entrance was in the centre of the stockade, lining up with the main road, judging by the marks in the earth where the wooden beams would swing open.

Judging by the size of the stockade's beams, it would be no easy task for their own cannons to make a dent, let alone break through. Calico Jack's crew were no fools, and Anne guessed that behind those massive beams were slats of iron holding them together.

Beyond the battlements, Anne could see the tops of some houses and a rather large one near the back closer to the sea, which Victoria claimed would be where Lance Nhil, Silver Eyes, resided. In the centre of the town, she could see another tall bell tower with another golden bell at the top.

"It's different than I remember," Victoria said, pulling away from the spyglass to look at Anne. "More fortified. Nhil won't go down easy."

"We were prepared for this," Anne said. "Fortunately, we're in control of the food supply."

"So, it is to be a war of attrition then?" William asked.

Anne nodded. "It is the safer way."

Pukuh slammed his spear into the ground and leaned against it. "What of the secret entrance Bellamy spoke of?"

"We can investigate it later, but from his description, and with the guards keeping watch, we may not be able to get enough of our crew in to make a difference."

Pukuh flashed a devilish grin. "It would only take a few to open those gates."

Anne couldn't help but return his smile. "We shall see. For now, send word to the *Queen Anne's Revenge* to get into position and have our crew move forward."

"Aye, Captain," William said before he left to relay orders to the crew.

"Victoria, head back to Alexandre and watch over the islanders. Tell our men to keep their distance. We don't know how far the sound of that bell tower will reach."

Victoria nodded and headed away from the town and down the main road to join with Alexandre and a small contingent of the crew watching over the entranced men and women from the island. They had gathered about one hundred and twenty souls, with the majority coming from the first village they'd gone to after meeting with Sam.

After Victoria left, Anne watched as the *Queen Anne's Revenge*, helmed by Christina with a skeleton crew, let loose the sails and moved to the harbour of the town. As they had discussed, Christina was to stay far enough away not to allow the cannons facing the sea to strike, but close enough to keep any ships trying to escape at bay.

After the ship began moving, the crew on land moved as well. They went to a field in front of the town, just far enough away to avoid any cannon fire from the battlements and began setting up their own cannons from the *Queen Anne's Revenge*.

The air was still with only a light breeze rolling across the small hills behind them every so often. It brought with it a waft of fresh earth and green grass. Anne couldn't remember the last time they had been on land for so long, and it felt strange to have solid ground underfoot and the salt of the sea only an aftertaste on the back of her palate.

She missed the creak and groan of the Caribbean pine aboard the ship, the din of laughter, boots cracking against the deck, the feeling of rigging between the hands. This island had its own beauty, its own charm despite the nature of its inhabitants, but it was not home. Home to her was the captain's quarters on the *Queen Anne's Revenge*.

But if she was honest with herself, she hadn't been that long ashore. The real issue was that which made that place home, the *person* who made that place home, was not there and hadn't been for a lot longer than she'd been ashore.

She looked down at her left hand, at the golden ring on her finger. The memento of a celebration of love. A memento of her love for her husband Edward, and his love for her. A memento of her real home.

Home was Edward's heart beating in her ear as she lay her head on his chest. Home was his smile that sent her heart racing. Home was his touch that made her shudder in all the right places. Home was his voice as he whispered his love when they were alone.

Her home was gone, and she had a job to do. Anne closed her eyes, took a deep breath, held it tight, and slowly let it go.

She opened her eyes and looked over the crew as they approached the marker in the field they had designated: the stump of a large tree, no doubt one of the trees that had been used in the construction of the fort. There were many such stumps around, but the forest it had once been a part of thinned out and ended at that one. It was also far enough away from the town that they had no worry of the cannons even if the cannonballs rolled a fair distance.

She saw Nassir guiding in the wagons holding their supplies, and the pieces of their own cannons they had taken from the weather deck of the *Queen Anne's Revenge*, three twelve-pounders and twenty eight-pounders in all. It left their ship less armed, but not defenceless, as it still had the thirty twenty-two pounders on the gun deck.

"Nassir," she called, "how long will it take you and the crew to secure the cannons?"

Nassir took a moment to assess their current progress. The tall, muscular man stroked his clean-shaven face, his dark skin smooth and supple like a rock worn over the years from the waves, such that he hardly looked his age. There was a hardness there, born of the hardships, tempered from loss only a loving father could know, but a softness too.

The crew had only just begun unloading the wagons and the cannons, but they had no limbers to set the cannons onto, so they needed to improvise. Some of the cannons would stay on the wagons, and the others would need something made by Nassir to hold them in place.

"We will have them by nightfall, provided there are no distractions." Nassir glanced to his right towards the town.

Anne followed his gaze. She could see movement on the wall, but it was calm. If she hadn't known that Silver Eyes' men were in a light trance, she would have thought it eerily quiet. "Let us pray there are none then," she said. "How are the men you're training?"

"They are well along but have much to learn. Perhaps some still do not value the word of a negro, but they listen in time."

Anne nodded. "If anyone troubles you, let me know, and I'll make rights of it."

"Understood, Captain," Nassir said, a wide grin across his face.

As though someone had been listening in on their conversation, the large bell in the centre of the town rang out. The strange tone, low and unnatural, then high and hollow, was nowhere near as loud as when she'd first heard it in the centre of the bell tower, but its effect was only slightly diminished. It shook her core and inexplicably made her bones itch. She had to force herself not to cover her ears, to get used to the sinister chime. If she let it take over her senses, then what would she do if it rang in the middle of a fight?

Some others in the crew had no such concerns and covered their ears to dull the sound of that unique bell. Anne could see all eyes drawn to the bell, and the crew stopped what they were doing to listen.

The bell kept ringing, and the crew kept still, watching. Anne needed to put a stop to it. She stepped on top of a few of the crates of supplies, pulled out a pistol and fired it into the air. The crack of the igniting black powder cut through the bell like thunder shaking the timbers of a home.

The crew came to their senses and went for their weapons, turning their heads this way and that to find the source of the gunfire. Slowly they noticed Anne standing tall above them.

"Do not let that bell take hold of you, lest you become one of the hollows." She had to yell to overpower the sound of the bell, and to reach each crewmate stretched across the field.

Her words rang true to the men, and none of them covered their ears any longer. They returned to work, setting up the cannons and supplies and trying their best to ignore the sound of the bell.

Anne, still on her perch, nodded approvingly before she remembered the crewmates watching the citizens of the island further inland. She pulled out her spyglass and looked down the road. She could see the group of them, the citizens tied up and the twenty crewmates watching over them from a distance. They were quite a way away, so it was hard to tell who was who, but there appeared to be none in a panic, and none of the islanders were struggling.

She did notice one person in the thick of the men and women, and she guessed it was Alexandre given his lack of care for his own wellbeing. He was ringing the handbell as he walked amongst them, seemingly as a precaution as she saw no signs they were affected by the bell tower at that distance.

"Captain!" William called.

Anne put the spyglass away and turned around. The wooden beams in the centre of the stockade swung open slowly, and thirty men ran out. Their weapons were drawn, and they were charging directly at them.

"To arms!" Anne shouted. "Muskets at the ready," she commanded.

The crew dropped what they were doing and grabbed muskets from the nearby supplies and out of the wagons. They lined up in front of the supplies in two rows, just as they had planned and just as Anne and William had trained them to do. One row dropped to a knee, and the other stood behind, both loading the muskets and readying to fire. There was enough distance and enough warning to give them time to load and ready before Silver Eyes' men were even close.

"Steady," William shouted, taking over for Anne as Anne watched the men approach through her spyglass.

The bell kept ringing over and over, filling the air with its otherworldly tone. It made the dead-eyed men approaching seem more a nightmare borne from the mist than real people on their way to kill them. On and on it rang, the rhythmic striking of the bell drowning out the shouts from the men approaching.

Anne could no longer feel the breeze in the air, as though the bell had whisked it away, and she felt a bead of sweat travel down her cheek. It was not a humid day, but the bell and the oncoming battle tensed her muscles like no other battle had before. These were no ordinary men they were about to face, and Anne didn't know what to expect.

William watched the oncoming enemy behind the two rows of men. They had to wait until the enemy was closer than three hundred yards before firing, but the closer they were, the more accurate the shot. Still, with the wall of men and muskets they had, there was no particular need for accuracy.

"Fire!"

William called the order at around two hundred and ninety yards. The wall of iron fired from the muskets, and smoke filled the air around them. Without the breeze, the smoke lingered and shaded their view as a light mist. They were still able to see the enemy approaching and saw the iron balls had met their marks.

The men hit by the iron slowed a step, but then returned to their charge unfazed. Their eyes looked like the entranced islanders, and their faces were unnaturally calm despite some of them shouting a war cry. It made their charge and their shouts seem rehearsed and wooden as though someone directed them to act in such a way.

"Fire!" William shouted again.

Another wall of iron shot forward, catching many of the men charging towards them. A few fell this time thanks to a few lucky hits to the skull, but the rest kept advancing.

The crew dropped their muskets and pulled out cutlasses and pistols. Anne put away her spyglass, drew her own weapon, and joined the crew. "Remember what Alexandre taught you," she shouted above the din. "These men are under a similar spell, but it's not as strong. We can break it with proper timing. Find an opening and strike!"

The crew didn't respond, too focused on the surge of men coming at them, but she hoped they heard her.

The battle began with a fury. The clang of steel on steel rang out as blades clashed. The crew of *Queen Anne's Revenge* outnumbered Silver Eyes' men by three to one, and their enemies were injured. It should have been a quick skirmish, but it was not.

The men they were facing were faster and stronger and had level heads, unlike their counterparts residing in the villages around the island. They struck with purpose, and even when the crewmates overwhelmed them with numbers, the enemy was able to strike effectively and efficiently to incapacitate or kill.

Anne gritted her teeth at the sight as she jumped into the fray. She joined William; injured as he was, he was having a challenging time of it.

The man he was facing had an injury as well: a bullet wound in the chest, but he seemed unhindered by it. He poked and prodded William with his sword, testing William's defences as William danced out of the way. The man was fast, but William was the better fighter.

William and Anne worked with each other, years of training combining in a beautiful ballet of blades. As William aimed for the man's neck, Anne swung her cutlass low and up in an arc towards the torso. The enemy swiped both blades away with a single strike. Anne and William moved with the enemy's sword, twisting and tangling them together.

William stepped in and moved his sword forward. The tip of his blade caught on the man's crossguard. He flicked his wrist in a firm, practiced motion, and the man's sword moved up with his. The man had no choice but to let go of his weapon.

Anne dropped her weapon, and she too stepped in with both her hands forward. Just as Alexandre had taught them, she smacked her hands together directly in front of the man's face as hard as she could. The sound of the clap, the proximity of her hands to the middle of the man's eyes, and the confusion of the action coupled together in perfect harmony.

The man took a few steps backwards as he shook his head. The hollow calm in his eyes and on his face was gone, and it was as if he had awoken from a dream where he had been falling. Anne had broken the trance, and the man was dropped back into the tangled thoughts of someone in the middle of a life-or-death situation. His hand reached for the wound in his chest as if he only just noticed the pain from the bullet.

Before he could choose to fight or take flight, William stepped forward again in a riposte stance and struck the man in the gut with his sword. William pulled the blade out and retreated a few steps as blood poured from the wound.

No longer under the protection of the trance, the man cried out in pain. He held fast to the wound, trying to keep it closed,

to stop the blood, and to keep his guts inside where they belonged.

Anne picked up her blade now that her opponent was no
longer a threat and turned around to help with the rest of the
crew. When she had a chance to look over the battlefield, she
noticed that, despite the rough start, the crew were turning the
battle around and using Alexandre's method to dispel the
trance. They were lucky the trance on Silver Eyes' men wasn't
as deep or as strong as the islanders. They had lost a few men,
but with the secret technique their enemies weren't prepared
for, as well as the superior numbers, they were winning.

"Captain, look," William called, pointing to the sea.

Anne turned her attention to the sea, to the *Queen Anne's
Revenge*. The ship was not staying away from harbour as they
had intended, but it wasn't landing ashore either. The ship was
heading towards the town.

*Please, God, don't tell me Christina thinks to take the fight into the
town.*

Anne watched as the ship came closer and closer to the
town's harbour. The cannons on the harbour, a higher calibre
than the ones pointed inland on the stockade, fired on the
ship. Most missed with the erratic bobbing of the ship, but a
few hit their mark and tore into their home.

The sound of battle around her brought Anne back to the
field, and she glanced at the crew once more. Her men were
finishing up the fight, with most of the enemy dispatched. The
uninjured carried the injured off the field to attend their
wounds as best they could be without Alexandre there. There
was no more threat, and the stockade gates were now closed as
well, indicating no further reinforcements would be sent their
way for the moment.

The sound of cannons pulled Anne's gaze back to the sea.
Their ship had turned now, no longer on a collision course for
the harbour. As the broadside faced the town, the cannons at
the bow fired off, but only two at a time. Each new shot had a

small delay between them as they fired into the town.

Anne could see clearly where the cannons were hitting, but not why. They weren't aiming for the cannons firing back at them.

What is Christina doing?

Shot after shot laid into the town, breaking apart some of the taller structures with the large iron balls. As the ship fired, they too took on more damage. Whatever Christina's intention, it was not a gamble Anne felt was worth the amount of destruction they were causing.

Then, with a thunderous clang, a cannonball hit the huge golden bell in the centre of town. The bell knocked against the top of the tower, breaking the structure apart with such force it sent the wood flying in all directions. The bell itself tumbled end over end in the air in a frenzy of movement and sound as the striker hit the sides of the bell over and over. After a dozen rotations, the bell fell to the ground, out of sight beyond the stockade, and rang out for the last time, the strange tone warped by the damage from the cannon and the fall, no longer the same haunting melody it once was.

The ship, their purpose fulfilled, turned away from the town and away from the defending cannons protecting the harbour. They let loose a few more volleys, hitting one of the cannon battlements and damaging one of the ships at anchor before the broadside was at too far an angle.

Anne shook her head, her anger replaced with mild frustration. Without the threat of the bell, either from the men and women it would trigger, or the haunting sound they had to deal with, it made the coming battle easier, especially if it was to be a war of attrition as they were thinking. If they had to stay there weeks, all the while listening to the droning of that bell, she suspected she would go mad.

Anne hoped that that was what Christina had been thinking with that attack. Otherwise, it had been a fool's errand, and merely a fool's luck. But it seemed luck was in ample supply this day.

With the bell destroyed, it lifted the cloud that had been hanging over the heads of the crew, and they burst out into cheers and hollers. The victory felt all the sweeter without that sound overpowering all thought. Now the air was filled with the noise of their making.

Anne smiled with the crew, happy at their boosted morale and with Christina's gamble. She also didn't doubt that Silver Eyes was watching them, and she suspected that he was very displeased.

14. SEASICK

Grace was furious.

Edward knew from the look on the captain's face that the arrival of the storm had incensed her core. With the storm now behind them, she overlooked the crew with disgust, battered and broken as they were, with many lying on the deck desperate for air and respite.

Edward was one of the few on his feet, but not by choice. He needed to keep that look of contempt, that anger, directed away from him, so he stood on shaking legs next to the helm, which Herbert now manned.

After Edward had killed John and he and Herbert disposed of the body, they'd gone above deck and into the storm. Grace had put Herbert in charge, and he filled the role as masterfully as he could under the circumstances. He shouted commands, held fast to the ship's wheel as wind and water tested his grip and endurance both, and guided the ship out of the worst of it.

As he did so, Edward was busy himself. He stayed as far from the quarterdeck as he could, as far from Grace's watchful eye as he could, and he did the one thing he seemed skilled at: he killed.

When the waves surged over the sides of the ship, and even the hardiest seaman's legs could have given out, he struck. It was so effortless; all he needed was a well-timed push. So easy to kill them. So easy, it was like breathing to him.

And it was there that Edward felt it again. The floating feeling of freedom. The same feeling when he was so far drowned into a bottle, he felt nothing else. The same feeling when he was so far beyond exhaustion, his body was moving on its own.

He was no longer in that storm, no longer subject to the

whims of the wind and waves. He had become the storm, and the sea. And the sea called for new visitors.

Edward threw at least four overboard in the storm. He lost count at some point because he didn't care for the lives he was expending, so it could have been more.

And judging by Grace's anger and disgust now that the storm had ended, she noticed the missing men amongst the crowd on deck.

"John," he heard Grace mutter under her breath. She was gripping the railing of the quarterdeck so hard her knuckles were white. She turned her rage in Herbert and Edward's direction, and he could feel his heart skip a beat. "Where's John?"

Edward just looked at her for a moment. His throat seized, and he no longer had that feeling of floating to help him. Whatever he drank to bring it on, it had left his body long ago with sweat.

"He's not here, and you were the last ones with him," she continued. "Where is he?"

Edward cleared his throat. It was just as Herbert had predicted. "I'm not the boy's keeper. How should I know?"

From Grace's expression, that was not the right answer. She turned her eyes towards Herbert and pointed at him. "My quarters. Now!" Grace turned to leave, the sight of her back brooking no refusal.

Herbert glanced over his shoulder, giving Edward a concerned look before heading to the quarterdeck ladder. Another crewmate took over the helm as Edward helped bring Herbert's wheelchair down to the weather deck and then down to the captain's cabin. There was no opportunity to talk with Herbert, no chance to go over the story again and ensure they were consistent.

Herbert went into the cabin, and Grace closed the door behind him. Edward stayed nearby and waited for whatever was going to happen.

Edward waited and paced and waited some more. He kept a tight grip on his cutlass, though he wasn't sure what good it would do. As he'd surmised before, if he killed their captain, the crew of the *Black Blood* would still be there to get revenge. They were on the open sea; there was no escape in the wooden box they'd stepped into. But Edward refused to lie down and die if it came to that. He would fight, and he would die. He would not let another choose what would happen to him, even his death.

A thought came to Edward as he waited, a way to avoid or at the very least postpone their deaths.

Edward's father, Calico Jack, could have killed him, could have killed all of them in that tavern weeks ago. Edward and Herbert had guessed that Calico Jack wanted Edward to kill him in some kind of test, just as the unlocking of the ship was a test.

If Edward told Grace who he was, there was a chance that she would keep them alive, at least long enough to bring them to her master. He looked at the ring, still adorning his left hand, simultaneously a threat and a marker of his connection to Calico Jack. If he needed to, it could prove who he was.

The noise of Grace's cabin door opening brought Edward out of his reverie. His hand went to his cutlass, but when he saw Herbert unharmed and under no immediate threat from Grace, he lowered his hand.

Herbert's face was forlorn, wearing a strange look of guilt or regret as he looked up at Edward from his chair. Despite his life and limb being intact, something unpleasant happened during their discussion, and it set Edward on edge more than he had already been.

"You," Grace called. "Inside."

After one final look at Herbert and a deep but quiet breath, Edward entered Grace's cabin, and she closed the door behind him.

Edward sat down in the chair across from Grace's and waited for her to sit. The anger that had been there was now gone, and she was emotionless as she stared at him.

"What happened ta John?" she asked.

Edward was silent for a moment. He had foolishly thought about everything but how to answer her questions. He chose to be blunt. "We lost a few to the storm. He's probably dead."

Grace's jaw clenched. "He went down ta fetch ye and never came back. You two did." Grace paused to let her words sink in. "What happened ta John?" she repeated.

"After he found us, we went straight above deck," Edward said. "I thought he was right behind us."

Grace tapped her finger on her desk. Her body was tense, each muscle taut and ready to snap like a snake. She didn't seem to care about any of the other crewmates who lost their lives at Edward's hands. She was only asking about John. That meant at least that she hadn't seen him throwing people overboard.

"I was watching for him. He never came back to the weather deck." Her expression changed. Her jaw softened, and she looked away from Edward.

"It was a storm. You probably just missed him." Grace didn't respond to Edward's comment. She just had the same faraway look now as she gazed at nothing. "Why are you only concerned about John? He was nice to my brother and me when no one else was, and I would be saddened to lose him as well, but from what I saw, we lost a few crewmates."

Grace turned to look at Edward again. "John's different."

She seemed content to leave it at that, but Edward needed to keep the conversation away from him and Herbert being suspect. "Different... how?"

Grace stared into Edward's eyes for a moment, and then she let out a sigh. "I told yer brother, I suppose I may'swell tell you, else ye'll hear it from him." She shifted in her chair, relaxing a bit, and her expression turning sorrowful. "John wus me son," she said.

"Your son?" Edward blurted out.

Edward's heart seized in his chest. Killing several of her crewmates was wrong enough. She killed one herself since they've been there. Killing her son was another matter entirely. He wasn't sure he could use his real name to forestall his death if she concluded that they had killed John.

"Aye," Grace said, long and drawn out.

After a moment of silence, she reached into the drawer of her desk and pulled out the liquor from before. She poured only for herself this time and downed the drink in one shot. There was no seeking pleasure in that drink, as Edward knew all too well. She wanted the numbness that it brought.

"Pirates came to me village when I was not twelve, maybe fourteen," she said. "I remember the bodies piled up in a ditch, all they owned stripped. Even the rich family wasn't safe." Grace took another drink, this time slower, and then she looked at Edward again. "Have ye ever been near a house set afire when the people are trapped inside?" Edward shook his head. "At first smells like nothing more than a roast. Then you smell the hair. Smells like shit. Reminds you what's burning, and you never forget that smell."

Edward sat in silence. He could already tell where the story was headed, trace the inevitable path that led a young child to have a son not much younger than herself, and a life of piracy, and a hardness born of experience.

He began to feel sick at his killing John, presumably her only son. Beneath the anger and now her strange façade of calm, he could tell that she loved John. It may have been from afar, but she still loved him. And Edward had killed him.

Grace continued. "I envied the pirates. They killed everyone I cared about, but I envied them for what they did."

"What?" Edward asked, perplexed.

"They made everyone equal," she replied. "Rich, poor, everyone was thrown in tha same hole when the iron took their lives." Grace swirled her cup before downing the last bit of drink. "I wanted that control." She took another moment and seemed to regain focus. "I wasn't poor, wasn't rich neither, but I was smart. I knew what was goin' ta happen ta the girls they didn't kill. So, I figured out who the captain was and… I made sure that he wanted my exclusive attention. The other girls weren't so smart. The men took their turns before discarding 'em, but the captain kept me for himself."

Edward had guessed the story already, but Grace's mention of the captain turned something in his mind.

"Jack musta saw something in me worth keepin'. Then, after I had John, and he found out, he made me a permanent crewmate." Grace shook her head as she bit her lip. "He'll not be pleased about this. Not one bit."

Edward felt crushed under a sudden weight, and his vision went blurry.

John had been Edward's half-brother, and Edward had killed him.

'I heard what you were saying about Calico Jack, about him being your father, about how you're going to kill him. Edward, I'm your—'

John had been about to tell him. It was also not so much a secret that John held some hatred for Calico Jack. John probably would have told Edward that he was on his side, and Edward killed him before he could get the words out. If only Edward had waited, if only he had trusted the young man a bit more...

"Ya look like yer about ta wretch on me table," Grace commented, bringing Edward back to the here and now.

"Just exhausted," he sputtered out.

"Go on, then, we're done 'ere."

Edward rose from his seat and left without looking back or saying another word. He closed the door behind him, ignoring Herbert's questions and calls. He rushed up to the weather deck, where the crew were just now beginning to start repairs on the ship, and he vomited over the side.

He was shaking, his head ached, and he felt his world closing in again. The trembling of his hand returned in full force, as though it had never left him. Images of the dead, those he'd killed and those who had died because of him, flashed in his head, and there was a new face added amongst them.

He slumped down to the deck and reached for the flask in his pocket.

15. LOOK INTO MY EYES

The night was eerily still and calm. The winds over the sea had abated, and the water was quiet save for the occasional breeze creating a light chop. Thick clouds off in the distance hid the moon from view. Somewhere, far away, a storm had stolen the winds away from this island and left it in darkness.

The clouds obscured God's eye, and the earth and sea lost his protection. There were only devils in the sea this night.

These devils knew nothing of fear, or hate, or pain. The harsh cold of the seawater did not sap their strength as it might have for other men, and it did not hamper their movement. The sea they moved through showed the barest hint that they were there, only the slightest ripple extended from their heads as they waded closer and closer to their quarry.

A tremendous wooden beast loomed in the distance in front of them, stilled by the serene sea it called its home. Though the beast was not alive, those moving around on it were. The bellows of laughter and the hollow boom of boots against the beast's frame cut through the silence of the night.

The leader of the devils, with eyes touched by silver that was not silver, guided his minions to the beast's side. Those aboard the beast had not noticed the ripples in the waves. Their ears failed to hear the subtle drip of water cascading off clothes and back to the sea as the devils climbed up the sides of the beast. Without God's eye, they were blind to the enemy in front of them.

The leader had watched his minions the day before, had seen how they had been defeated. With his superior eyesight, granted him by one of the fingers of Midas, he knew how the wicked creatures of the light wrested control over his minions from him. And though he knew not a way to counteract it, he knew how it was done, and that was all he needed for his dark plan to succeed.

He and his minions boarded the beast, covered by the dark of the night and their dark clothing. One after the other, each of his men captured those who called the beast home, locking their arms and covering their mouths to stop their cries and their means of disabling his control.

After they had secured the beast's back, he went over to each man they'd captured. They squirmed and fought, but his minions were stronger, and so there was no escape. He gripped their shoulders, staring into their eyes, whispered the secret words he had learned over time, casting his spell over their mind to make them his.

Some fought, their minds stronger than others, but even the strongest were no match for his power. He had learned the secret ways long ago, practiced on many minds, and each one fell to him in the end.

All but one. The one who had given him his eyes. The one who had given him his new name and had let him loose on this island. That one had his own power, his own eyes that the fewest of the few possessed, that allowed him to resist. No, that allowed him to *conquer*. His blood was the blood of kings, and no man could overcome it.

One after the other, the men fell asleep. They would awaken later and serve a higher purpose than they had before.

Something unexpected stopped the leader of the devils from his work. A door opened to the beast's innards, and a young woman, two men—one holding a fiddle—and a wolf stepped out.

There was a silent moment where the three figures glanced across the ship, assessing the situation. Then, when they realized what was happening, they pulled out their weapons. The girl held twin daggers, one defensively to her side and the other up and ready to strike, while the man with the fiddle pulled out a pistol, and the other man his cutlass.

"Tala, *tuer*!" the young woman shouted.

The wolf, answering her call, ran forward and attacked one of the leader's minions. In one swift motion, it struck the neck, tearing a chunk of flesh away and letting loose a torrent of blood.

The leader ignored the wolf and raised his fist in the air. He needed no words to command his minions, and they obeyed the silent order in unison. They all pulled knives from their belts and placed them under the necks of the subdued men.

"Stop!" the girl shouted.

The leader held his hand in the air, unwavering, and he stared at the girl. He didn't want to continue the command if he didn't have to, as that was not his plan, and so he waited for the girl to act.

After another moment, the girl realized there wasn't anything she could do and lowered her daggers. "Tala, *venir*," she said. The French verb meant 'come,' a command to the wolf, which it obeyed by stopping its attack and returning to the girl's side.

The leader opened his palm and lowered his hand, then pointed at the three, and his minions went to restrain them. The wolf growled but remained stationary.

Now that he was closer, the leader was able to take a better look at the girl in command.

Her features, lit from a lantern in the cabin they had just exited, were pleasing to the eye. She was blond with a hint of rouge, as a tranquil field of wheat in the red light of dawn. Her body was well-toned, a fighter's body, youthful and shapely as a budding rose that could one day bloom into motherhood.

All those they had captured so far looked to be good fighters, trained and ready for battle. They would make useful additions.

The leader pulled the young woman's chin up to face him. Her cheeks flushed with anger and embarrassment.

"Look into my eyes."

A new day began in their stalemate of a battle.

Anne awoke from her first rest in some time and assessed their battle preparations and provisions with new eyes.

Nassir and the other crewmates had worked hard through the night and prepared a defensive wall of cannons. The makeshift, stationary limbers would hold the cannons and prevent them from flying away after each blast but were challenging to change the angle of. To be effective, they needed two men on each of the smaller cannons, as opposed to a single man had they still been at their home on the ship.

Their provisions, gathered from the many farms they had visited, would sustain them for quite some time if needed, and they could also collect more. If they couldn't win by force or by stealth, which Anne would find out about soon, then they could win by starvation. No matter how powerful the trance Silver Eyes' crew were under, they could not avoid the need for food indefinitely.

A few paces back from the line of cannons aimed at the town, Anne had set up a table with a few chairs for her, William, and some of the other crewmates to discuss strategy. She noticed William sitting there, and a bowl of food and a drink waiting for her. Pukuh was standing beside William, chewing on a piece of bread with meat and cheese on it.

Anne sat and quickly ate the modest food to break her fast. She didn't want to waste any time to discuss the investigation of the secret entrance Sam had provided the key for. She still found it challenging to eschew habits formed during her royal upbringing and waited until she finished swallowing before she spoke.

"What of the tunnel into the town?" Anne asked.

William glanced at Pukuh over his shoulder, then gave his report. "The tunnel, as Sam said, appears to be for the soldiers in need of a flanking attack. However, it has fallen into disrepair due to negligence and arrogance. It could collapse at any moment."

Pukuh scoffed. "No matter. We'll not be long there," he said.

William appeared exasperated, though to anyone but Anne, who had been studying his minute expressions, he looked as placid as ever. "It is as our friend says. We shan't be in the tunnel long, so we could possibly end the battle tonight under cover of darkness."

"Why must there always be waiting with you white people? Now is the time to strike back. We kill their leader and dine in his puny castle before the sun is high."

William didn't respond; he had probably heard the same argument from Pukuh before she awoke. The two simply waited for Anne, their commander and current captain, to speak.

Anne, for her part, being well-rested and high off their recent victory, saw no purpose in rushing into doom. That Sam knew of the tunnel meant Silver Eyes knew of the tunnel.

"Pukuh, are you familiar with the phrase 'the better part of valour is discretion'?"

Pukuh took a bite from his bread, meat, and cheese. "No," he replied, his cheeks full.

"It is from one of our great playwrights, and it means that caution is better than blind bravery."

Pukuh nodded. "Ah, I see. So, the savage is not smart as you are."

Anne was taken aback at Pukuh's comment as she had only known the Mayan prince to be a kind and affable man. "My apologies, Pukuh, that was not my intent. I am merely trying to—"

Pukuh held up his hand. "Save your air for later. If Edward were here, the Silver man would have his head on my spear on the walls now."

Pukuh's raised voice brought the attention of the crewmates nearby, and many were visibly uncomfortable and glancing at the scene over their shoulders.

Anne took a moment to gather herself, then stared into Pukuh's eyes. "You may be right. Edward may have finished this by now, but Edward is not here. In his place, I am your captain, and I give the orders to the crew of this ship." She paused for a moment to let her words hang in the air. "I understand your frustration with how I am approaching this matter, and I'll take it under review. Having said that, I can assure you that sooner rather than later, that spear of yours will see its fair share of blood. Can I count on you to be there when the time comes?"

Pukuh didn't reply, he simply stared Anne down for a long moment. She held his gaze, unwavering, as she sat stock still in her chair.

Another moment more, and Pukuh grinned. "You'll get your spear, princess," he finally said.

Anne returned the smile. She had never thought of him as a savage, as he put it, but she knew that their interactions so far had been brief at best. Perhaps this was his way of testing her, not knowing her very well. If it was, it appeared she had passed.

"Captain, look!" a crewmate called, his finger pointing to the sea.

Anne turned in her seat and followed the crewmate's gesture to the *Queen Anne's Revenge*. It was no longer circling the seas around the town as they planned. It had dropped anchor. That alone would not have caused too much alarm, as they had been able to damage the ships at harbour yesterday. There was no threat of Silver Eyes escaping now. What did cause alarm was the longboats of the ship carrying the crew to shore.

A tingle up Anne's spine forced her up from her chair. A dozen thoughts flashed through her mind as to what would cause the crew to leave the ship behind, but she was powerless to know now.

Her instinct guided her where knowledge could not. "Something's not right," she muttered. "Prepare for battle!"

Confused at first, the men drew their weapons and those

not manning the cannons grouped up with Anne. Anne drew her own cutlass and headed towards shore.

William ordered the men to form up, making a line two strong. The high from yesterday's victory turned into a sour note as the crew realized what may be happening.

Anne pulled out her spyglass and watched as the longboats hit the shore, and the crew aboard them jumped off in a sprint towards the field in front of the town. Christina and Jack were there, both had weapons drawn, lips curled back in a snarl like some animal ready to kill. Tala, a real animal, was keeping pace with Christina.

It was their eyes that gave Anne another shiver. Their eyes were hollow. They had been put under a trance by their enemy sometime in the night.

"They're under a trance," Anne shouted to the crew around her. She stepped forward and turned around to face them, so all eyes were on her. "But we can break it. We know it works. Try your best not to harm them, but don't let yourself be killed either." The crew objected, confusion and denial overtaking reason. Anne held up her hand. "This is no time for debate. Prepare yourselves." She went back to her place in the line before she had to field any other objections. "Bring some of the men off the cannons, we'll need all the hands we can get," she said to William. William nodded and left to issue orders to the crew manning the cannons.

Anne turned around as she took a few deep breaths and faced down her crewmates on the way to kill them. The entranced crew's rapid pace set a cloud of dust behind them.

William and some of the other crew returned to join the battle. "Spread out! Start moving," Anne shouted. "Split them up so you don't get overwhelmed."

Anne moved forward to meet Christina, and the other crewmates did as she commanded. As the targets spread out, the entranced crewmates followed suit, slowing their pace to attack.

"Tala," Anne heard Christina say as she came closer, "*tuer!*"

The wolf quickened her pace and lunged at Anne. Anne didn't want to harm the beast and rolled out of the way. She put herself at an angle away from Christina and Tala so she could face both, though not flawlessly.

Anne could hear the battle all around her, chaotic and discordant. Blades and bodies clashed as dust from upturned earth filled the still air around them. She could see William trying to get close enough to Jack, but he and another crewmate were on the attack and keeping him at bay. Pukuh was similarly having a challenging time, not only dealing with having only one hand and not being able to break the trance but also having to hold back so as not to harm his fellow crewmates. Nassir had joined in the battle, but he was inexperienced and kept his distance to distract rather than attack.

Christina lunged at Anne, slamming down with her right-hand dagger. Anne blocked with her forearm. The force rippled through her bones. Christina was using all her strength, her mental limits gone with the veil to the subconscious pulled open. If Anne wasn't careful, Christina could break Anne's arm or her own.

Anne yanked her hand over and clutched Christina's right forearm tight. Christina swung low with her other dagger. Anne dropped her cutlass and caught her opponent's wrist. Just as Anne was about to twist and disarm her friend, Tala charged at Anne's side. Anne bent her and Christina's bodies, blocking and pushing Tala back.

Between stopping Christina from attacking and keeping Tala at bay, Anne couldn't end the trance. They were locked in a dance, and none of the crew were nearby to help her.

"Tala, *arrêter*!" Anne's command didn't work. The wolf only obeyed Christina and Edward.

Christina looked crazed and feral, nothing like the sweet girl with the mild temper she knew. Her eyes, though looking straight at Anne, didn't carry the same recognition of a sane person. Silver Eyes had somehow put his talons in her and made her think her friends were her enemies, but Anne knew they could break the trance. There simply hadn't been time to turn them into the state the islanders were in. Alexandre had said it would have taken months to get them to that state. If only Anne could find an opening to break the spell…

Movement at the town's wall drew her eye. The gate had opened, and more of Silver Eyes' men were exiting and heading towards the battle.

Dad dammit! We don't have the manpower for this right now. Anne dodged another strike from Tala and kept her hold on Christina by a hair. "William!" she called.

William, just managing to sort out Jack, turned to her call and started running.

"No!" she yelled. "The cannons, the cannons!"

William looked over at the cannons and then noticed the men approaching by foot. He began shouting orders and pointing towards the cannons as he moved that way. Several of the crew and even some newly conscious crewmates joined in to gather muskets and man the cannons.

"Christina!" Anne shouted. It was taking all her strength to hold on to the young woman. "It's me. It's Anne. I know you're in there. Wake up!"

Christina's eyes changed, coming into focus. She stopped moving, stopped resisting. She appeared confused but still distant, as though she were half-asleep.

Pain seared Anne's right leg, and a force pushed her to the side and away from Christina. Anne fell to the ground and lashed out towards her lower leg. Tala, at the moment Anne had let her guard down, had bitten down on her calf and shin. She'd ripped through her clothes, through the muscle on her calf, and to the bone on her shin. Anne punched the wolf, shouting commands and expletives at the beast in French. Tala snarled, tugging at Anne's leg and refusing to let go as it ripped her leg to shreds.

The pain overtook Anne's mind, just as the bell had when she had been right underneath it. She screamed in vain, punching and punching Tala to no avail. She needed Tala off her, or

189

she would die, she knew it. Anne reached into her belt, pulled out her knife, and slammed the blade into Tala's skull down to the hilt, killing the wolf instantly.

Anne ripped the beast's jaws off her leg, another roaring pain surging up her right leg, through her pelvis, and up her spine. She reared back, all thoughts lost in that storm of pain.

She pulled herself back from the pieces the pain had broken her into and mustered her will. Her whole body shook with the effort to bring herself to her feet, and she nearly collapsed as soon as she stood.

Christina was looking at her and Tala's lifeless body. She was still in a daze, her mind still trapped. Some part of her seemed to know what was happening, even in that dream-like state, and tears were streaking her face as she gazed at Tala and Anne.

Anne, her right leg useless, limped her way to Christina. She leaned on the younger woman for support, then clapped right in front of her eyes.

The spell released, and Christina took a sharp breath as though waking from a nightmare. "Wha... what happe..." She looked around at the scene of the battle, over to Tala's dead body, and then burst into fresh tears. She covered her mouth and pulled back from Anne, but Anne needed to hold onto the young woman for support.

"Christina, listen to me," Anne said weakly, trying to keep a hold of her consciousness.

Christina's eyes were moving quickly over everything, shock taking over her senses. She was breathing too rapidly and becoming hysterical. She looked down and saw Anne's injury and began to cry harder. "Your leg, oh Anne!"

"Christina, Christina!" Anne called. "Look at me." She grabbed the woman's face and gently took her attention back. Christina's eyes still didn't focus on Anne. "Look into my eyes," she said. The words triggered something in Christina, and Anne finally had her attention. "This wasn't your fault. You did nothing wrong."

The young girl was a mess. She wept, with no way to stop the tears. Anne pulled her tight and held her as she cried. The battle raged on around them as Christina's tears and Anne's blood fell to the ground.

Cannons, muskets, swords, smoke, shouting, sweat, pain, blood. William's mind filtered through all the noise to focus on only the most essential things needed in the time of battle. He had been trained to do so, and he was adept at it.

He had not been trained to fight an enemy incapable of feeling pain. He had not been trained to fight his comrades. He had not been trained to hold back in battle.

And he had not been trained to suppress his emotions. That came from years of practice. And in that, he was struggling.

Anne had ordered him to act, and he acted. They were winning the battle, but only by the thinnest of margins. Their only saving grace was their surgeon's technique. On all other fronts—the number of men, morale, and even training, save for a few exceptions—they were on the losing side.

The cannons and muskets kept their enemies at bay while they fixed more members of their crew who had fallen under the devil's spell, and with each person who was saved, it added to their numbers.

"Draw swords!" Some heard his command and drew their swords and cutlasses with him. "Charge!" William led the men into the fray just before the enemy would be too close.

William had been called The Arching Light, a name given to him by others in the royal guard for his speed and the way light shone off his blade with his perfect form. Here on the battlefield, as a pirate, he knew his sword did not shine, and he was no source of light. Outside of training, in a real battle, his sword turned red.

William needed to end this quickly and ensure Anne's safety. He slashed, stabbed, kicked, punched, and elbowed one man after the other. His dance of death was muted. There was no beauty in it, only the purest form of battle. Parry, thrust, parry, sidestep, thrust. There was no chaos, no wasted movement, and no thought. Memory carried his blade and his body as one to where it needed to be, memory from his unknowing mind built over years of experience and training.

When it was over, he had killed eight, sending their souls to whatever afterlife their actions warranted.

William assessed the situation, taking stock of their numbers. The enemy had sent a similar number to what they had the other day, but with Anne's quick reaction, they had managed to fend them off. There were still some left, but the crew could handle the rest.

William turned his attention back to Anne and Christina, and as he approached, he saw the two in an embrace. Relief washed over him, but he didn't slow his pace.

Though they had lost many men so far and had many more injured, the other crewmates were turning those put into a trance back to normal. Soon, the battle would be over.

As he drew near he noticed Tala, dead and off to the side of the two women. Her muzzle was bloodied, a sure sign she had inflicted grievous wounds on someone. He looked Anne over for injuries and quickly noticed her right leg bleeding profusely. He quickened his pace, and his heartbeat soon matched.

Christina noticed him coming, and she pulled away from Anne's embrace. "Anne's injured. It's my fault. I'm sorry, I—"

William held up a hand. "Bring Alexandre to the ship, most of his supplies are there."

Anne's face had blanched from blood loss. "I am well," she protested. "I simply need some assistance walking at present." William scooped her up, lifting her off her feet. "This wasn't what I had in mind."

Christina wiped tears from her face, took a breath, and nodded at William before running off to find Alexandre.

William took Anne to the shore where the longboats had

landed. He gingerly placed Anne inside the boat, taking care not to bump her leg. Despite his diligence, he noticed her wincing and stifling a cry of pain. William thought the only thing keeping her awake was the pain.

After Anne was secure, William rowed the longboat back to the *Queen Anne's Revenge*. The two of them were silent for the ride, neither broaching the nature of the horrific injury she had received, nor the battle which was finishing inland. The noise of crossed blades, shouts, and pain had faded away to a whisper on the wind by the time they reached the side of the ship, replaced by the soft whistling across the weather deck, and the lapping of waves against the side.

William secured the boat to the side of the ship and then picked Anne up again. "Apologies, Captain," he said as he hoisted her over his shoulder.

Even at this, she didn't say a word, which told him that she knew the severity of her own injury. This made his heart race even faster.

William climbed up the side of the ship, his muscles burning with the effort. After a careful few minutes, he had her aboard, but he dared not put her down now. He took her below deck and into the surgeon's room and placed her on the long table in the centre. He helped her lie down and went to work before Alexandre arrived.

William was no surgeon, but he knew a concoction that would be useful for pain mitigation. He grabbed a bottle from the storage cabinets, one of the only bottles in the bunch clearly labelled, which William thought dangerous, and gave the liquid a sniff to be sure.

William handed the bottle to Anne. "You must drink this, Captain."

Anne cocked her brow. "What is it?" she asked, but she began drinking before he answered.

"Gin," he replied as she took a large drink and reeled back at the sharp taste.

He thought of cleaning the wound with the gin and dressing it, but he knew how particular Alexandre was. He didn't want to risk his ire, nor the possibility of making the situation worse. Instead, he wrapped a cloth just beneath her knee and tied it tight to stanch the blood loss, sat down in a nearby chair, and then they waited.

After a moment of silence, Anne spoke. "William?"

"Yes, Captain?"

"What kind of a man was my uncle-in-law?"

Anne spoke of William III, the king before her mother took the throne. The question caught him off guard, as they had not talked much of their lives before joining Edward's band of pirates.

William looked away from Anne as he reminisced. "I loved him," he said. "He was more than a king to me. He was like a father."

"He must have been a great man to have such high praise from you."

William still didn't know how to respond. He settled on a nod and "He was." It felt... insufficient.

There was another pause, then after another drink of gin, Anne said, "Why didn't you save him in the Triangle?"

It took a moment for William to understand just what she was referring to. William had been a kingsguard and had been framed for his king's murder, so he'd fled. Years ago, the *Queen Anne's Revenge* had entered the Devil's Triangle, where the crew had experienced strange events. William, along with Sam Bellamy and a woman they'd thought was their enemy at the time, were seemingly transported to the time just prior to the king's murder. It was thought to be a dream, but dream or real, William had chosen not to change what happened and let his king die again.

"How...?"

"Sam told me. He told me that you didn't want to risk changing history but never told me why. He said to ask you, but I never did because I thought it was too personal."

William rose from his seat to look into Anne's eyes. Her

pallor hadn't improved much, but the gin seemed to be helping.

"I didn't stop his murder because of you," William said.

Anne arched her brows, a question unuttered but implied.

"I've never seen you happier than aboard this ship. Yes, there have been some hardships"—he cast a glance at her leg—"but you have made friends here, shared laughter here, and you were even married here on this ship."

William took his chair and pulled it closer so he could sit next to Anne. He sat a moment, staring off at nothing, then looked Anne in the eyes again.

"I remember meeting you when you were twelve," he said. "I was a new kingsguard then, just a few years before your uncle-in-law's death. You didn't scowl, but you never smiled. You smiled in the way that they trained you to, but you never truly smiled. Except once, when you were with the ladies in the kitchen, and you started a fight with the food they were preparing." William took Anne's hand in his. "If you would have stayed royalty, I have no doubts you would have made a wonderful ruler, a wonderful queen. I'll admit that that was what I had hoped would happen at first. I hoped I might bring you back to take your place in the palace, but I realized you belong here with these people. This is where you are you and not what someone else told you to be. This is where your family is."

There was another moment as William's words sank in, then Anne spoke. Then she squeezed his hand. "And your family too, I hope?"

William couldn't help but smile. He thought to say something affirming her question, but the words felt hollow in his mind. Too hollow to convey the feelings which held his hand firm to hers. By the look on her face, this was all he needed to say in answer.

The sound of boots slamming against wood above them took them away from their reminiscing. After a moment, Alexandre, Victoria, and Christina all entered the room.

Alexandre and Victoria wasted no time in preparing to treat

Anne's wound. Alexandre first grabbed scissors and went to Anne's injured leg.

"And how is *le patiente*?"

Anne lifted the gin bottle in the air. "Excellent," she said before taking another drink.

"I see you've started already. How thoughtful."

Alexandre began by cutting away Anne's clothes from the wound. Using a deft hand, he cleared the area around the wound and then took away the pieces that had became stuck to the skin as the blood dried. After a few careful minutes, however, Alexandre stopped and stepped back slightly.

"What is it?" William asked.

Alexandre stayed still in thought. His face scrunched and deadly serious. "Victoria, prepare for amputation."

The words sent a wave of shock through William's system. Anne and Christina both looked just as shocked as he.

Christina, already in hysterics over being entranced, looked ready to burst into tears again. "Why?" was all she could muster.

"The damage is too severe. Bone fragments entered her muscle. It is impossible to remove them all. They will, at best, cause paralysis. At worst, rot."

Alexandre retrieved a sizeable curved knife and a thick piece of wood. He handed the wood to William. Victoria was shuffling around the small room, gathering things they would need after the amputation was complete.

There was no way around this, so William steeled himself. Alexandre was a consummate professional, unparalleled in the study of medicine. If he said they needed to amputate Anne's leg, there was no use arguing. Anne would survive this, there was no way she wouldn't.

William looked down at Anne. "Take another drink, Captain."

Anne, she too nearing tears, took a long drink of the gin, then handed the bottle to William. William set the bottle aside and placed the piece of wood in her mouth.

"Hold her steady, all of you."

Christina and Victoria both came to the table and put all their weight down on top of Anne to hold her still during the surgery. William placed his hands on her shoulders as he stared down at her.

Deep in her eyes, he could see fear. It was rare for her to be afraid, let alone show it, and if he were honest with himself, he too was afraid. She needed strength now more than anything else.

She lifted her head up and looked at her injured leg, part of which she was about to lose. "No, Anne," he whispered softly. "Look into my eyes." She laid her head back down, and tears streaked her face. "It's going to be all right."

16. NASSAU

Edward hadn't slept properly in days. His body felt heavy, as though he were thirty feet below the sea. Moving, breathing, just existing, was gruelling and painful. He wanted it to end. And so, Edward did the one thing that helped him sleep and made him feel less pain, less leaden, less everything: he drank.

It didn't matter when; Edward drank all hours of the day, and it showed. His speech slurred from time to time, he lost his sea legs, and the cloud the booze gave him sapped his strength.

Strangely enough, his fighting ability had improved. Because of various blunders during his shifts, as well as a few misunderstandings on Edward's part, he brawled with a few of the crew. The drink helped him withstand even more punishment than he already could and made his movements unpredictable. His opponents hadn't known how to handle him under normal circumstances, and the drunkenness only made him more dangerous.

Herbert caught Edward after he had taken a rest. He was still dealing with the effects of having drunk the night before but was no longer intoxicated.

"Edward, this must stop," Herbert said.

Edward's head pounded in his ears, and his stomach lurched with each movement. "This is far too early for such talk, Herbert. Let me eat and drink, then we shall discuss whatever it is that must stop."

Herbert scowled. "It is precisely the drinking that I am referring to," he said. He glanced around him, then moved his chair closer to Edward before speaking in a whisper. "I know that you are mourning the loss of John. I know you two were… closer than you previously thought, but if you continue this, then—"

"What? I won't be in well enough shape to kill more of my family?"

Herbert's face went stark white and his eyes nearly bulged out of their sockets. "Keep your voice down, you fool!" he whispered harshly.

Edward didn't feel the same urgency as Herbert's tone called for, but he didn't say anything else. Instead, he reached into his pocket and pulled out his flask.

Herbert reached over and swiped the flask out of his hand. Edward tried to grab it back, but Herbert kept it out of reach. He put it in the secret compartment of his wheelchair.

"Give that back," Edward said.

"That's going to get us both killed."

Edward, his head still pounding, tired, body aching, was like a packed cannon, and Herbert was the linstock. It only took a touch for him to explode.

He reared back and punched Herbert square in the jaw. Herbert spilled out of his chair and tumbled to the deck.

Edward picked up the wheelchair, not bothering to check if Herbert was all right, and tried to open the secret compartment. "How do you work this thing?" he muttered to himself.

Herbert punched Edward on the side of the knee. He collapsed and fell to his knees, grimacing in pain. Herbert pounced and wrapped his arm around Edward's neck to choke him. Edward pulled against Herbert's arm, but Herbert's grip was secure.

"There's lead balls ready to fire from that thing, you idiot!" Herbert's words came out in haste from the strain, but he managed to be only loud enough for Edward to hear.

The other crewmates of the *Black Blood* noticed the fight and cheered the combatants on. The two of them rolled and tumbled on the floorboards as hoots and hollers goaded them to continue.

Blackbeard's Family

"You think you can beat me in a fight, you bastard?" Edward poured his all into pulling back Herbert's arm.

Herbert brought his other arm up and locked his grip. "Just because I don't handle rigging all day doesn't mean I'm weak."

Edward's neck was in a vice, and he couldn't breathe. Pulling Herbert's arm was useless as he had superior upper body strength and a better position. So, Edward pulled his arm up, then slammed his elbow into Herbert's ribs. Herbert grunted, and his grip wavered. Edward brought his arm up repeatedly, smashing his elbow on Herbert's bones. Though each blow loosened Herbert's hold, it provided no chance to breathe or escape.

"By these copper legs o' mine, you boys better stop yer fightin' else I'll shoot the lot of ye."

Grace O'Malley stormed through the crowd that had gathered, looking down on the two she thought were brothers having a squabble.

Herbert released Edward from his hold, and Edward rolled off him, sputtering and coughing to catch his breath. Herbert went to his chair and got in it.

"We're about ta land in Nassau and you boys're about ta meet Calico Jack. If ye want ta survive the experience, I suggest ye stop fuckin' about." Her hands were on her hips, and her expression daunting. "Herbert, get ta the weather deck. The helmsman needs relief."

"Aye, Captain," he replied as he pushed himself forward to the ladder.

"As fer you," she continued, looking at Edward, who was sitting on the deck and rubbing his sore neck, "ye've been useless of late. If ye want me ta put in a good word, take stock and get ta work. Otherwise, take yer chances overboard. Ye'll 'ave better luck with the sharks than with Jack, I can tell ye that much." The other crewmates chuckled, and some muttered agreements. Then she turned her attention to them. "Did I ask any of ye ta say somethin'? Back to work!"

Grace and the other crewmates dispersed at once, leaving Edward alone on the sole of the deck in the crew's quarters.

Edward's body still ached, but now he also felt the red flush of embarrassment join with it. He gritted his teeth, slammed his fist on the floorboards, and went to the weather deck.

Herbert was already at the helm, so either he'd carried his wheelchair himself or someone else had helped him. He glanced Edward's way when he appeared, then turned his attention back to steering the ship.

Off the bow of the ship, Edward could see the dark shadow of their destination, Nassau. It wouldn't be long before they arrived. It wouldn't be long before he had to kill again; not long before he had to kill more of his family.

Edward, without the numbing effects of the rum, decided to pour himself into the work aboard the ship. He tried to distract himself from the arresting thoughts his mind wouldn't let go of—thoughts of killing his best friend, Henry Morgan, his stepbrother John, and the countless people young and old he had ended over the years.

Haunting him too were the faces of those he had let die through his own weakness. His old quartermaster, John, returned to him. If he had just killed Kenneth Locke instead of leaving him to die, then John might have lived.

John's last words came back to him again as they had the last time he'd thought about the man. *'Your father is in the Caribbean, Edward.'* As Edward thought over the words and what they had meant, something itched in his mind.

If John knew my father was alive and he knew that he took the name of Calico Jack, then he knew what my father wanted all this time. He was the one who handed me the first clue to finding the keys of the Queen Anne's Revenge. *John was trying to protect me, guide me, and push me to pass the tests. Was he also sending my father letters, telling him of my progress?*

Edward's head hurt, but now for a different reason.

No, that can't be. Calico Jack attacked Bodden Town after *we got all the keys. If he was to be the final test, then he couldn't have done it any sooner, and John died before we got the last key. It was someone else. Someone else in the crew must have told him we finished. Could it have been Victoria? No, she joined in Port Royal after I acquired the ship. Unless that too was a lie. She and John could have co-ordinated together to…* Edward shook his head violently and regretted it just afterwards. *It's no use thinking of that now. Focus on the work. The work, man!*

Edward returned to his duties, trying to clear his mind in the endless repetition afforded him by the menial labour. With considerable effort, he was able to clear his mind enough to relieve his need for the booze. Before he knew it, the ship had its sails furled and coasted into the harbour towards a nearby port.

The *Black Blood*, being a brigantine, loomed over the smaller sloops and even smaller ships in the harbour. There were very few that matched the *Black Blood's* size, and only one that Edward could see that surpassed it. If his ship had been there, it would have been out of place in the harbour, as it often was. The *Queen Anne's Revenge* was an anomaly amongst pirate vessels, being a three-masted light frigate.

Herbert guided the ship into port, where the crew were ready to secure it to the mooring of the wharf.

Edward took in his surroundings. The town of Nassau wasn't large, but it was bustling with activity. From the many ships in the harbour coming and going to the noise in the town itself, Edward could tell it was a hub for trade.

The buildings were centred around the main wharf they had settled into, where several larger ships were also moored. Many of the buildings close to the wharf were well built and well established, made of hardwoods and atop cleared ground. Further out, the buildings were shabbier, fashioned with inferior cuts of wood and straw roofs overhead. A few smaller piers where longboats could unload smaller cargo saw better housing or business for trade, but only a few.

The swaying palms dotted the landscape, with some poking out above the taller buildings in front of the wharf and progressively becoming denser the farther one looked. Beyond the buildings, Edward could see forested vegetation with pockets of clear-cutting for roads and the homes around them.

To his left, west of town atop a slight hill, he could see an old fort with two high walls overlooking the harbour. It could be a deterrent for attacking ships at that elevation, but beyond it was even taller hills that would make inland defence impossible. Edward noticed cracks in the foundation and holes in the walls from cannon fire. He would be surprised if it were still in use.

The crew lowered the gangplank, and a swarm of hawkers came down the pier to sell their goods. Before they even set foot on the gangplank, Grace was standing there looking down at them. Without a word, the hawkers backed away and left.

After they left, Grace spoke to her senior officers, then called Edward over. "Before I introduce ye ta Jack, I'll be headin' over ta tell him what happened ta John. Ye won't want ta be anywhere near him then. Stay aboard the ship, I'll come back ta get ye if the time is right. Otherwise, we may need ta leave in a hurry."

Edward tried to hold back his anger. Would his father be so incensed if *he* died? Considering the many times his father, either directly or indirectly, had attempted to kill him, he doubted it.

Grace took Edward's silence as affirmation he'd heard her, and she left the ship. The two senior officers, stoic and quiet as ever, both stayed aboard and blocked the gangplank access. When some of the crew approached, trying to leave for shore, they stopped them.

Edward went to the quarterdeck, where Herbert had been watching. The crew had abandoned their duties now that the ship was moored, and the two were alone.

"We need to get off the ship, but Grace ordered everyone

to stay aboard."

Herbert's anger was evident, but he looked past Edward to the two men guarding the gangplank against the horde of crewmates. Though they outnumbered the two senior officers by twenty to one, with even more below deck, the crew were only making a play at trying to leave. None dared to take it as far as to attack the senior officers. So complete was Grace's intimidating force that it was there even when she was not.

Herbert let out a deep breath. "We could try to convince the crew to go ashore, but looking at them now, I don't think they have the spine in them to go against Grace."

"So, a distraction, then?"

Herbert nodded and stroked his chin. "But what kind of distraction would pull both of them away from their post?"

Edward mulled it over, he too reaching up to his chin before his lack of a giant beard made the physical act of ruminating somehow more distracting. After another moment, he shook his head and shrugged his shoulders.

"I'm just going to start a fire," Edward said finally.

"Wait, what?"

"Stay here, I'll not be long."

Edward heard Herbert stumble to say something else as he walked down to the weather deck. He didn't have time for further debate. They needed to get off the ship one way or the other, and he didn't care if he destroyed Grace's ship in the process.

Edward went below deck and found two lanterns filled with oil. He spread some of the oil in one of the corners of the ship, then over some other cargo, and lit it on fire when no one was looking. He chose a few other spots where the fire could spread but not be put out quickly. It was just enough fire to cause a panic but not enough to burn the whole ship down. Or, at least he thought it wasn't.

Before anyone could see the fires beginning to engulf the ship, Edward went above to the quarterdeck again.

"We should probably stay back so they don't see us waiting around," Edward said, pointing to the stern.

Herbert pulled his wheelchair back from the edge of the quarterdeck, and Edward followed before crouching down to be out of sight from the senior crewmates. They waited a few minutes until they head shouting below them.

The shouting, indistinct and scattered, continued for another moment longer before a few crewmates ran above deck. "Fire!" one man shouted. "Fires below deck. It's spreading."

The crewmates above deck answered the call and rushed below, but not all left to investigate. Ten crewmates, and the two senior guards, all stayed behind. Edward cursed under his breath, thinking he should have lit more fires.

Another minute more and smoke began rising through the opening to the deck below and through the grated hatch covers near the ladder. The shouting grew louder and calls for aid filtered through the noise.

Edward watched as the crewmates who'd stayed behind changed from being complacent to concerned until they went into action. The guards, too, looked at each other and rushed to help the rest of the crew below deck.

Herbert wheeled himself forward to the edge of the quarterdeck as black smoke billowed up from below. "Edward... how many fires did you set?"

"No time for that, we have to leave."

Edward picked up Herbert's chair, with Herbert still in it, and took him down the quarterdeck steps as far from the ladder and grates as he could. The effort put pressure on his head, making it pound again. He let Herbert back down on the gangplank before pushing the wheelchair at top speed. There was no point in stealth given the level of noise below deck. In no time, the two were off the *Black Blood* and onto the wharf where a crowd was gathering towards the sight of the smoke.

Edward kept pushing Herbert forward and through the crowd towards Nassau. He rushed onto the main road, a large dirt and mud track wide enough for carts, ignored the terrible odours emanating from every person and every corner, and entered the nearest tavern.

Inside, Edward finally stopped running and looked down to see Herbert breathing heavy and holding onto his wheelchair like driftwood in a storm.

"Are you well, Herbert?" he asked.

"No thanks to you. I know we needed to get away from there, but once we were in the crowd, you could have slowed down." Edward grinned and shrugged. After Herbert caught his breath, he took in his surroundings. "What are we doing here?"

Edward stepped up to the bar in the tavern and ordered two glasses of whiskey. After taking the drinks in hand, he answered Herbert's question by lifting them up into full view. He motioned for Herbert to follow him, and the two went to a corner of the bar out of view of the windows and entrance.

The two sat in silence, slowly drinking the whiskey as they calmed their nerves. Edward hoped that none had seen him lighting the fires and that the crew were able to put it out. Earlier, he didn't care, but now that it was done, he would regret it if the ship burned down. They'd managed to keep their identities hidden so it wouldn't do to have Grace and her crew looking for them because they torched her ship.

After a few moments, Herbert spoke. "This was a mistake, coming here."

The comment took Edward aback, and he didn't know how to respond. "What?" was all he managed.

"Us coming here was a mistake," Herbert said. "Because of me, you killed your brother, and who knows how things are going with our crew. How are we to even find them again? And then we're supposed to kill your father, without a plan, without help, with no way to escape."

Edward gripped his glass harder. "You mean *me* coming here was a mistake."

It was Herbert's turn to be confused. "What?"

"Look, I—" The words choked in Edward's throat. "I know I'm messed in the head, but I meant what I said. My father has done horrible things, and he wants me to kill him. Some twisted final test of his I'll never understand. So, I'm here to end it before he hurts anyone else I care about." Edward took another drink from his whiskey, letting the burn take over his mind.

"He... he wasn't all bad."

Edward looked up from his glass at Herbert, who was staring into his own glass intently. He had a small smile on his face.

"When I was young, before my accident, he was the first one to show me how to read clouds, how to man the helm, how to read a map. It was all basics, but for me, it meant a lot." Herbert took a long drink of his whiskey. "He has done horrible things, but he wasn't evil." He looked up at Edward, pain in his eyes. "Was he?"

Edward couldn't think of what to say. Calico Jack had always been Herbert's entire world. Revenge had been his reason for taking to the seas. It had once caused him to steal away the *Queen Anne's Revenge* in pursuit of Jack and leave Edward behind. For him to say the man wasn't evil felt strange.

"And you know what the worst part of it is?" Herbert's voice cracked, and he had tears in his eyes. "I don't even know if I was right this whole time."

"About what?"

"Gregory Dunn, the one you got that gold from to make your sword and rings, said that I was his favourite. And I remember that I used to get money sent regularly to me by someone, but then it suddenly stopped. Sometime after I left, Dunn became Jack's Gold Division Commander. They're the ones in charge of the money."

Edward was putting the pieces together. "You think he... stole it? Stole the money my father sent to you?"

Herbert shook his head. "I don't know. But what if he did? Then it means your father didn't really abandon me because he thought I was useless. All I've had since I lost my legs was hate, and when you came along, I had hope again. What if the reason for that hope is a lie?"

Edward gritted his teeth. "And what if it's not?" he seethed. "What if that money was from someone else? What if you don't remember things right? He still left *me* when *I* was ten; he still became Calico Jack." Edward was nearly shouting. It took everything he had to hold back his anger and keep his voice low. "Grace told you her story, the bodies piled up, the girls taken, hell, even Grace herself. You must have known about it already, you were there." Edward took the last drink and slammed the glass down. "I don't care if he wants us to do it, he needs to die."

Herbert nodded and looked defeated. Perhaps the drink was hitting him harder than he'd thought it would. "I know. We're in too deep to swim back to shore now." There was another moment of silence before Herbert took the flask out from his chair and threw it across the table to Edward. "Look at us. Pathetic, aren't we? We're about to kill your father, a man we both loved and hate, and here we are trying to find the courage to do the deed at the bottom of a bottle."

Edward let out a dark chuckle as he pocketed the flask. "Lately it seems to be the only way I can find it." He rubbed his eyes and slapped his face. "Apologies for my outburst earlier. I'll not drink anymore until the deed is done."

Herbert nodded. "I'm sorry as well. I could have handled that better. And," he added with a wide grin, "I too promise not to drink anymore until the deed is done."

Edward and Herbert both laughed together, the first time that they had in a long while.

"Well, I see ye both're gettin' along well enough without me."

A familiar voice drew the two men's attention, and when

they looked up, they saw a ghost in the flesh. Edward rose half from his seat at the sight of the man in front of them.

"S—Sam!" the two of them said in unison.

"I heard ye bastards thought I was dead. Don't ye know ye can't kill a man what looks this good? Why, just think of the ladies whose hearts would break."

"Sam!" Edward said again as he ran in to embrace his long-lost crewmate, Samuel Bellamy.

"Whoa, whoa, Captain, ease yourself. Don't bring any attention this way. As I understand it, you're here to kill the big man. Wouldn't do ta ruin the surprise now."

Edward pulled away from Sam. "How do you know what we're here for?"

Sam walked over to one side of the table and sat down. Edward joined him and sat back down to hear Sam's story.

"I met yer wife nearabouts a week past. She got me up ta speed with what you ran off ta do, and I agreed to come help."

The news that Anne knew where Edward was, and that Sam had come in her stead, was almost as shocking as the revelation that Sam was alive.

"I know," Sam said. "I had the same dumb look on me face. She's facin' off against Silver Eyes ta save the island he took over and keep him distracted. If ye ask me, she made the wrong move, but the woman's got standards, that much is true."

Edward nodded. If the people on that island needed her help, Anne wasn't the type to let them die, nor leave a job half-finished. As much as he yearned to see her again, this was probably her way of telling him to finish things as well.

"So, what about you? What happened after I escaped Cache-Hand?"

Sam waved his hand. "We got no time fer that. We'll small-talk later. Right now, we need to take care of yer pa," he said. "So, what's the plan?"

Edward and Herbert looked at each other, then back at

Sam. "We don't have one. We just got here."

"I thought we might scout his villa and come up with a plan from there."

Sam chuckled. "Are... are ye boys tellin' true? Ye have no plan?" Sam shook his head and rubbed his face. "Well, there ain't no chance of ye getting ta him in his home. Too heavily guarded, so best leave that out. Ye need ta strike when he's outside. Me crew and I can help ye with an ambush, we jus have ta find the right time."

"You have a crew?" Edward asked. Sam gave him a stern look of disapproval. "Right, focus," he said. "That won't work, we don't have the time. Grace O'Malley will be looking for us soon, so it's now or never."

Sam's eyes bulged nearly out of their sockets. "Grace fuckin' O'Malley'll be lookin fer ye? The hell did you boys do?"

"We joined her crew to get here, and we're supposed to go meet Jack soon as new crew members," Herbert explained. "And could you not call us boys anymore? We're older than you."

Sam ignored Herbert's comment. "Wait, you're supposed to meet Jack?" Edward and Herbert both nodded. Sam looked at them both as though the next trail of thought were self-evident.

Edward shook his head. "No, it's too dangerous. You said yourself, his home is well guarded. As soon as he sees either of us, it's over. Our only opportunity is a surprise."

"I'll handle the guards. I'll have me crew start a small riot o' sorts, something he won't be able to ignore. You use that chance ta finish him off and get outa there, head ta me ship the *Whydah* and we'll head back to yer wife. Done and done."

Edward hunched over in his seat, thinking it over in his head. He looked at Herbert, who also seemed to be testing the plan in his mind. Herbert saw Edward looking at him, and he shrugged his shoulders.

"I suppose it will bring us directly to him, rather than us

waiting for him to come to us."

"Aye, it's the best plan we got," Sam said before standing as though it were settled. "Ye better get back to Grace's ship, she's not a woman ta be left waitin'."

"Tch," Edward spat. "You don't know the half of it." He held out his hand to Sam. "Good to have you back, Sam. We'll be counting on you."

Sam shook Edward's hand. "As it always was." Edward and Herbert both went to leave, but Sam stopped them. "Almost forgot this," he said as he took his cutlass off his belt and handed it to Edward. The hilt was covered in cloth, but once Sam pulled it out from its sheath, he saw the familiar golden gleam of his cutlass shining out.

Edward reached for his blade, the familiar gold that was not gold calling to him, but he pushed it back towards Sam. "I can't. If any saw it, they would know something was wrong. You hold onto it for me."

Sam nodded and put the cutlass back on his belt. "Don't die, Captain."

"Same to you, Sam."

Edward and Herbert headed back to the *Black Blood,* still moored to the wharf. The crowd that had been gathering before was gone, and the ship looked, at least on the outside, undamaged. As they approached, however, they saw Grace on the weather deck, and she looked quite displeased.

When they came closer, a crewmate pointed at them, and Grace turned around. She seemed surprised, but her expression changed at once, so it was hard for Edward to tell if he'd read her right.

"Ye boys have fun in town disobeying orders?"

Edward and Herbert stayed at the bottom of the gangplank. "We were thirsty, so we thought we'd grab a drink in town," Edward said.

Grace nodded, her usual calm feeling strange to Edward at that moment. "Aye, and what of the fire on my ship? Ye wouldn't know anything about that now, would ye?"

Edward glanced at Herbert. "We were above deck when it started. And the other crewmates seemed capable of handling it, so we let them take all the glory."

Edward knew he was playing a dangerous game, but it was all he could think of at the moment. He was hoping their imminent meeting with Calico Jack would be more important than them leaving the ship during a crisis.

If Grace was angry, she didn't show it outwardly. "We'll discuss this later. Now, you need to meet Jack." She marched down the gangplank and joined them on the pier. "Come," she said as she walked past them.

Edward took a few silent breaths at the narrow escape, and he and Herbert followed Grace into town once again. She led them down the main road, past the many houses, taverns, brothels, inns, and various businesses of the town before stopping in front of a gated two-storey villa.

With its wrought-iron fence, open lawn, pure whitewashed wooden exterior, and two floors, the villa looked like the home of a wealthy magistrate. It reminded Edward of the home of the Bodden Brothers in their town Edward had taken over— the town his father as Calico Jack had attacked, setting this series of events in motion.

The main difference here was the level of security. There were five guards Edward could see at the front of the property, two at the gate, two at the door, and another on a balcony on the second floor. Edward guessed there were more both outside and inside.

Is my father not supposed to be a king here? Why does he need so many guards? Is he simply paranoid?

Edward had no time to think about it, as Grace led them inside the gate. She didn't take them to the front door and instead led them to the side of the villa. There was another entrance there, with a lone guard stationed at the ready. When he noticed her, he opened the door for her, and she headed inside.

Edward and Herbert followed her, and it was then that Edward realized why Grace had been acting slightly strange. Inside the room, a half-dozen men had muskets trained on the two of them. At the back of the room, there was a cell with an open door.

Edward raised his hands in the air, and someone threw Herbert to the ground beside him before the door was closed behind. The guard from outside had his weapon out and trained on them now as well. There was no escape.

"Inside," Grace commanded, gesturing to the cell.

Edward walked forward, his hands still in the air, and entered the cell. Herbert crawled into the cell beside him, and they closed and locked the doors shut.

"Not the welcome I expected," Edward said.

"Cut the shit," Grace spat. "I know who you are, Thatch. And you, Blackwood."

Edward glanced down at Herbert, who was sitting at the bottom of the cell looking up at him. "What gave us away?"

"A six-foot-two behemoth with Jack's eyes and a cripple helmsman. It weren't that difficult to piece together, even after giving yerself a shave." Grace stepped closer to the cell. "Now tell me true. Did ye kill my John?"

Edward didn't answer. He gritted his teeth and lowered his head. "I didn't know he was your son."

Edward saw Grace's hand ball into a fist. She slammed it against the bars of the cell, and the iron rang out. She pointed a shaking finger at Edward. "He was a good boy. He was yer brother! He didn't deserve that."

"I know."

"You know what I know? I know it's gonna kill Jack that ye weren't up ta snuff, but I'll enjoy seeing you hang. That much is sure, Thatch." Grace looked on the verge of tears, from anger and from a future relief she was envisioning, Edward thought.

The sound of gunfire rang out outside of the villa's prison.

Judging from the volume, it was nearby. Sam's crew were implementing the distraction as planned, unaware Edward and Herbert weren't anywhere near Calico Jack.

Grace looked daggers his way. "Is this your doing?"

"We just arrived here, how would we have had the time?" Edward said, thinking on his feet. "You have a town full of pirates, and none of them fight?" Edward sat down on a hard chair in the cell with a loud thump. "This must be a paradise if you manage that."

Grace's jaw flexed with anger, and she stormed out of the prison. One guard stayed behind to watch them, and the rest left with Grace to handle the situation outside.

Edward leaned back, resting his head against the stone wall at the back of their cell, and closed his eyes. The sounds of more gunfire and fighting filtered in through a window at the ceiling near the door.

"Now what?" Herbert asked, frustration clear in his tone.

Edward opened his eyes and folded his arms. "We're pirates, right?"

Herbert nodded but looked confused.

"We'll just have to steal this victory back from them."

17. BREAKING POINT

Anne had been in a daze of high fever, the time passing without her knowledge. She could only half-way remember the rare bits of clarity through the haze. The sun and the moon through a window. Movement at her periphery. Many muddled faces visiting her, helping her eat, changing her bandages. A young girl—Christina, Anne thought—sobbing as she held Anne's hand and apologized. For what, Anne was too delirious to remember.

When the fever broke, she woke in a cold sweat, both famished and thirsty. At her bedside waiting for her was bread and water, which she devoured. Her head still ached, and her whole body was weak. Even her jaw muscles strained to chew the bread.

She took in her surroundings as she gathered her strength. She was lying in her bed aboard the *Queen Anne's Revenge* in the captain's cabin. It was the same as it always was—table and chairs, dresser and bookshelf, Edward's clothes hanging on a rack on the wall. The only new thing was two crutches near the foot of the bed, and some of Alexandre's medical supplies on a bedside table.

Then Anne remembered why she was there lying in her bed weak from fever for God knows how long. Her leg. She didn't want to look at it, as though the longer she went without seeing it, the less real it was. As though if she never looked down, it had never happened. But real life didn't work that way. Not looking at a problem doesn't make it go away.

Anne pulled her blanket away in one swift motion to get it over with, and there it was. Covered thick with cloth tied tight was a wound just beneath her knee. There was no blood,

215

which was both a good and bad sign. It meant that it had healed enough that it no longer needed frequent changes, but that also meant some time had passed in her delirium.

She knew that someday soon, she would feel hollow without her right foot, but for now it remained a curiosity. A painful, ugly curiosity.

But more than anything, it made her angry. Angry at her momentary lapse that had allowed the injury to happen. Angry at herself for killing Tala, Christina's poor wolf, who hadn't known any better and had died for it. Angry at Silver Eyes and his wicked skill that turned her comrades and friends into enemies. Angry that she'd chosen to stay here out of some foolish sense of duty, and what that foolish sense had brought her.

Anne pulled herself up, her hands shaking to keep her body steady. A painful minute later, and she had her upper body slumped forward. Even with that little movement, she was sweating and felt dizzy. After catching her breath and waiting for the room to stop spinning, she turned her body sideways and placed her left leg on the deck.

The cold of the wood beneath her foot felt pleasant, as her body still felt hot, especially her wound—another reminder of her loss, her weakness, her enemy. More anger arose to fuel her weakened muscles.

With care and a lot of time, Anne pulled herself over to the end of the bed and took the crutches in hand. She had little experience with crutches. She had broken a leg in her earlier years, but she had been forced to be bedridden or into a wheelchair rather than allowed to stalk the halls of the palace in crutches. She had seen them used before, though, and thought it couldn't have been that difficult.

What made it difficult wasn't her lack of knowledge, it was her lack of strength. She was able to get herself balanced, and at rest she could lean on the crutches for support, but her leg wobbled and shook as though it would give out with each step forward.

Then came the door to the cabin. There was simply no

crafty way to stand to reach the handle. She planted her foot down and in a swift motion, grabbed the handle and pulled the door ajar. She backed up a bit and used one of the crutches to knock the door open enough for her to walk through.

With one obstacle out of the way, she was able to exit the captain's cabin. She already had sweat soaking her brow and the small breeze coming from the weather deck down to the gun deck was a welcome respite.

Strangely, none of the crew were in the gun deck. She could hear voices coming from the bow, and movement from Alexandre's room, but no sounds were coming from above or below.

Anne swung herself forward to the bow. With each plop of the crutches on the wooden floorboards, she found herself acclimating to her new situation. It felt strange not planting her right foot down with each step forward, strange to not feel the cold of the wood or the air on her toes, but she pushed the feeling aside. She needed to ignore the curiosity for now. Now she needed to know what had happened as she'd slept.

She entered the surgeon's room too quickly and nearly fell over when she tried to stop herself. Nassir was there to catch her.

"Careful, miss," he said.

After righting herself, she tried to thank Nassir, but her throat seized, and she began coughing. The coughing only emphasized how thin and frail and hungry she was. With each cough, her stomach heaved as though it would cave in.

Victoria came up beside her, a cup of water in hand. Anne took the cup and drank it down in great gulps. She coughed one last time, wiped her chin, and thanked both Victoria and Nassir as she handed the cup back with a shaking hand.

"How long was I asleep?" she asked as she made eye contact with Nassir, Victoria, and Alexandre.

Alexandre answered. "Eight days."

She had guessed it to have been some time, but the news floored her still. She rebalanced herself in her crutches as she absorbed Alexandre's words.

"Silver Eyes?"

"He still lives," Alexandre said. "We have been starving him and his men, as per your orders. William held back from attacking through the tunnel until you awoke. The men are eager to see this ended, but he held them back."

Anne's anger bubbled forward. "Good, I want to see him die for myself," she spat.

Her tone must have alarmed her companions, as they all became silent. She tried to soften her tone. "Worry not, Alexandre, I recall our promise. You will have the honours of the final blow; I simply wish to see it happen."

Alexandre nodded. "*Merci*."

Anne looked down at the table, and she understood why Nassir was here in the surgeon's room. On the table lay a nearly complete imitation of a leg. Though it was not within her realm of study, Anne knew of medicine and recent advancements, especially amongst the wealthy who could afford the best of care. The device on the table was of the newest design and would allow her to walk as it didn't lock into place and instead had hinges to mimic the movement of the leg.

The sight of it was enough to bring tears to her eyes. She reached out to touch the apparatus, and then she looked at the three in the room. "Thank you," she said before wiping her eyes.

"It is nearly complete, but your wound won't support it yet. You will need another week to heal before it is safe."

"Understood," Anne said as she dried her eyes.

The gesture warmed her heart, but it did little to quell her anger at the man responsible for her injury. It only served to focus her mind away from her lost limb and towards a way to finish the battle with minimal casualties.

"Where's William?"

"He's ashore, managing the crew," Victoria replied. "I'll take you."

After a few more words of thanks to Alexandre and Nassir

218

for their craftsmanship, Anne left with Victoria to go ashore. It took quite a bit of time to get above deck, and with each minute wasted, she grew increasingly impatient, but she managed the ordeal with little incident.

On the weather deck, Anne did see a few crewmates on watch, weapons at the ready and cannons nearby loaded. William must have overseen some of the deck cannons returning to the ship after the incident with the crew.

The crew left their posts to greet her and ask after her well-being. Though there was evident concern in their eyes, none were insensitive about her appearance and frailty. Anne tried to rush things along, the delays irritating her despite her crew's concern. After the crew were done seeing how she was, they helped her and Victoria into a longboat to take to shore.

In the boat, it was just Victoria and Anne. Anne rested as Victoria rowed the boat to shore. It would be a short trip, and Victoria was capable enough, but Anne wished she had the strength to help just to make the trip that much quicker.

With nowhere to go, Anne's irritation stewed within her, and the sight of the town and the fortified walls off in the distance only served to incense her further. Knowing that Silver Eyes was in his villa unharmed and unburdened by what his actions had wrought made her skin itch.

Anne needed to calm herself, and so she decided to look at Victoria instead. It was the first time in a while that the two were alone, and the first time in a while that Anne actually took note of the woman.

Despite all knowing her nature as a woman, she kept her black hair short enough that most would mistake her for a boy. Her clothes, too, showed little of her femininity. Anne had an inkling of the reasons.

She had heard about what had happened to Victoria at Calico Jack's hand. She saw the way that she shirked away from most men, nay, all men save Alexandre. It was not from a lack of ability; with her lithe form, she could kill a man three distinct ways before he had his belt unbuckled. That kind of skittishness reminded Anne of Edward at times. Times when memories came unbidden into the mind. Times of turmoil, of pain, of helplessness. It seemed that even for her, the years had not healed the wounds put upon her.

"How do you deal with the anger?" Anne said. Victoria stopped rowing for a moment and looked at Anne. Anne realized that she had said what she was thinking aloud without the usual preamble. "Apologies. What I mean to say is… with all that you've been through, how do you deal with the anger from it?"

Victoria was silent for a moment, and then she began rowing again. "Anger's a shield at your front and wind at your back. It'll get the job done, but it won't last long. Once it's gone, you'll wish you had it protecting you still." Victoria tapped on her temple. "Use it while it lasts."

Anne nodded and didn't ask any further. The two women remained in silence for the rest of the short trip.

On shore, Christina, Pukuh, Jack, and William were all waiting along with a small contingent of the crew. William helped Anne disembark.

William said no words, but from the look in his eyes, Anne could tell that he was remaining strong for her sake. He probably blamed himself for not being there to help her but would not say the words in public.

Anne placed a hand on his chest as she came down from the longboat and gave him a warm smile that she hoped would tell him all that he needed to hear. He took hold of her hand and squeezed it gently as he placed it back on her crutch. To everyone else, it would look as though he were simply helping her back into her crutches. It was his way of remaining close yet respectful.

After settling herself, Christina came up to her. She was already in tears again and hugged Anne tight. Christina began whispering apologies and sobbing into Anne's shoulder, and Anne tried her best to console the young woman. "Worry not." "It's just a leg." "The one I blame is Silver Eyes."

Then, after Christina had calmed herself enough to pull away from Anne, Anne turned it around by giving her own apology. "I'm sorry... for Tala."

Christina shook her head so vigorously Anne thought it hurt the girl. "No, don't apologize. I should have trained her better."

Anne rubbed Christina's shoulder. Though she was holding it in, it was clear that the loss of Tala pained Christina. They had been inseparable since meeting near Pukuh's village. Anne remembered how the two of them had fought a bear and won, just to bring back medicine to save Anne when she was sick. If not for Tala and Christina, Anne would have died.

"You trained her well. She was a true warrior, and she will be missed by all." Anne pulled Christina in and embraced her again for a moment.

Jack also offered his apologies, lamenting his weakness. Anne gave him the same words she gave Christina, reassuring him that it was no fault of his. She leaned in and whispered to him, "Now more than ever, the crew and I need your music. Keep their spirits high until this is over."

Jack smiled. "I understand, Captain," he said before stepping back to let others have their chance to speak with her.

After pulling away, Pukuh was standing there with his arms folded. He looked her over, barely glancing at her missing leg, his face inscrutable. "You look like death."

Anne couldn't help but laugh, and it was both joyful and painful in her state. "I feel it."

"Soon, it will become a part of you. This, I know," Pukuh said, touching his right shoulder, the stump that used to be his right arm.

"I shall have to take you at your word," Anne said. "For the time being, I suppose I'll look and feel like death."

"It was praise," Pukuh said. "Death is my namesake. I mean you look ready to end this."

"I was ready eight days ago," Anne replied. "So, let's end it, shall we?"

Anne had run through the various scenarios in her head before the battle with her crew. She did the math, and if not for her injury, she would have ordered the use of the secret tunnel long ago. Doing so would have cost them several crewmates, and there was only one way around the problem. It was a cruel method, and before she had only thought of it as a last resort, but now, in the throes of her anger-fuelled mind, she didn't care about the morality.

Others did. William, Alexandre, and some of the crew objected, but their voices were few. William eventually followed her orders as he always did and carried out the first part of the plan. Alexandre realized quickly that there would be no swaying Anne, but he was visibly angry. If Anne had been in the right state of mind, she might have rethought her actions, but she was not.

After William and some of the other crewmates returned from their task, Anne gave the signal.

They removed a large cloth covering one of the golden bells they had taken with them from one of the villages on the island. It, unlike the one Christina had managed to destroy in Silver Eyes' town, was whole and intact. The sound it would produce would have its desired effect.

The crew laid the bell down, so the open bottom was facing the town, then looked at Anne for final confirmation. Anne waved her hand in a striking motion, and the crew lifted the bell's striker and slammed it down.

The sound of the bell was loud in her ears, with the same pull as it had had before. She was able to resist the numbing effect it had, but she did have to close her eyes. She wondered just what the metal was, the same ore that her ring and Edward's cutlass were made of, that could produce such a tone.

After the bell's tone died away, the crew struck it again. This time, Anne forced her eyes open to watch the town. Silver

Eyes' men were stationed along the perimeter as before, and they remained unchanged, unfazed by what Anne thought would be a strange development.

Again, and again the crewmates struck the bell, but nothing changed. At least, not on this side of the town.

Soon, Anne could hear sounds of fighting within the town in between the striking of the bell. The crew didn't let up, because Anne didn't tell them to, and the sounds inside grew with each strike. Shouts, snarls, gunfire, and clashing swords, a bizarre counterpoint to the ringing of the bell.

After some time, the fighting came to the stockade. Those fighting Silver Eyes' crew were not the crew of the *Queen Anne's Revenge*. Those fighting were the crazed, entranced villagers they had previously been trying to save. Triggered by the bell, they would attack anyone, even their masters.

The cruel, immoral act that Anne had chosen to commit was to use those poor souls to do the fighting for them. They had taken the entranced villagers, unable to refuse, into the tunnel and locked the entrance behind them. Then with the bell turning them mad, there was nowhere to go but into the town. There, they fought Silver Eyes' men.

Exhausted and enraged, Anne just wanted it over with, and with the least casualties to her crew as possible. They had suffered enough; *she* had suffered enough, and she wanted it to be over.

She had considered leaving, briefly, but her anger wouldn't let her leave before she'd had her revenge.

They kept ringing the bell as the fighting continued. There was no doubt that Silver Eyes' men had access to a handbell like the one that Sam gave them, but they knew that it wasn't permanent. As they continued ringing the bell, they ensured the fighting would continue.

When the sound of the fighting died down to almost nothing, Anne ordered the crew to stop striking the bell. Then they brought the cannons forward.

In the eight days that Anne was unconscious, Nassir had

built a few limbers from the wagon parts. That gave the cannons more maneuverability and stability and enabled the crew to take them in closer to the stockade. And, without their enemy manning the stockade's cannons they had no fear of retaliation.

They fired the cannons at the stockade's entrance, the large iron bouncing off the massive wooden beams. With each hit, the beams cracked increasingly until they finally gave way under the force. The entrance now open, the crew were free to enter the town and finish off Silver Eyes' men.

Anne, in no shape to fight, stayed behind as the crew entered the town to finish the job. She hated waiting, but she knew better than to be involved with their enemies who had already been stronger and faster than her *before* she was injured.

William, too, stayed behind as Christina, Pukuh, Victoria, and Alexandre all entered the battle. Jack wasn't far behind, a drum in hand, playing a rousing beat for the fight.

And so, the two waited as they listened to the sounds of the battle growing once more. William seemed content to remain in silence with Anne, but after a few minutes, Anne became restless.

"Do you think less of me for this?" she asked.

William, silent for a moment as he looked at Anne and then back at the town, replied with a simple "No." After another moment, he elaborated. "Alexandre may be upset, but he was making no progress in freeing those people. With time, perhaps he could have undone the trance put upon them, but we don't have such time. We couldn't have taken them with us either. This will ensure victory and the least casualties for us. You made the right decision."

Anne had expected him to say as much, but it disappointed her still. He had objected to the plan before; there was no way he wholeheartedly agreed with her decision. He was trying to ease her mind at that moment.

She knew deep down that she would regret the decision, she could feel it. At the moment, it was as Victoria said: her anger shielded her, protecting her from the guilt which would weigh on her later.

More time passed, and again the sounds of battle waned. Anne decided then to enter the town with William and the few crewmates who had stayed behind with her. With her still on crutches, it took some time to reach the town.

Bodies littered the roadway, the fronts of buildings, and the alleyways. It wasn't a large town by any means, and so between the hundred and twenty villagers they had gathered, and however many of Silver Eyes' men had been left, you couldn't make it five steps before encountering one of the dead.

Thankfully, it hadn't been long, and so the stench of death was light. It smelled of fresh blood and gunpowder as smoke still whirled around the town.

The only activity was from their crewmates keeping watch nearby, and the sound of shouts from farther off. Some of their enemies appeared to still be alive and making a last stand.

Anne recognized a woman, one of the villagers, reaching a bloodied hand towards them. Her legs had been cut or torn off during the fight, and her hair was matted with blood. She was still, even in that state, entranced and trying to reach them to attack.

"I'll handle this," William said. He pulled out his sword and put the woman out of her misery.

Her eyes stayed open, staring at Anne. Those hollow eyes from the trance remained unchanged in death. Whether under Silver Eyes' spell or free from their mortal coil, their eyes were the same.

Christina ran over to them as they walked through the maze of bodies. "We have Silver Eyes surrounded. He's holed himself up in a fancy house. Come, I'll show you the way," she said.

Anne, William, and the other crewmates went through the small town, around all the dead bodies, and to a small but opulent house near the centre of town. It was located beside the bell tower, and it appeared as though the two buildings were joined.

Jack was outside the home catching his breath. He had a weapon drawn, and his fiddle slung across his back. He waved as they approached.

They entered the home, and Christina took them to the back where Alexandre, Victoria, and Pukuh were standing guard next to a door.

"Let's end this," Anne said. "Kick down the door, but be wary."

Pukuh grinned and nodded, then did as Anne ordered. In one swift kick, the door busted in, swinging wildly. Pukuh rolled off to the side, away from the entrance.

Nothing happened. No one ran outside to face them. No pistols fired off into the air. No traps sprang. Only the sound of the door swinging back from hitting against a wall.

"Enter," a voice called from inside.

The lot waiting outside the door glanced at each other, unsure of just what game Silver Eyes was playing.

"I can assure you this is not a trick. I know when I am defeated."

Anne motioned for the others to enter, and one after the other they went into the room. Anne was last, taking her time to stay steady in her crutches. Each step forward sent her heart racing a mite faster, to the point that she could feel it pounding in her ears by the time she came up beside William.

Inside the simple room, a study with a large window overlooking the sea, their enemy, Lance Nhil, sat leisurely in a chair facing them. He was of a darker complexion, close to Pukuh, and looked to be from the Near East with thick and short brown hair and a full beard. He would not have looked out of place in an Ottoman palace in Constantinople, or perhaps as a refined captain of a Barbary corsair vessel.

His eyes shone from the sunlight streaming through the great window behind him and made them appear a solid silver. There was something strange about the colour that Anne couldn't place, an otherworldly quality about his eyes that made him look, for lack of a better word, inhuman. They were as beautiful as they were haunting.

"That's him," Christina seethed. "He's the one who came aboard the ship."

Lance looked at Christina, and he appeared to recognize her. "Ah, yes, the pretty girl from the ship. I am surprised you survived," he said with a smile that sent shivers down Anne's spine. "*Alqamar*," Lance said—the Arabic word for moon.

Christina's hands dropped to her sides, and her face lost all emotion.

"William, get Christina out of here!" Anne shouted.

William put away his weapon and took Christina's out of her hand before she could do anything with them. Thankfully, the trigger didn't send her into a frenzy as before. William was able to lead Christina out without fighting her, and Victoria left with them to help.

That left Pukuh, Alexandre, and Anne in the room with him. Pukuh and Alexandre both were keeping their distance, and Anne was the farthest away, as she could do little in her condition.

"Tell me, where is Edward? Where is Blackbeard?"

"I would worry about yourself right now," Anne spat back. "He's off killing your captain."

Lance shook his head. "A pity. He was supposed to come here first. The young always love to rush things." Lance sat there in silence for another moment before turning his attention back to Anne. "You pitiful thing, you've lost your leg." He rose from his chair. Anne pulled herself back instinctively and nearly fell. She caught herself at the last second, and her face flushed red hot with anger. "Do you fear me, girl?" Lance took a step forward.

Alexandre's rapier stopped Lance's advance. "Apologies, *mon ami*, but you will not be taking another step."

Lance looked down at the rapier tip at his chest. He reached one hand up to the blade and stroked it. "Such a fine blade." There was a snapping sound. "Sleep," Lance said, and

Alexandre's arm went limp.

Lance had brought his other hand up in front of Alexandre's face while attention was on the blade and had done what he did best. He put Alexandre in a trance, his eyes hollow and out of focus. Alexandre kept his grip on his weapon, but the tip was now dragging on the floor.

Pukuh growled and leapt forward, striking with his spear. Lance stepped to the side, grabbed the spear and pulled it forward, bringing Pukuh closer before punching him in the gut. Pukuh doubled over in pain but kept hold of his spear. Before he could jump away, Lance grabbed Pukuh's shoulder and pulled him close. Lance whispered something in Pukuh's ears, and he froze in place.

Then Lance turned to Anne. She tried to back away, but this time she did lose her balance and fell backwards to the floor. She panicked and scrambled backwards away from Lance's advance.

Lance leaned forward, reaching towards her. "Look into my eyes," he said.

Anne, whether through defiance or fear, closed her eyes tight. Sweat and tears poured down her cheeks. She couldn't move, she couldn't even scream.

Silence. Lance's hand hadn't touched her, he hadn't whispered his spell into her ears. She opened her eyes. Lance was there, towering over her, about to touch her shoulder. Pierced through his neck was Alexandre's rapier. It was the precise kind of strike that only Alexandre in his full state of awareness could have done.

He removed the blade in one smooth motion, and blood shot out from the wound. Lance, somehow still alive, grabbed his wound as he turned around to see his killer before tumbling to the floor. When he saw Alexandre there, a small smile at the corner of his lips, Lance's eyes widened even more, which gave away his last thoughts as plain as day.

Alexandre put away his rapier, reached over, and helped Anne to her feet and back into her crutches. "Alexandre, how did you…?"

"Come now, after all this, you think I could be put under his spell?"

Anne accepted Alexandre's simple explanation, and Alexandre went to help Pukuh out of the trance. She looked at Lance in his last moments, his beautiful silver eyes marred by blood from him straining to stay in the world of the living. The look of confusion mixed with his pain pleased her, more so than she liked to admit. She was happy that he could be taken down a level before he passed. It was the least he deserved after all he had done.

Alexandre brought Pukuh out of the trance, and they both came up to her. Satisfied, she was ready to move on. "We're done here. Let's go home."

18. THE PIRATE WITH THREE NAMES

"So good to see you again, boys," Edward's father said. "Especially you, Herbert. How long has it been? Ten, eleven, twelve years? I'm sure you've kept track," he said before cackling.

Edward and Herbert were led into the study of Calico Jack's villa, a large room on the second floor with several tables filled to the brim with papers, letters, and books. On the walls hung several trophies, including a golden horn like the one his father carried at his side, and a strange hand that Edward thought must have been fake. Or at least he hoped it was.

The double doors on both sides of the study leading to balconies were open, letting in a breeze free from the smell of filth that lingered at street level in Nassau.

Edward's father, true to his third name, wore a suit made of coarse green cotton with a floral pattern around the trim. It didn't fit with his imposing figure and scarred features. One scar, running from his right eye down to his mouth, made him look a monster in human form. Edward recalled that his wife had given him that scar.

"So, what am I supposed to call you? Benjamin Hornigold, Jack Rackham, or your real name, Albert Thatch? Or would you prefer to keep it simple, and I call you *Father*?"

Edward, his hands bound in front of him, tried his best to keep calm, but it was proving difficult.

"Let's stick with Jack for now," the man said, still smiling.

"Why are we here?" Herbert said. "Why don't you just kill us and get it over with?"

Jack folded his arms. "All in due time, gentlemen. All in due time." He stared at the two of them for a moment before unfolding his arms and walking over to a cabinet, waving a finger as he talked. "You know, I was really rooting for you this time. Grace told me how you got aboard her ship and nearly had her fooled, too." Jack took out a few glasses and some dark drink. "She wouldn't admit it, but I imagine if you hadn't killed your brother, she wouldn't have figured it out. Even I can't recognize you since I last saw you with that thick beard." Jack poured the rum into the glasses in equal portions and brought two of them over to his captors. "Oh, that's right, you're a little tied up now. Just open your mouth, and I'll pour it down."

"I'll pass," Edward said. He desperately wanted to say yes, but he remembered his promise.

Jack looked at Herbert, and Herbert simply stared at him. He shrugged. "More for me," he said before downing one of the glasses in a single gulp.

This was not the father he remembered from his youth. Edward remembered a kind, gentle man who loved to play and teach him about sailing. A man who would go on walks with him, name the stars for him. A man who would tell him stories before sleep, comfort him, drop everything for him. A man who loved him.

This man was wholly and completely Calico Jack, a pirate who seemed to love himself and the sound of his own voice. His old father was dead.

"To answer your question: you're here because I thought we could talk a bit. I wanted to hear about what's happened to you over the years before it's too late. The gallows are being prepared as we speak, so we'd best get on with it, gentlemen."

"Your spy didn't give you enough information?" Edward asked.

Jack arched his brow for a second and then grinned. "A spy? Now, what makes you think I sent a spy aboard your ship?"

"John, at the very least, knew everything. Victoria is another. They could have been working together to send you information."

"I see," Jack said as he rubbed his chin. "Just those two, hmm?"

Edward's jaw went slack. There were more than just John and Victoria? Some of his most loyal crewmates had been with him from the beginning since he'd set out to be a whaler. From there, they had gone to Port Royal, and there John got them more crewmembers, many of whom were also still on the crew to this day. Edward supposed with his father's reach it could have been any port, but Port Royal was the closest to their home island. It would have been simple to have some other crewmates ready to join them there, including Victoria.

But Edward remembered that Sam was the one who had suggested they head to Port Royal, not John. Could Sam be a traitor too? How did he get involved with his father's crew after their run-in with Cache-Hand? It all seemed too coincidental.

There was no way to be sure, and right now, Sam and his crew were their last hope to escape this situation. He had to believe in Sam and not give up any information that could tip their hand.

"Tch," Edward spat. "As Herbert said, just kill us and be done with it. I'm tired of the games you've had us playing these past years."

Jack shrugged. "Well, if that's what you wish, who am I to object?" He whistled as his gaze turned to one of his guards keeping watch at the door.

Edward turned his head to look behind him. The guard pulled a pistol from his belt and aimed it at Herbert. Edward shouted and jumped at Herbert to knock him out of the way. There was a loud shot and Herbert roared as the iron ball seared into his back.

The guard began reloading his pistol. Herbert, his hands tied in front of him, couldn't grab hold of the wound to stop the bleeding. He pulled himself tighter as he stifled shouts of pain between heavy breaths.

"Stop!" Edward shouted at the guard, then looked at his father. "Stop it, you bastard!"

Jack raised his brows again and placed his hand on his chest. "Me? Isn't this what you wanted? You both begged for it." He shook his head. "Now who's playing games?"

The guard finished loading the pistol and aimed it at Herbert again. Edward pivoted, ready to tackle the guard, but he pulled the pistol back and put it away. Edward looked at his father again, and he was holding his hand up. The guard walked back to his post.

"So, speaking of John," Jack began as though nothing had happened, "could you tell me what happened to him? I know he's passed, but details were scarce in the reports."

Edward gritted his teeth, unable to hold back his anger. Herbert was bleeding out, but still holding on and conscious. "Herbert's going to die. We need to stop the bleeding." Edward pressed down on the wound, doing his best to keep the pressure on it. Herbert groaned but didn't scream.

"He'll survive long enough for the execution." Jack took another drink from the second glass of rum he had gotten. "Now, answer the question, if you please."

"Shut it. I'm not going to talk to you as if you're still the man who was comrades with John. You took on the man who killed him as a crewmate."

Jack pointed at his son. "Don't forget that he also tortured you half to death," he said. "I couldn't let that kind of talent be squandered. Locke... or what was it he called himself? Chest-Hand? Money-Mitten? Box-Fist?" Jack shook his head as he scratched his face.

"Cache-Hand," Edward said.

His father snapped his fingers and pointed at Edward. "Cache-Hand, that's the one. He made for a good, if unexpected, test for you a bit ago. Twice. He paid back his usefulness. Now you, on the other hand. What a disappointment you've been."

"Why? Because I haven't killed you yet? If you want to die so badly, do us all a favour and kill yourself."

Jack burst out laughing, a howling, cackling laugh. "That's good, I like that. Where was that anger when I stabbed you in the back? You had your wife carry you away like some useless drunk. In fact," he stroked his chin again before running a finger down the scar along his cheek, "she was the one who gave me this wound. Maybe she should be the one in your place. She seems far more capable than you. She could have been queen by now if not for being declared dead, what with her mother's passing."

"Anne's mother passed away?" The news floored Edward and broke through what had been happening up until then.

Jack stopped stroking his scar and looked at Edward. "Yes, almost a year ago," he said. "Does she not know? Where is she right now? Did you leave her behind?" He waved his hand. "No matter, perhaps after you've failed, she'll try her hand at revenge." Jack placed the empty glass on the table. "It doesn't seem you want to talk with your dear father, so let's get this over with."

Jack walked past Edward and Herbert and left the room.

Edward was still reeling over the news of Anne's mother. She had been a thorn in their side and announced Anne had died as a means to tell Anne she had been disowned, but deep down Anne still loved her mother. If he made it out of this alive, he would have to break the news to her.

The guards picked Edward up off his feet, and one of them pushed him towards the door. Edward stumbled forward as he looked over his shoulder towards Herbert who was still bleeding from his back. The other guard picked him up with no regard for his wound, and Herbert let out a yelp of pain.

The guards brought the two of them out of the room and down the stairs to the first floor. Jack was already gone, headed to the gallows ahead of them.

Herbert's wheelchair was at the foot of the steps. Edward

remembered the weapons Herbert had hidden, as well as the secret weapon built into the wheelchair by Nassir. It could be crucial to getting out of this alive. He needed to get Herbert into the wheelchair, even if he was injured.

After they descended the stairs, and it became clear the guard was just going to carry Herbert the whole way to the gallows, Edward stopped.

"Let Herbert have some dignity in his last moments," he said. "Put him in his chair, for God's sake." The guards didn't listen and pushed Edward forward. What could he say for them to listen? He couldn't make it sound like he was desperate.

"Just put the boy into the wheelchair and be done with it," someone said from the front door of the villa.

Edward turned around to see Grace standing there. As usual, she looked ready for a fight wearing her copper greaves, which Edward guessed were loaded and prepared to fire.

"You'll be pushin' 'im, though," she said, pointing at Edward.

The guards put Herbert in his wheelchair, and he winced from the wound. From what Edward could see, the bullet didn't go all the way through and was still lodged inside. It would get infected if they didn't treat it soon.

The guard pushed Edward back to the wheelchair. He looked down at his locked hands and then at Grace. He opened his mouth, but Grace put up a hand.

"Don't even try it," she said, her tone as filled with annoyance as her face showed. "Ye can still push him with yer hands tied. Ye think me daft, boy?"

Edward closed his mouth and didn't say another word. He pushed Herbert's chair forward, and Grace left the door open and went ahead. Behind Edward, the guards were following on his heels.

Edward pushed Herbert over the lip of the door and down the steps towards the villa's gate. Outside, he could hear loud shouts of many voices from the centre of Nassau. From beyond the gate, some ways down the road, a crowd had begun gathering.

Edward looked up at the other buildings crowding the street, and he could see all eyes were on him and Herbert. It hadn't taken long for news about the execution to spread.

Once outside the gates, with the noise of the looming crowd providing some protection, Edward leaned down to whisper to Herbert. "Are you well?"

Herbert was sweating and visibly in pain. "Well enough," he said.

"Get it ready," Edward said.

Herbert looked up at him, looking confused. Edward motioned with his eyes to the compartments in the armrests of his chair. Herbert nodded, then went to work.

First, Herbert had to shuffle around, stifling groans of pain as he did, to get his blanket, which had ended up underneath him. He pulled it up and unfolded it to cover his legs and hide what he was doing with his arms.

Edward kept pushing Herbert forward, keeping with Grace's pace. He didn't want to risk her paying more attention to them at that moment.

As they went down the road, the crowd that had gathered became thicker, with more bodies standing in the street waiting for the hanging. As they came closer, Edward could see the podium.

The noise grew louder as people began noticing them approaching. Those in the crowd were more varied than Edward had thought they would be. Many looked to be sailors—pirates, Edward could tell—but some women and men appeared to be more respectable. Traders, business owners, some people of import, and even some children about. But pirates outnumbered the others by ten to one, so it was clear that pirates ruled the town. And Edward's father was their leader.

Herbert looked up at Edward and nodded. The weapon

was ready, but if they unleashed it now, they wouldn't get far. As soon as they had been captured, their opportunities had narrowed to only one choice.

The only way out alive was to kill his father and end this. Grace and his father's words confirmed that it was what he wanted. *'I know it's gonna kill Jack that ye weren't up ta snuff.' ' Maybe she should be the one in your place.'* His father had set all this in motion as a test, that much he guessed, but they had confirmed it. *'By the sound of the Golden Horn!'* Their rallying cry. He was their leader, and he wanted Edward, his son, to kill him, and it was all a test. It wasn't much of a stretch to see that the test was whether Edward was strong enough to become his father's successor.

If Edward killed his father, there was a chance that the pirates wouldn't kill him in return, and he would become their new leader. It made a twisted kind of sense to Edward, and it was their only real chance to survive. Everything else led to death.

Grace was the only wildcard. They had killed her son, and she hated them for it. He knew from her story that she probably didn't have any real affection for his father. If it looked like he was about to escape or win, she would probably kill him afterwards. Edward had to kill Grace first.

Edward was so deep in thought that he didn't see the oncoming missile as it hit him in the face. A bystander had thrown a rock his way. He reeled back but stamped his foot down to stay upright. He stood back up to his full, towering height and looked for the aggressor. Soon he found the man, who had gathered another rock to throw, but when Edward's eyes met his, he stumbled and dropped it. He cowered at Edward's gaze. Edward noticed others in the crowd who had gathered the courage to throw something because of the first volley, and he stared each one of them down.

Whatever power Edward held in that gaze of his made the people in the crowd sink into themselves with fear despite him heading for the gallows in bonds. He didn't question it and turned his gaze to the men and women on the other side of the road for good measure. He could feel blood trickling down the side of his face where the rock had hit, but he didn't wipe it away.

The crowd parted as they came closer and closer to the gallows, giving them a straight path to the wooden structure. Edward could see his father there, waiting for him, and another man who would operate the lever. His father moved to the side and motioned behind him, beckoning Edward towards the noose hanging at the top.

When they were not thirty feet from the gallows, Edward noticed Sam there in the crowd. Sam winked and grinned at Edward, then looked down to his hip. Edward followed his gaze and Sam tapped on the cutlass at his hip, Edward's golden cutlass, and then he tapped his wrists.

It was all the confirmation Edward needed. He could count on Sam and his crew to help them through this. Relief washed over Edward, but the feeling was brief. He steeled himself for what was coming.

Grace passed Sam, staring daggers at him. Sam shrugged and laughed. The failed distraction from earlier had blown over, but not without a loss of Sam's position. Grace turned her attention back to the gallows in front of her, ignoring Sam.

Sam pulled the golden blade from his sheath. The strange golden metal sang. Edward put his hands out and held the rope tying his wrists taut. In one swing, Sam cut the rope in two. It was no match for the razor edge of Edward's blade. With another flick of Sam's wrist, he cut the bonds from Herbert's hands as well.

Then Sam tossed the cutlass to Edward. He caught it and swung around in an arc behind him. He sliced open the two guards behind him in one stroke. They fell to the ground, instantly dead.

"Now, Herbert!"

Grace had turned around just as Edward had killed the guards.

"You're not the only one with a secret weapon, you bitch!" Herbert shouted.

Herbert pulled on a cord within the arms of his wheelchair. The cord was attached to several small flintlock mechanisms inside the arms. The flintlocks fired off all at once, sending iron balls out the front of the wheelchair.

Grace jumped out of the way and to the ground. Some of the iron balls missed, but a few caught her in the stomach, and she clutched the wounded area. She gritted her teeth and rose to shaking feet. She grabbed onto the cords in her copper greaves and pulled.

Edward grabbed Herbert out of his wheelchair and jumped as Grace's weapons fired. Edward didn't feel anything hit him, but he heard Herbert groaning in pain. They tumbled to the ground together.

"Herbert, were you injured?" he asked as he got to his feet.

Herbert coughed. "I can't feel my legs."

Edward shook his head. "This is no time for jesting." Edward looked over his friend, and it appeared that he was mostly uninjured.

Edward rose to his feet to see Grace standing there, still clutching her stomach as she bled out. "Sam, protect Herbert."

Sam came over, another weapon drawn. "You got it, Captain. Now kill yer da so we can get out of here!"

Sam's crew had surrounded the gallows and were keeping the rest of the pirates at bay. The earlier shouts of a crowd eager to see a hanging had been replaced with women screaming and the battle cries of pirates loyal to Jack. Something felt off about it all though, as though there should have been more fighting and more noise than there was. For the number of people who had gathered there, it felt subdued.

Then Edward looked up at the gallows, and he could see his father had his hand raised. When Sam's crew noticed what was happening, they stopped provoking fights but remained at the ready.

Then Jack jumped off the podium to the ground below. "Grace, are you well?"

"Well enough," she said, though the sweat on her brow and the blood from her stomach told another tale.

Jack pointed at Sam. "Kill Sam," he said.

Grace took a few deep breaths and pulled out a cutlass from her belt. "Gladly."

Jack stepped away from Grace to give her some space, and Edward followed. He held his blade forward, pointed at his father and ready to strike or defend.

Edward felt ready. His body was healed, better than it had been before he had been stabbed. The demanding work on Grace's ship had paid off. He had more stamina, more strength, and he felt more agile. The only point he felt weak on was his swordsmanship. He hadn't been in an actual fight in ages, but his golden sword with the eagle pommel, the one he'd had for several years now, felt right in his hands.

Jack unbuttoned his calico jacket and tossed it to the ground. He then took off his white undershirt, showing his toned body underneath. Though he was at least twenty to thirty years older than Edward, his body looked like someone of Edward's age. Other than the unprecedented number of scars across his body, it would be hard to tell his age just from his frame alone.

But it was his father's eyes which told the story, and the true nature of his strength. It also gave Edward an answer to why, aside from his towering height, people cowered at his gaze. His father's eyes, more than any other part of him, conveyed an air of strength. Looking into those eyes was like looking into the eyes of Death—a swift inescapable death. It conjured the feeling you get in the seconds before waking up from a nightmare where you're falling.

He had felt the same feeling many times. The first was

when he'd seen the man who called himself Plague, and since then, Edward realized he felt it along with the unbidden thoughts of those he'd killed, the torture he'd endured, and those who had died because of him. He knew that feeling well, so well that it had become a part of him.

And yet, Edward still fought on despite it. His father's gaze held no power over him because he experienced it daily.

"I find it quite interesting, the way we think alike, son," Jack said as he gently pulled out a blade from a sheath at his belt. It, too, was golden like Edward's and sang a similar, eerie song as though it were a yawning beast waking up from a long slumber. "Only *my* son would think to make a blade from this metal."

"We're nothing alike," Edward shouted back. "You use people, rape little girls, and kill innocents."

"Oh? Acting holier than thou, are we? I know of your deeds. I've heard all about them. You have a silver tongue you use to manipulate others into doing your bidding. Your crew has done horrible things to innocent people, and to get your ship back, you fired cannons at the homes of innocent people at Portsmouth. Or do you forget your own actions?"

Jack rushed in, slashing wildly at Edward. Edward ducked and dodged the blows. Jack was testing him with a flurry of strikes, and Edward managed to avoid them. His father was skilled, and Edward could tell that he was only warming up.

Edward cut through and retaliated, pushing his father back. He channelled the feeling he'd had aboard Grace's ship, the feeling of floating on air far above everything else. It wasn't a completely freeing feeling like when he was exhausted beyond all reason, but it was enough.

"I remember everything," Edward said, his tone and mind calm. "Every face."

Jack laughed. "Do you also remember where you got the metal to make your blade?" he asked before thrusting forward.

Edward parried the strike, slid forward, and slashed down

at Jack's head. Jack turned his body and took a step to the left out of the way. Edward followed through with another slash to the body. Jack jumped back and out of harm's way.

"Was it not from the body of one of my commanders? Gregory Dunn? What kind of a man takes the arm off a dead man and turns it into a sword?"

Jack leapt towards Edward and came down hard with his blade. Edward parried again, pushing his father's sword off to the side. The clash of the blades sent sparks flying with the strange harmony they produced together. Jack punched Edward in the jaw. Edward turned his chin with the punch and twisted away.

"What kind of a man turns another man's arm into gold?"

"I gave Dunn a gift from Midas. He desired wealth more than anything else, so I gave him enough to last a lifetime if he only sacrificed an arm."

"You think you're some Greek god come to earth? What kind of a trial is that for a person? What kind of a man sends his son off to die to solve a bunch of puzzles all around the world? What kind of a man tries to kill his own son?"

Edward took the offensive. He thrust forward, aiming for his father's stomach. Jack knocked Edward's blade aside. Edward spun around, using the momentum, and went to a knee as he attacked in a wide arc. Jack jumped over the blade.

"What kind of a man faces those trials? Someone willing to stand up to a challenge. You could have walked away so many times. You had so many opportunities. And look at you! You're stronger now than you ever were." Jack lowered his cutlass. "You're stronger than *I* ever was." Jack stood there for a moment, his face changing, softening. "Do you remember what I told you when you went into the Devil's Triangle?"

Edward's guard faltered. "What?"

"When you met me in the Devil's Triangle, on the *Freedom*. We were in the captain's cabin, though I imagine it looked quite different from how I left it for you. For me, it was." Jack looked down at the ground in thought. "It must have been eight, no, nine years ago."

Edward remembered the moment vividly. The crew had landed on an island in the Devil's Triangle and walked into a strange mist, and he'd gotten separated from Anne. Then he'd seen a vision of his father. Many had seen strange events, some from their past, some from a loved one's past. Edward and the others had debated whether what they had seen was real, or if it had been a hallucination.

"It can't be," Edward said. He had never told anyone about what had happened to him. Not even Anne knew. There was no way that his father could have heard about it from one of his spies.

"I told you that I was proud of the man you had become. You told me about your adventures, the keys, everything. I had been Calico Jack for a time by then, and work had already begun on the trials and the keys. It was then that I knew this was the right path to take." Jack held his hands out to his side and closed his eyes. "Now, end it, Edward. End it, son."

Edward looked at his father, arms open and eyes closed, calling on Edward to kill him. Edward lifted his cutlass and pointed it at Jack Rackham, at Benjamin Hornigold, at his father, Albert Thatch, who had raised him, for good or ill, to be the man he was today. The one who had put him through so many trials, both fantastical and horrifying; trials that had made him stronger, but had also caused him so much pain; trials that had allowed him to meet his captor who made him want to die, but also his wife who gave him a reason to live on.

"I…"

"Do it, Edward!" Herbert shouted from behind him.

"Do it, Ed ya bastard!" Sam said, his voice strained.

"I… can't," Edward said. He dropped his blade to the ground, and it fell with a clang.

"What?" his father said, opening his eyes to look at his son.

"I can't do it. Despite everything you've done, I love you. I can't do this." Edward felt hollow. "Please, just stop this madness. We don't have to fight each other. This is a fool's errand."

"Pathetic," his father snarled. "How did I raise a boy so weak as you? We don't have to fight each other? Everything has been building to this moment, you snivelling little shit. I don't have... When I'm gone, someone needs to rule here, and you're supposed to be that someone." Jack took a deep breath, rubbed his temples, and let out a sigh. "Then I suppose I'll have to settle for second place. Perhaps after I kill you, your wife will try to get revenge. If she manages to kill me, she could be a queen yet. Better a queen of pirates than the alternative, I'd say."

Edward's thoughts went back to Anne, and just what his father was saying. He was going to try killing Anne next. Edward knew that Anne would seek revenge, there was no way she wouldn't. Edward, in his current state of mind, cared little for his own life, but he still cared deeply for Anne. He loved her more than he loved himself. He also loved her more than he loved his father.

The thought of Anne dying took over his mind, and a wave of great anger washed over him. It stripped away the floating feeling he had been holding onto during the fight. It ripped from his body the arresting memories that haunted him. Rage took over.

Jack stepped forward and thrust his blade at Edward's chest. Edward rolled out of the way, grabbed his blade midroll, and slashed his father's stomach. His father couldn't dodge out of the way, and the blade sliced through him from front to back.

Edward bounded to his feet and turned around to clash blades with his father again, but Jack had fallen over and was bleeding out from the wound on his stomach. It was a mortal wound, Edward was sure.

Edward ran over to his father and pressed on the wound.

"No, no," Albert said. "Go get Herbert." Edward, his mind in shock, going from enraged to his instinct to save his father, couldn't hear him. "Go, go," he said again. This time Edward heard.

Edward got up and turned around to see Herbert sitting up, watching everything. Sam was nearby, wounded and breathing heavy, but alive. Grace was lying in a pool of her own blood farther away.

Herbert was listless and pale, but from the tears in his eyes, he knew what had happened. Edward picked Herbert up and brought him over to his dying father.

"He's here, Dad, Herbert's here."

Albert, his face soaked with sweat, and already paler than Herbert, was barely clinging to what little life was left in him. He reached out and touched both of them.

"I'm proud of both of you. You've become so strong," he said. "Herbert, you became a fine helmsman; better, I heard, than any I knew in my lifetime." The pool of blood beneath the three of them was growing and covered his father's whole body. "Edward, I'm sorry for what I made you do, but I wanted this. Don't blame yourself." Albert reached into his pocket and took out the driftwood seashell necklace that had once belonged to Edward's mother and handed it to him. "It's yours now. Don't lose it, it's the only thing of hers left."

Edward, his hand shaking, took the necklace and nodded. His memory of his mother was faint, but at that moment it felt stronger than it had before.

Albert's voice was fading fast, and he had trouble keeping his eyes open. "And I forgive both of you for John. He was a good boy; he wouldn't fault you for what you did." Albert couldn't keep himself up any longer, his strength waning. "I'll see him soo..." Albert's voice trailed off, and his eyes closed.

"Dad?" Edward called, but his father didn't answer.

Herbert pulled Edward in close and embraced him. Edward couldn't help but weep for his father's death. Despite everything that he had done, he still loved him, and Edward mourned.

The two sat in the middle of the road in Nassau for several minutes, the crowd around them silent. Then a chant began, starting with one person in the crowd, then another, and another, until it felt like the whole of Nassau were speaking as one.

"By the sound of the Golden Horn!"

"By the sound of the Golden Horn!"

"By the sound of the Golden Horn!"

The chant continued unabated. Edward pulled away from his tearful embrace with Herbert to see all eyes were on them. All eyes were on him.

Edward looked upon his father's body again. The familiar golden hunting horn, from his father's time as Benjamin Hornigold, was tied around his waist. Edward loosened the horn, took it in hand, and rose to his feet.

He took a deep breath and sounded the horn.

19. WATER AND BLOOD

In the week since leaving the island, Anne started to acclimate to the prosthetic Alexandre, Victoria, and Nassir had made for her. It felt altogether strange and uncomfortable and itchy where it secured to her thigh with a leather, corset-like strap, but she could walk in it, and that was what mattered most to her.

She still had a problem with her gait and putting the right amount of weight on it, but she had the rest of her life to perfect that, so it didn't bother her.

She also liked the privacy that it gave her, as she could wear a boot and cover it with her pant leg. If she were standing still, none could tell that she had lost her foot. None save her. Though she supposed for some in their profession, it could be seen as a badge of honour, she saw it as a sign of weakness.

They left Los Huecos after gathering and burning the bodies of the dead, as well as the main town that Silver Eyes had occupied. The crew agreed to break and toss the golden bells into the ocean. Whatever strange power they held was better off at the bottom of the sea with Davey Jones.

If Anne never heard them ring again for the rest of her life, it would be too soon.

They set sail for Nassau, and before setting anchor, sent out a scouting party by longboat. They came back after hearing word that Blackbeard had killed Calico Jack.

The news nearly caused Anne to collapse. She had been holding a secret weight, secret even to herself, over the thought that Edward might have perished in his attempt. The weight lifted, and her heart felt free. She was eager to land and see him again.

Only then did she take in what the news meant. Edward had killed his own father. The same father whom he, from day one, had insisted was alive and was partially the reason for his being at sea in the first place. The same father for whom he'd held such complicated emotion after learning the truth about who he was.

Anne's heart broke for Edward as she thought of how hard it must have been to end his own father's life. It also made her scared. He already had a drinking problem from the nightmares that haunted his waking thoughts. What would this new trauma do to him?

"What news of my brother?" Christina asked, clutching the carved rose at her neck.

The crewmates shook their heads. "No mention of 'im. Sorry."

Christina nodded, but her face looked dire. It seemed to Anne like she too had been holding onto a secret weight of her own.

Anne went over to Christina and touched her back. "I am sure your brother is safe and well. Take us into the harbour, and we shall see for ourselves."

Christina managed a weak smile and a nod before she took the helm and issued orders to the crew. She deftly guided the ship into the harbour before ordering the anchor lowered.

Anne, Christina, William, Alexandre, and Victoria were the first party to head to shore in a longboat with some other crewmates. Jack, Pukuh, and Nassir stayed behind, choosing to go later.

As they approached the pier near the centre of town, they noticed Sam waiting for them at the dock. Sam helped moor the longboat, and the crew disembarked onto the pier.

"Sam, happy to see you well and uninjured. Our scouts tell us that Edward killed his... killed Calico Jack."

Sam nodded, his face dour despite what should be good news. "Aye," he said. "You were right ta send me off ta help. Ed woulda gotten 'imself killed if not."

"And what of my brother?" Christina asked once more, stepping forward, her eyes desperate.

Sam's face still held fast to its grim demeanour. "I'll take you to 'im," he said, but would say no more.

Christina didn't seem relieved by the news that he was still alive, and why would she when Sam seemed reluctant to give any more information?

Sam took them through the town, full of revelling pirates as far as the eye could see, and explained what had happened. He gave a brief telling of Edward and Herbert's time aboard Grace O'Malley's ship.

Sam also explained that Edward killed Grace's son who also turned out to be Edward's brother, but they hadn't known it at the time. The news sent Anne's heart racing. Not only did Edward kill his own father, but he killed a brother he hadn't even known he had. Edward's mental state had been hanging on a razor's edge *before* all this had happened. She hoped he was coping with it well, but she felt more fear than anything.

Sam's recounting continued, explaining how they met in Nassau and hatched a plan that backfired due to Grace knowing the truth of Edward and Herbert's identities. Then Sam had regrouped and saved Edward from the gallows, allowing Edward to finally finish off his father.

After a funeral for his father—a muted affair from Sam's estimation due to what happened afterwards—they gave Edward the official title of Magistrate for Nassau and the unofficial title of King of the Caribbean among the pirates. There was a ceremony, which really was just him being named Magistrate and Edward blowing his father's golden horn again, and afterwards the pirates partied for several days and nights.

Benjamin Hornigold and Jack Rackham would live on through Edward, their names and their legacy taken over by him as if his father had never died. That was what Edward's father had wanted for him, what he had tested him for: to prove he was worthy of taking over those names by the republic his father had created. They'd learned that it was the only way Edward's father could force the other pirates to come to an agreement over their next leader.

Anne surmised that on the surface, it functioned as a democracy, but behind the scenes, it was an oligarchy. Edward needed to be savage to rule through force if needed and keep the pirates in line.

After the ceremonies, Sam continued, Edward did his best to catch up on the administrative side of his father's business. Or, at least, that was what he told everyone. Sam knew that Edward was in mourning and spent his days and nights reading things left behind in his father's study as his new staff kept him plied with liquor. He hadn't left the study since the ceremony.

They eventually reached a large gated villa near the edge of town. There were many guards around the premises, but upon noticing Sam, they opened the gates and allowed him entry.

Upon entering the villa, Sam pointed to a room on the first floor. "Herbert's in that room, Christina."

Christina, her face still filled with worry, rushed off without another word. Sam looked at Alexandre and motioned his head towards the room, and Alexandre and Victoria both understood the message and joined Christina.

Anne's heart sank further. That Sam wanted Alexandre to see Herbert meant something terrible had happened to him in the battle. He was still alive, perhaps, but in what state of living was he?

"Come, I'll take ye two ta the captain," Sam said.

"Does he know I… we've arrived?" Anne asked.

"I sent one of me men off when I saw the *Freedom*… ah, I mean the *Queen Anne's Revenge* sailing in," Sam said, then muttered, "That's going ta take some gettin' used to."

Anne and William followed Sam to the second floor of the villa to a room at the back. The other crewmates decided to stay behind and visit Herbert first. A guard opened the door for them and let them enter a large study.

Anne saw Edward sitting in a chair at a table layered with papers, charts, and various oddities. The sight of him, alive and well, took another weight off her, and she felt she could breathe normally again.

After the relief, she noticed his beard was almost completely gone. There was hair there, just not at much as she remembered. It made him look younger and less menacing than he had previously.

Edward looked up from some papers, and when he noticed Anne, his eyes opened wide. He rose from his chair and nearly ran over to her. He scooped her up in his arms and spun her around. He had the widest smile on his face, and his eyes had misted. He pulled her close, and they kissed and wrapped their arms around each other as they let out all the built-up passion from their time apart.

After a moment, he settled himself and rested his head on top of hers. "I missed you," he said.

Anne laughed. "I can see that," she replied. She nestled her head into his chest. "I missed you too."

He smelled of booze, but it was not so pungent as to be intolerable, and Anne decided that now was not the time to broach the subject. It was a time for reunion and time for her to be there for him.

Anne lifted her head up and looked into his eyes. She placed her hand against his cheek, feeling the warmth on her palm. "Sam told us what happened. Edward, I—"

"Let's not speak of it," he said. "There will be time enough for that later." Edward looked behind her to William and Sam. "Where are the rest of the crew?"

Anne stepped back awkwardly due to her leg and answered, "Most are on the ship. Some came with us. Christina, Alexandre and Victoria are visiting with Herbert."

Edward had heard her, but he was looking at her feet. He must have noticed the awkward way she had stumbled backwards.

Anne let out a sigh, wishing that she could have held it for a time when they were alone. Perhaps if she dispensed with it sooner than later, it would be simpler.

Anne knelt and lifted her pant leg up above her knee, showing the prosthetic. "Sam told you of our battling Silver Eyes? Well, the battle did not go as planned, nor as simple as I would have desired."

Edward knelt, joining his wife, and examined the prosthetic. "How did this happen?" His words were short, and his tone a mix of concern and sadness.

Anne shrugged her shoulders. "It's a rather long story. There will be time enough for that later," she said with a grin.

Edward nodded and smiled as well, a bit of relief in his eyes. "This is a remarkable design. Did Alexandre make this?"

"Yes, he, Victoria, and Nassir all had a hand in it."

Edward continued his appraisal, and then he lifted a finger up. "I have just the thing to finish the design and make it even better." He rose to his feet and went to the back of the study and began rummaging through some things.

Anne kept her pant leg rolled up, but she stood up as well, waiting. After a moment, he came back, holding a pair of copper greaves in his hands. He showed them to Anne and handed one to her.

"These are from one of Calico Jack's commanders, Grace O'Malley. She won't be needing them anymore, given that she's with Davey Jones now. They have a secret weapon inside them which fires off bullets out the front."

Anne inspected the greaves, taking note of the weapon inside. "That is ingenious." She handed the greaves back to Edward, and he laid them on a nearby table. "Can you tell me what happened to Herbert? Sam wasn't forthcoming, I assume because Christina was with us," she said as she glanced over her shoulder at him. Sam had his arms folded and shrugged.

Edward's face soured, and he stroked his chin. "He was injured before we fought with Jack, and, well, perhaps it would be best to see him for yourself. I would wish to speak with Alexandre and Victoria soon besides."

Edward left the study and led Anne, William, and Sam to the room on the first floor where Herbert was. The crewmates who had gone to see him were waiting at the door, and they greeted Edward with joyful but muted expressions, which quickly reverted to sullen. Edward opened the door, and a distinct smell of rot mixed with chemicals and herbs met Anne's nose.

Inside, Alexandre and Victoria were standing in a corner near the door, there was an attendant at the other corner, and Christina was sitting beside a bed where Herbert lay. Christina was weeping as she held Herbert's hand.

Anne rushed over to see Herbert's eyes open and alert. He was still alive, but judging from the looks on the faces there, it was not a good prognosis.

She placed her hand on Christina's back, and Christina looked at her. Christina opened her mouth to say something, but she burst into fresh new tears. Anne leaned down and hugged the young woman as she sobbed.

After a few moments, Christina was able to compose herself, though not entirely.

"Glad to see you well, Anne," Herbert said. His voice was hoarse and weak, and with each breath, there was a guttural noise from his throat.

"I am happy to see you as well, Herbert. We sorely missed you these past weeks, but your sister makes a fine helmsman. She managed the ship well in your stead."

Herbert smiled, but then had a coughing fit. He coughed hard for a full minute before he was able to stop and then he took a few deep breaths. "That is good to hear. The *Queen Anne's Revenge* will be well cared for."

Christina's head sank, and she gripped the folds of her pants until her knuckles were white. She didn't need to hear it spoken aloud, for it was clear that Herbert was not long for this world. There was nothing Alexandre could do for him in this state. Whatever injury he suffered must have been infected, and they had failed to treat it in time.

Anne touched Christina's hands, and the young girl looked up at her. Her eyes, filled with grief, pleaded to Anne, begging her to do something.

She looked at Herbert, unable to bear Christina's gaze. "We will let you alone with your sister," she said.

Anne and the rest left the room. Outside, Anne questioned Alexandre.

"So, there is truly no hope? What of the herb from Pukuh's home that you used on me those years ago?"

Alexandre waved his hand. "No two infections are alike, you should know this," he said. "Herbert's has reached his lungs. Even should we use the medicine, it would only prolong his suffering. There is no cure for him."

Anne shook her head. "How long does he have?"

Alexandre crossed his arms in thought. "Perhaps a few days, perhaps a week. It is hard to say."

Edward appeared unfazed. He had been with Herbert from the time the infection began and appeared to know that it was dire. Alexandre was his last hope, but not one he had been holding out for, it seemed.

"Victoria, I'd like to speak with you alone about a matter involving my father. Join me in the study," he said. "And I suppose, Alexandre, you may join, as I know trying to keep you out will be a futile matter." Edward looked at Anne. "Not to worry, my dear, this won't take long."

Edward left, and Alexandre and Victoria followed behind him, leaving Anne and William waiting. Anne wondered just what it was that he wanted to talk with them about.

Christina, alone with Herbert, couldn't hold back the tears any longer and began crying again. She felt as though she had done nothing but cry for the past week and a half. Crying over what she had done to Anne, crying over her weakness that had allowed it to happen, and now crying over her brother's inevitable demise. She hated it.

Her hands instinctively went to her rose necklace. The

necklace became a totem of loss and serenity. When she touched it, she felt calmed. It brought her comfort as she ran her finger along the intricate grooves.

Ochi, her first love, Nassir's son, had given it to her as a gift—a gift expressing his affection for her. She had been wearing it ever since.

Ochi had died. She had loved him, and he had died, and a piece of her died along with him.

Everyone close to her was dead or dying. She hated it.

She ripped the necklace off her and pulled it back, ready to throw it against the wall. She gritted her teeth and looked at the wall, but she couldn't do it. She lowered her hand onto her lap and looked at the rose again. She traced the lines, the curves of the small petals made by a skilled hand, a hand cut short before his prime, and she calmed herself.

She wiped her eyes and glanced at her brother. "What am I going to do when you're gone? You are all that I have left in this world."

There was a moment of silence, then Herbert said, "Do you mock me?"

Christina's jaw dropped. "How could you say that?"

"I recall I said those exact words to you once before," Herbert said before a few weak coughs. "And you said to me 'We are—'"

"Your family," Christina finished.

Herbert nodded. "You were talking of the crew. You have so many aboard that ship who care for you, who love you, and would die for you."

"The crew doesn't share my blood; you do. The crew weren't there for me when Mother and Father died; you were. The crew didn't support me by joining a merchant ship as a powder-monkey before being captured and crippled on a pirate ship; you did. The crew didn't raise me; you did."

Herbert waved his hand. "Blood brought us together by chance. The crew chooses to be with you. And if we're getting into specifics, I would say this crew raised you just as much as

I have. I think Anne could hold some stake in that claim if pressed upon it. You two are like sisters."

Christina chuckled. "I suppose you're right."

There were a few more moments of silence, and then Herbert spoke up. "So, are you getting more comfortable with sailing?"

Christina spoke with her brother about how Anne wanted her to become helmsman, and her time with the ship, as well as the details of their adventure. She recounted the entranced islanders, knocking down the bell with the cannons, getting put under the spell and what had happened to Anne because of it, and finally the sailing to Nassau.

As she recounted the story, she saw him smile, and it warmed her heart. Up until then, he had seemed to be in so much pain. By the end of her telling, they were both holding hands again, and Christina was no longer crying.

After a few moments of silence, Herbert spoke again. "Christina, I need to ask you for a favour."

"Yes? What do you need?"

There was a long pause as Herbert sought for words. He didn't look at her, and instead out the window next to his bed. "I don't want to let this affliction ravage my body any more than it has. It will only get worse from here."

Christina pulled her hand away from her brother's. "What are you saying?" she asked, but she already knew the answer.

"How many spies for my father are aboard the *Queen Anne's Revenge*?

Edward, Alexandre, and Victoria stood in the study— Edward's father's former study. Edward kept a hand at his hip, ready to draw his weapon at a moment's notice. He didn't know what Victoria would do at this line of questioning.

Victoria stood silently for a moment before answering. "Half, perhaps a bit more than half. I'm not their keeper."

"And you've been sending him reports with our status, our whereabouts?"

"Yes," she replied, her face like stone.

Edward's rage reached a tipping point, and he pulled out the blade from its sheath. "Tell me why I shouldn't kill you right now."

Alexandre and Victoria both had their own weapons drawn, Victoria a short sword and round shield, and Alexandre a rapier.

"I doubt you could," she said first. Then she followed up with, "I wasn't the only one sending letters."

Edward calmed himself and dropped his stance. "No... no, you weren't." He put his cutlass away, and the other two followed suit. "Tell me why you did it. According to you, you hated my father, so why follow his orders and spy on me? Why report back to him?"

"Simple," she said. "Your father wanted to die, and I wanted him dead. It was an uncomplicated decision."

Her flippant attitude was making him angry once again, but he couldn't fault her for wanting the man dead. After all, Edward was the one who'd killed him. His father seemed to have a knack for bringing people together and setting them apart.

Like father, like son. "So, what am I to do with you then, hmm? If I cast you away, then by rights I should be casting away half my crew. By that reasoning, this whole bloody island was loyal to my father and his ends, I can't rid myself of all of them."

Alexandre stepped forward. He had the same slight smile on his face, the one that showed no genuine emotion. "Perhaps I can be of assistance. We were planning on leaving after this matter was settled, so we shall depart of our own accord."

The revelation took Edward aback and confused him. "You were planning on leaving the crew? I thank you for saving me the trouble, but why?"

"As I said when we first met, I was here for the entertainment. I enjoyed watching you over the years, but I have had my fill. Your wife may be able to illuminate you as to the breaking point that came about during her *aventure*."

Alexandre and Victoria turned around to leave and headed towards the door to the study.

"Hmph," Edward scoffed. "And what about that question about me that was puzzling you so? Do I enjoy the smell of blood?"

"Ah, yes, I found the answer to that some time ago."

Edward's jaw dropped. "And? What's the answer?"

Alexandre grinned. "What indeed," he said, and then he headed out the door.

The crew held Herbert's funeral on the deck of the *Queen Anne's Revenge*.

Before Alexandre and Victoria left, they heard about his passing and decided to attend and use it as an opportunity to say goodbye to the rest of the crew.

Sam also joined with some of his crew to pay their respects.

It was the first time in quite a while that Edward had been aboard his ship, but the circumstances were far from pleasant. He had already prepared mentally for Herbert's passing, but the suddenness and the manner were unexpected.

Only those who were on land in Nassau knew the truth of what had happened. They told the crew that he had died of illness from an infected wound and kept Herbert's head covered to hide his final shame. None of the crew who knew the truth blamed Christina for helping her brother end his life and end his pain, but it was a shock nonetheless.

Christina remained composed as best she could for the funeral, but her eyes were red, and she either kept one hand on her rose necklace or clutching tight to her pant leg. She told Edward that she couldn't bear to say anything given what she had done. Edward thought the poor girl wouldn't have made it through more than a few words either way.

And, so, the task fell to Edward. Edward walked up the ladder to the quarterdeck slowly. He could feel all eyes on him, and he thought it funny that some time ago, the thought of speaking in front of such a large crowd terrified him. Now, the crew, and him also, thought nothing of the act.

Edward looked at the immense helm, Herbert's domain. He touched the familiar wood, staring at it for a moment. He could almost picture Herbert holding it, his wheelchair positioned at an angle so that he could reach the massive wheel. The thought made him smile.

"You know," he began, changing what he had planned to say, "this wheel is almost as tall as I am." Edward held his hand out, gesturing to visualize the height difference. It reached his neck at its highest point. "And yet, Herbert, our helmsman sat half that height." Edward moved his hand down, below the railing of the quarterdeck. "One would wonder if Herbert was manning the helm, or if the helm was manning Herbert." Edward's comment made the crew laugh. Then he pointed at the wheel. "Day in and day out, Herbert struggled with this beast, and he won." He clenched his fist. "He won every single day in his battle to ensure that each one of you got to where you wanted to go. To make sure that each of you was safe from storms. To make sure that we won any battle we had at sea." Edward let the words hang in the air for a minute. "Each one of us, at some point or another, owed our life to Herbert. And now we won't ever get the chance to repay that debt."

Edward needed a moment. And from the looks of it, so did many in the crew. His eyes were watering. He wiped them and took a few deep breaths.

"Herbert was my brother," he said. "We may not have shared blood, but he was my brother. We fought like brothers, too, as you're well aware." The crew chuckled again, and Edward could see a few wiping tears away as well. Anne, comforting Christina, wiped her eyes. "He was our brother. We were his family." The crew shouted in agreement. "Now, with his vengeance complete, may he rest in peace." The crew roared again at Edward's declaration.

Edward nodded to Pukuh to begin the final ceremony. As he had done before for others in the crew, he placed a piece of corn and a small piece of jade in Herbert's mouth: food for the journey he was about to take, and jade to pay for passage. Then he said a prayer, which the other crewmates joined in by bowing their heads.

The crew placed Herbert in a longboat and lowered it into the sea. They tossed a torch inside before letting it loose on the swells. As his body drifted out, some in the crew fired off muskets into the air. After three shots, they stopped, and it meant the service was over, but many continued to watch as the longboat went farther and farther out to sea, the fire reaching higher as it and Herbert drifted from the earth.

"So, Silver Eyes was putting everyone in a trance?"

Anne nodded as she took a bite from some food they'd brought into their cabin. "It's a shame you weren't there to see it. It was hard to imagine that the islanders could be so far gone from a simple trance, but I suppose it's a testament to your father's crew."

Edward and Anne, as well as the rest of the crew, had decided to stay aboard the ship after the funeral. They had a feast where many drank to Herbert's honour and recounted his time at the helm. Some even lamented being against him at first but gaining respect for him due to his tenacity.

After the feast, and after Anne saw Christina to her bed where she finally slept after some mournful drinking, Edward and Anne had retreated to their cabin where they sat leaning against their bed, a plate of food in front of them and a lantern nearby. Anne told Edward about what had happened on the island, and how Silver Eyes had controlled the crew to attack them.

Edward shivered at the thought of the men and women of

the island, hollow-eyed and out for blood, and stronger than one with their full senses.

"What say we take a trip to the Devil's Triangle?" Edward said with a grin. "We can switch places: you join Herbert and kill my father, I'll take the ship and go after Silver Eyes."

Anne gave Edward a dark look. "Don't jest about such things. We've already been there once, and once was too much." She shook her head. "I cannot believe that what we saw there was real. If that's true, then we cannot go back. If we were to change something in the past, then it could have untold effects on the present. Our present, at least."

"That's not how I see it," Edward said. "Think about it. We were already well into our journey for the keys when we entered that mist. My father said that my visit to him secured his doubts about what he was going to do. And, you said William did the exact same thing that he had done in the past: he left the room where his king was and didn't go back in to stop his murder. The present was the same in both situations. Going back didn't change anything because it played out exactly as it had. Even if we go again, whatever happened would have already happened in the past, and the present would remain the same."

Anne raised her brow. "But what about Sam and Miss Alston?"

Edward opened his mouth to respond and then closed it again. He looked off to the side as he thought it over. Sam and Theodosia Burr Alston, whom at the time they had thought was their enemy, had been with William in his vision of the past. They had most certainly not been there with William when he had been a royal guard, so them being there must have changed history.

"My dear, I'm far too intoxicated for this right now. You've just rattled my brain a bit too much."

"Eat something, Ed," Anne said, handing him some meat and bread.

Edward ate the food offered, and despite wanting to move

on from their time in the Devil's Triangle, a thought occurred to him. "You've never told me about what you saw that day," he said.

Anne looked at Edward for a moment, her red curls draped over her shoulders as she moved her head. She looked away and at the wall. "I, like you, saw my parents. Both of them. I didn't know where I was at first, but I quickly realized it was one of my mother's houses. I hid when I heard someone coming, and it turned out to be my mother. She had just given birth to my brother George, but he died minutes after." Anne leaned her head back and looked at the ceiling above. "I would have been eight at the time, far too young to remember the details, but I do remember the fights. My father tried his best to console my mother, but she rebuffed him. My mother's friend, Sarah, came next and comforted my mother in her time of need. Then my aunt visited, and Sarah left. Instead of comforting her, my aunt berated my mother for her relationship with Sarah. They fought, shouting at each other the vilest things." Anne closed her eyes for a moment. "That was the last time they saw each other."

Edward watched as Anne told her story. Her expression was a mixed shadow of pity and anger that had simmered and evaporated over the years but still existed in the ether.

He remembered what his father had told him about Anne's mother. She had passed almost a year ago. He hadn't told Anne about it yet, but he knew he should. Before he could, Anne continued her story.

"I never did put the two together, but I realize now why my leaving was such a betrayal to her, why she chose to declare me dead as a way of disowning me and sending an assassin to make it true. Though they fought, my mother loved my aunt, but my aunt was so cruel to her. That's what made her an overbearing, overprotective and controlling woman. The cruellest irony is that that's what pushed me away." Anne glanced at Edward and let out a sheepish chuckle as she wiped the mist from her eyes. "Sorry, Ed, it's the drink talking. I didn't mean to drown you in melancholy."

Edward laid his hand on Anne's and looked deep into her eyes. "Never apologize for opening your heart to me. I am your husband, remember? We're supposed to share in the burdens too, not just the joys."

Anne leaned forward and kissed Edward, then the two embraced. Anne held him tight, and Edward could feel the slight damp of fallen tears against his back.

"I love you, Edward," she said.

"I love you too, my Anne."

They sat there for a moment in silence. Anne repositioned so that she was leaning her back into his chest, and she held Edward's arms wrapped around her body. The stars shone outside, giving a small bit of light into the cabin along with the ever-dimming lantern in front of them.

"Besides, there's no use worrying about the dead. It's a lesson we'll both have to learn, it seems," Anne said suddenly.

Anne's comment shocked Edward. "What?"

She turned a bit and looked up at Edward. "Yes, I suppose I never told you. Back when we were in Porto Bello, I learned that my mother passed away."

Edward's jaw dropped in shock. "You knew?"

Anne sat up and turned around to face Edward. "Wait, you knew about it too?"

"I just found out recently. I was trying to find the right time to tell you about it." Edward let out a sigh and ran his fingers through his hair.

"Well, I suppose I've saved you the trouble," Anne said with a laugh.

"I suppose so."

They sat in silence once again.

After a moment, Anne shook her head. "We're quite the pair, aren't we?" she said.

Edward cocked his brow. "I recall I said the same to you once. What do you mean by it?"

"Though you weren't aware at the time, you had an overbearing, controlling father who tried to kill you, the same as my mother. Fate is the mother of all coincidences. I take that as more proof we were meant to be together."

Edward smiled at his wife. The thought that they were meant to be together, though their shared circumstances may have been the inciting incidents, warmed his heart.

"Anne, I want you to have this," Edward said as he reached into his pocket. He pulled the driftwood seashell necklace and handed it to her. "It was my mother's. My father had it with him. I think it would be better if you kept it safe."

She examined the carved necklace with care and reverence, gently touching the curves in the porous wood. After a moment, she put it around her neck.

"How does it look?" she asked.

"Better than it would on me," he replied with a grin.

Anne laughed with him. "You've never talked about your mother before. Tell me about her."

Edward told Anne about the only memory he had left of his mother: her beautiful, long black hair, as black as onyx, and wavy like the summer sea. Then he recounted the stories that his father had told him about her and finished with his father's comment about his mother not being meant for this world.

Anne gave him a warm smile, then touched the necklace. "I'll keep it safe and wear it with pride."

She turned around and laid her head in Edward's lap. She held his hand across her chest, and they sat there for a time. Edward watched the stars outside the cabin as the waves splashed against the hull, the familiar sound pulling at his core and reminding him of what he missed on his ship.

The familiar smells of the sea air and the Caribbean pine that lined the ship from stem to stern, as well as his wife's warmth in his lap, calmed his mind. For the moment, despite the loss of his father and his brother Herbert, he was at peace.

"So, have you thought about what we'll do from here?" Anne asked.

Edward looked at his wife, her eyes deep green like the

ocean, her gleaming red hair shining in the light of the lantern. The small freckles around her face and her rose-coloured lips made his heart race.

"I have a few things in mind for us to do tonight," he said with a cheeky grin. Anne smacked his hand, but she couldn't hold back a smile and a blush. Edward kissed his wife, then looked out the window to the stars again. "We're free from our horrible parents, and we're pirates. We can do whatever we want."

EPILOGUE

It was a stormy day, and Edward holed himself up in his father's study reading through the mass of notes and letters, ledgers and journals left behind. He was trying to find some purpose behind the noise, trying to stay afloat in the business his father had created.

Suddenly, the doors to the study swung open on a gust of wind. Edward looked up to see an older man with salt and pepper hair and a pipe sticking out of his mouth at the entrance. The man held no weapon, but Edward drew a pistol all the same.

Edward stood up from his seat and pointed the pistol at the man. He held his finger at the ready but didn't fire. "Who are you? What are you doing here?"

The man looked Edward up and down, as though appraising him. "So yer the egg, eh?" he said in a gravelly voice. "You'd better have been worth all this. I lost my eye because o' you."

Edward, from this distance, could just barely make out the slash on the man's left eye and cheek. His eye looked clouded over.

"I'm afraid you have me mistaken for another," he said. "Now, I'll ask you to leave unless you want to die."

The man nodded and stepped forward, unfazed. The sound of a peg leg snapped against the wood of the floor. "Aye, you have some fire in you, that's good," the man said. He looked around the room, then when he eyed a cabinet nearby, he stalked over to it and opened it up to find a bottle of liquor. "You remember the man you fought, Edward Russell? What was the name that fool

266

called himself? Ah, yes, *Plague*. What a joke. At least when people call me a foolish name, it wasn't my idea."

The mention of the assassin Edward had fought piqued his interest. He didn't lower the pistol, but he did approach the man. "What about him?"

The old man pulled the cork of the liquor out with his teeth, spat it away, and took a long drink. "I'm the reason you won that fight, little egg," he said. Then he motioned with two fingers from his left shoulder in a line to his right hip.

It took a moment to remember, but Edward recalled that Plague had had a wound in that same spot. The wound had only been hours old when they had fought, and Edward surmised that without that wound, he very well might not have won his fight. Only those who were with Plague, or on Edward's crew, knew of that wound.

Edward furrowed his brow. "Who are you?" he asked again.

"I'm William Kidd. Some fools call me The Tsunami. I'm a friend of yer father, and I'm here to help you with what comes next."

THE END

OTHER BOOKS
BY THE AUTHOR

The Voyages of Queen Anne's Revenge Series:

BLACKBEARD'S FREEDOM

BLACKBEARD'S REVENGE

BLACKBEARD'S JUSTICE

BLACKBEARD'S FAMILY

The Pirate Priest Series:

BARTHOLOMEW ROBERTS' FAITH

BARTHOLOMEW ROBERTS' JUSTICE

BARTHOLOMEW ROBERTS' MERCY

BARTHOLOMEW ROBERTS' SPIRIT

The Collection Series:

BLACKBEARD'S SHIP (Includes Books 1&2 of The Voyages of Queen Anne's Revenge & The Pirate Priest)

BLACKBEARD'S BLOOD (Includes Books 3&4 of The Voyages of Queen Anne's Revenge & The Pirate Priest)

ABOUT THE AUTHOR

JEREMY IS CURRENTLY LIVING IN NEW BRUNSWICK,
CANADA WITH HIS WIFE HEATHER, AND THEIR
TWO CATS, NAVI AND THOR.

Jeremy's first foray into the writing world was during a writing
competition called NaNoWriMo, where the goal is to write a
certain number of words in the month of November.

After completing the novel he started, and some extensive
rewrites, he felt it was worthy of publishing and self-published
his first novel, Blackbeard's Freedom in September, 2012.

After writing over ten books under two names, his passion for
writing hasn't wavered over the years, and hopes to one day
make it his primary career.

Let everyone know what you thought of his novels by leaving a
review. He loves getting feedback on his books, and loves to
hear from fans of his work.

Want to pirate one of Jeremy's novels? Visit
http://www.mcleansnovels.com/free-book-link for a free copy
of one of his books.